D0445096

star

BETHANY FRENETTE

HYPERION
NEW YORK

First Edition
1 3 5 7 9 10 8 6 4 2
G475-5664-5-12228
Printed in the United States of America

This book is set in Garamond Premier Pro.
Designed by Marci Senders

Library of Congress Cataloging-in-Publication Data
Frenette, Bethany.
Dark star/Bethany Frenette.
p. cm.
Summary: "Audrey, the sixteen-year-old daughter of a superhero, must
access powers she never knew she had to defend Minneapolis from terrifying
demons that have emerged from Beneath"—Provided by publisher.
ISBN 978-1-4231-4665-0 (hardback)—ISBN 1-4231-4665-4 ( )
[1. Supernatural—Fiction. 2. Psychic ability—Fiction. 3. Demonology—
Fiction. 4. Mothers and daughters—Fiction. 5. Superheroes—Fiction.] I. Title.
PZ7.F889345Dar 2012
[Fic]—dc23   2011053078

Reinforced binding

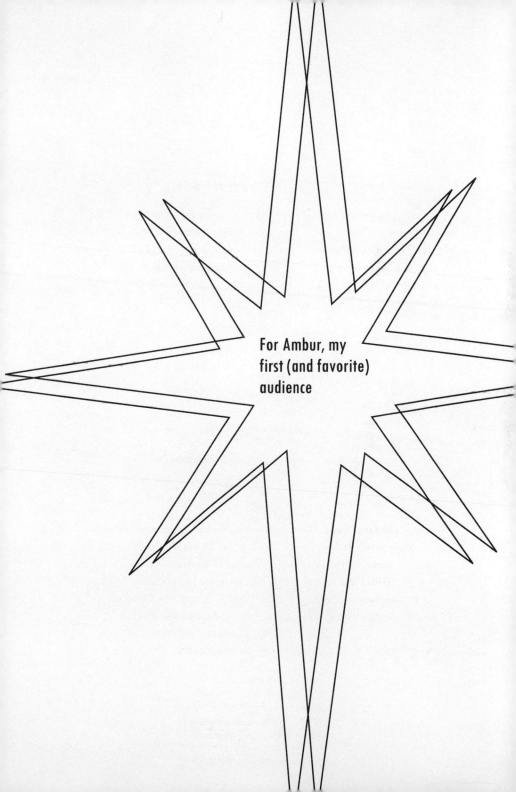

For Ambur, my
first (and favorite)
audience

dark star

You know when you have that dream?

The one where you haven't been to math class all year, and suddenly you're taking the final exam? Or the one where you're about to go on stage, and not only have you forgotten your lines, but for some reason you aren't wearing pants?

This dream wasn't like that.

In this dream, I stood on the roof of a building, looking down across the city. Minneapolis. My city. I knew those streets, the high-rises, the corporate offices reaching skyward. There was heat at my back, but no light. In a city of nearly four hundred thousand people, the silence felt heavy. Dead. The towering buildings sat dark around me. Empty streets trailed off into ramps and freeways, touching the edge of the horizon. The sky was starless, blank and bare. I stood and breathed and all around me the silence gathered. The darkness gathered.

Then.

A band of light. A circle spreading outward, touching the buildings, the sidewalks, the idle buses and taxis scattered in the streets. A flash, and gone. Dark again.

Then noise. Noise that broke through my body, through the night, through the darkness and the stillness and the heat at my back. Like an explosion far below, beneath the roots of the trees that lined the parks, beneath the streets and the sewers and beneath the oldest secrets the city held. Beneath.

One by one, the buildings crumbled. Not like dominoes, or a line of cards—nothing so innocent as that. Glass shattered. Bricks fell. I heard the creak and groan of metal and concrete as skyscrapers toppled. Then the hotels collapsed, and the apartment complexes, the bars and restaurants and shops. Tree branches splintered. Streetlights bowed. The river went dark and dry, and the air filled with the scent of blood. Only I remained. And I knew. I had done this.

I looked down.

Fire.

Fire in my hands.

If Gram had been alive, she'd have reminded me that most dreams aren't prophetic, even if you have a Knowing. She'd have reminded me of nightmares I'd had as a child, dreams of monsters that crept out from shadows with cold, unblinking eyes—and, as it

4

turned out, Gram said, those dreams never came true. She'd have reminded me that having a Knowing didn't mean it was always right.

But it wasn't every night I dreamed I'd destroyed an entire city. I woke shaking, a chill of dread filling my lungs. It was still dark—barely. Outside, the first gray of morning pushed back the darkness, and I heard the chatter of birds in the trees. I rose from my bed and moved to the window, placing my hands on the blinds.

I heard a voice and spun around, searching the half-light of my room. Someone had spoken. Someone had spoken my name, and then—

A whisper.

"I'm going to tell you a secret, Audrey. Don't forget."

"Gram?" I asked, seeking, not seeing.

"Look for the light."

I was still dreaming.

Then, as the dream moved on: "What do you remember?"

What I remember best about Gram is walking.

Summer mornings, we walked down sleepy streets where traffic wasn't heavy. We followed trails that led into parks, looping around lakes, feeling the early sun on our skin. We went just after dawn, the time of morning when the sky is the color of lilacs and the light is just beginning to crest. Every summer, from the time I was eight until the year she died, we walked.

And as we walked, she told me secrets.

"Audrey," she would say, smiling. "Listen. I'm going to tell you a secret."

I'd lean toward her, feeling the difference in the air, as though her words cast a spell around us. Secrets had a kind of magic, she often said—but only when kept. "Don't tell," she'd say, even if it was simply a memory, or a thought she didn't want repeated. And I would nod. I understood about secrets. How to hold them close. How to keep them. It was one of those things I'd grown up knowing.

Some of the secrets were real.

"I'm going to tell you something very special," Gram said, one morning when I was eleven. "I'm going to tell you who you are."

"I'm Audrey," I said.

She smiled, pausing in our walk to cup my face with her hands. "Yes. But that's not the name you were born with."

I was young, but not too young to understand the implications of this. I fixed a little frown on my face and looked up at her. "I was adopted?" I asked. My best friend, Gideon, was adopted, but it had never occurred to me that I might be, as well.

Her laughter was soft and musical. "No. You're not adopted. But you are hidden." And then, to put me at ease, she took me home and showed me my birth certificate.

Esther Audrey Whitticomb.

I looked up at her, still frowning.

"That's you, of course," she said. "I thought it was time you knew your own name."

Panic formed, a lump in my throat. She'd said I was hidden, but she hadn't said *why*.

"Gram," I said. "Was I a mistake?"

She pressed her hands over mine, those smooth hands just beginning to wrinkle. Gram was never old the way grandmothers in movies are, but she was beginning to look stretched, a little worn out. Her hair was still blond, with only a hint of gray, and she wore it long, in a braid that fell down her back. But some part of me—my Knowing, maybe—told me that our moments were being counted off, a tally run through. I knew I should remember every detail, everything she told me. And when I asked her if I was a mistake, she smiled and held my hands when she answered.

"No, sweeting, you weren't a mistake. But you *are* a secret. The very best kind."

She never would explain what she meant by that.

"What do you remember?"

Everything, Gram, I wanted to tell her. *Everything you've told me.* I remember it all. Walking. The ground beneath my feet. The swell of a storm. The red summer sky. Secrets and mistakes.

But the dream was fading. And the light warming my eyes wasn't the light she wanted me to find, but the sun.

I'd overslept. Again.

The truth is? Even without things like hidden names and Gram's whispered secrets, my life wouldn't have been normal.

You can't be normal when your mom leaves the house every night as soon as dusk falls and returns with the first blue of dawn, like some kind of vampire, or when she's strong enough to bend the barrel of a shotgun with barely a flick of her wrist. When your mom's a superhero, normal isn't even in your vocabulary.

Of course, Mom never liked the term *superhero,* but I've seen enough cartoons and read enough comics to know it's an apt description. And she'd strictly forbidden me from calling Leon her sidekick. They were Guardians, she explained. Guardians of the Twin Cities—even though she has trouble remembering things like dental appointments, and Leon's just some skinny college kid who works at a bakery.

Guardian. Superhero. I'd long ago decided they were basically the same thing. Guardian was simply the preferred term. I mean, Mom even had an alter ego. The Cities didn't know her true name, so they gave her another one. They called her Morning Star.

That was Mom's other face: a hooded figure moving in darkness. She was called vigilante, hero, menace, myth. Most adults I knew claimed not to believe in her, but at school I heard talk. Whispers and exaggerations, mostly, things Mom couldn't have possibly done—like stopping a train with her bare hands, or saving entire neighborhoods from the spring floods. Morning Star was a fantasy, a story told to children. Like Santa or the Tooth Fairy. When pressed, I claimed to be a disbeliever.

Officially, Mom worked for a private security firm in downtown Minneapolis, H&H Security. Unofficially, she did the whole Guardian thing, and we lived off of her inheritance and investments. When I was eight, we'd moved into this monster of a house that was left to Gram, so Mom didn't have to worry about snooping neighbors. To most of the world, we've always just been Lucy and Audrey Whitticomb, normal mother and daughter.

Which just means we have to work even harder to keep the secret.

We aren't always successful. My friend Gideon found out about Mom when I was in third grade. Mom had been driving us home from martial arts when a truck ran a red light. It didn't hit us hard, but it was enough to toss me forward against the seat in front of me. As soon as we were through the intersection, Mom pulled over and scrambled to get us out. She opened the door next to Gideon by yanking it right off the car.

After that, we kind of had to tell him.

Mom worried over that for weeks. She wasn't certain Gideon would be able to keep the secret. But Gideon hadn't gone through a comic book phase like I had, and even though he'd liked cartoon superheroes as much as any little boy, he was smart enough to know that some secrets are better when kept. He never said a word to anyone.

I'd known all along it would be all right. Ever since Gideon and I met, I could tell he was special. He was the person who first made me aware of my Knowing. In second grade, when my family moved back to Minneapolis, Gideon was in my class at the elementary school. I walked in, and there he was, sitting in the front row, smiling—a boy like most little boys I'd known, with a mop of dark hair, face full of mischief, and legs covered in scabs. But all around him was light. A brilliant, shining light that radiated out of him, like a sun caught in a snow globe.

Gram told me later I was reading him, that I had a Knowing. Gram had it, and Mom had it a little, and I had it too. Certain people, Gram told me, I would look at and *Know*. Others I might be drawn to or repelled by. And I knew then, immediately, before the universe had spent another fraction of a second, that Gideon and I would be friends. No other Knowing before or since had ever been so strong. I'd never seen his aura again, but I knew it was there—just as I knew he would never reveal our secret.

I'm not sure why Mom worried. Even people who have no Knowing at all seem to understand about Gideon. When we were little, no one ever teased him. He never got bullied or had his head dunked in a toilet or whatever else the little cannibals in elementary school come up with when they decide to eat their own. And year after year, Gideon was invariably teacher's pet.

You'd think this would have made everyone hate him. But no; he lived with the curse of being almost universally adored.

I didn't even hate him for being wide awake and cheerful on a Monday morning, eating pancakes in my kitchen when I walked downstairs still tired and shaken from my dream.

And I didn't hate him for looking at me, sighing, and then saying, "I see you're continuing this trend of rolling out of bed and into yesterday's clothes. Also, we're late."

I poured myself a glass of orange juice and sat down beside him, rubbing my face with my hands. Even on good days, mornings do not contain my most shining hours. That morning, I'd done pretty much what Gideon accused me of: climbed out of bed, pulled on the pair of jeans I'd left on the floor, tossed my hair into a ponytail, and then grabbed the first clean shirt I'd groped my way to in the closet.

"You could've woken me up," I said, grabbing a fork to steal his pancakes.

"And risked another black eye? Not a chance."

"Even I'm not that brave," my mother said, glancing up at me. She and I looked alike, with the same brown eyes and small, straight noses; but while my hair was a mess of brown curls, hers was straight and blond and very nicely drawn into a bun. She also appeared far more alert than I felt, even though she'd been awake all night.

I gave her a little wave. She was seated across the table, flipping through a magazine and dousing her pancakes in syrup. Since she slept afternoons and was gone most evenings, breakfast was our main meal together. She leaned forward and poked my shoulder, asking, "Everything all right?"

"I had a dream about Gram," I said, shivering. I thought of brick and cement, tall buildings crumbling. But it was Monday morning, and the kitchen was bright with the early sun. I didn't want to think about dark dreams. I took a sip of my juice and said, "She thinks you should let us go to the cabin this weekend."

I'd long ago discovered it was impossible to convince a Guardian to take a vacation, even for a weekend. Because Mom spent her nights prowling dark alleys and dirty streets, she was pretty much convinced the world was evil, but I had persuaded her that Gideon and I should be allowed to go to the family cabin up north— preferably before winter set in and the whole place got buried in ten feet of snow. Since it was already the middle of October, we didn't have much time left.

Two days ago, she'd changed her mind.

Now she didn't even look up from her magazine. "My teenage daughter alone for three days with a boy. In a cabin on a lake. I am thinking... no. Thanks for playing."

"I'm sixteen, not twelve. Anyway, Gideon doesn't count as a boy."

"Hey." He stabbed my hand with his fork. Syrup ran over my fingers.

I ignored him. "And even if he did, you're gone all night anyway. We could be having just as much sex as we wanted to right here."

Mom glanced up at that and gave me one of her looks. One of those looks that meant my comment had gone over about as well as my suggestion that she try wearing something a little less obvious than a black hoodie with a bright white star on the back. (Rule #47 of living with a superhero: *Don't* mess with her costume.)

"Mom," I said. "You know Gideon and I are just friends."

She returned her attention to her magazine. "Mmhmm. Still not happening."

"Well, the thing is—it hasn't really been my place to say it, but the truth is, Gideon's gay."

That led to more fork stabbing.

Mom smiled. "I've spent too many years hearing him moon over that Brooke girl to believe that one. But good effort."

"It's a new development," I said, moving my hand safely away from Gideon and scooting to the other side of the table. "But if you're not worried about us, why can't we have the cabin? You're not planning to use it, are you? Don't you have nefarious schemes to thwart and evildoers to punish?"

"You're late for school," Mom said.

"You're dodging the question."

She closed her magazine and slapped it against the table. "Because I'm your mother, and I said so. Does that still work? How about—because I'm stronger than you and can lock you in a cage if I want to?"

"Child Services might have something to say about that," Gideon said, apparently forgiving my earlier remarks. That went along with my inability to hate him: he never held a grudge.

"It's not a good time, Audrey," Mom continued. A slight frown had worked its way across her brow. I could tell from her tone that she was about three seconds away from another of her "the world is full of death and danger" speeches, so I decided to strike first.

"I'd be safer at the cabin than in Minneapolis. Nevis has a population of eighty-six, and I'm pretty sure the last time someone was murdered there was *never.*" Actually, I had no idea what its population was, but that sounded close enough.

"We could always be eaten by bears," the ever-useful Gideon suggested.

I smacked him on the back of the head. "You're really not helping."

"And you're really not winning this argument," Mom said. "I don't want you away from the Cities right now. I need you close to home."

That caught my attention. "Why? Is something going on?"

"Nothing you need to worry about," Mom said, which was her standard answer whenever I asked about her work. Before I could press the issue, she rose from the table and headed out of the kitchen, pausing at the doorway to call back over her shoulder. "I've got a meeting this afternoon, but stick around after school. We need to have a talk."

"That doesn't bode well," I told Gideon as I got into his car.

The early air was cool, but I felt the humidity in it, the threat of heat to come. The end of summer was dragging its heels, even though the trees had all gone orange and brown and the streets were littered with leaves.

"What?"

"A Talk," I said. "Capital *A*, capital *T*."

"Sounds like someone's in trouble."

I sighed. I had an idea what it was about. Mom's partner-in-crime-stopping, Leon, thought I shouldn't be telling fortunes at school. And he'd been rather vocal about it recently. "Leon's trying to get me to stop bringing my Nav cards to school. He says people will ask questions."

Gideon shrugged. "It's not like you're telling the future," he said, pulling onto the highway that ran past our houses, toward Whitman High. It was after eight. We'd be twenty minutes late even if he sped, which Gideon never did.

Starting the week with a tardy notice and yesterday's jeans: another thing that did not bode well.

As for telling the future...

"I'm not," I agreed.

"You can't do that, can you?"

"I predict this will not be the last tardy notice we receive from Whitman," I said. I didn't tell him about my dream, the void that pressed in on me, a night without moon or stars. That had felt like some sort of future, sitting out on the horizon, waiting.

"What's Leon's problem, then?" Gideon asked.

"He says I'm using my powers too blatantly."

Powers. That was what Leon called my Knowing. What he called my mother's strength, and his own bizarre ability to transport himself various places. Lately I'd been wishing he would accidentally teleport himself somewhere very far away. Like maybe the sun.

"You're not selling fortunes for lunch money or anything," Gideon said. "Besides, no one takes it seriously."

"And even if they did believe it, they'd think it was the cards, not me."

Gram had given me my Nav cards five years ago. There were only a few dozen sets of the cards in the world, she told me, and half of them had been lost. She owned one of two sets located near the Astral Circle—and she had given me hers.

Gram always told me our abilities were gifts. She thought they should be encouraged, treated with reverence. The Nav cards were a way to enhance my Knowing: a deck of fifty-one cards that allowed me to focus my thoughts and energy into a particular task. I liked to see into people, and I doubted anyone would start asking questions. Except for Gideon, I hadn't told any of my friends about my Knowing—and most of the other students at Whitman High *already* thought I was weird.

Which was actually becoming more depressing by the day. Aside from a brief stint of popularity in middle school, I was once again known only as Gideon Belmonte's Best Friend.

Not that Gideon's likability had done him much good. The girl he was convinced was his soul mate was the one girl who barely knew he existed: Brooke Oliver, a beautiful blond Barbie doll. I'd thought they were supposed to start making them look like real people, but apparently Brooke hadn't gotten the memo.

"Are you even paying attention?"

I looked up. We'd pulled into the parking lot at Whitman, and Gideon was frowning my way. The lot was empty except for a few stragglers and two boys sneaking cigarettes behind the cars. Coils of smoke drifted up in the early light. "What? Sorry."

"Zombie Audrey rises again."

I touched my hair. The ponytail had it somewhat contained,

but the clinging heat made its curl turn to frizz. "I'm not that bad. What were you saying?"

"Friday? Drought and Deluge? Tink said you weren't sure, since you were trying to get the cabin."

"Oh. Yeah, I can be there. It doesn't seem like Mom is going to change her mind." The Drought and Deluge was a club downtown that allowed minors every Friday, served watered-down soda, decent appetizers, and less-than-decent music. I wasn't a great dancer, but when it was dark and crowded enough, it didn't really matter.

"And she said something about wanting to talk to you in Homeroom."

"Which we've already missed," I pointed out as Gideon pulled into a parking space. "You should really let me drive."

"I will. Once you get a car. Or, you know, *a license.*"

"Corner backing is a completely made-up skill," I countered. "It shouldn't even be on the test."

"Don't feel bad. Not everyone can fail a driver's test three times. That takes real talent." Gideon put his car into park. The engine made a long, rattling gurgle, and he patted the dashboard fondly.

"At least I don't drive like I'm ninety," I shot back, hopping out of the car before he had a chance to respond.

I looked at my watch as we hurried toward the office. It was the beginning of first period—precalculus with Mr. Alvarez. I sighed.

Mr. Alvarez wasn't known for being overly charitable, and he tended to smell like chalk, two things that put him low on my list of favorite people. And even though he was only in his mid-twenties—the youngest teacher on staff—he didn't seem to remember anything about attending high school. He delighted in destroying egos and piling on homework.

So I wasn't surprised that when I entered the room, trying to slip quietly to my seat in the back, he looked at me and said, "Nice of you to join us, Whitticomb. Oblige us, if you will, by solving the problems on the board."

I grimaced and walked to the blackboard. I still felt rattled from my dream, and the numbers before me were a blur, just a series of slashes and curves, nothing that formed any sort of pattern. It might not be fire and destruction, but this was enough like a nightmare that I glanced down to make sure I was still fully clothed.

"Whitticomb?"

"Just checking," I mumbled.

I couldn't even delight in the fact that Mr. Alvarez had already ruined his dark pants with chalk.

Whitman High was a large school, and growing. The

dark brick building had been constructed back when my grandmother was still a young girl; by the beginning of my junior year,
it seemed the school wouldn't be able to hold all of its students
much longer. As a result, the lunch area was usually overrun, and
the inner terrace crowded. Trying to weave through the obstacle
course of chairs and unruly jocks meant keeping a tight grip on
your tray and praying to keep your balance. I picked my way carefully through the throng, because dropping a hamburger on my
shoes was exactly what this day didn't need.

The horror of precalc had been followed by eleventh grade
English. Ms. Vincetti had forced us to read our essays aloud in
small groups, and I was stuck with the most boring girl on the
planet and a boy whose cute-but-befuddled head never managed to
absorb even the most basic rules of grammar. Surviving till lunch

had seemed an impossible task. Reaching our table unharmed was nothing short of a miracle.

I set my tray down and sat beside Gideon, pressing my head to the table. Probably not my smartest idea: the tables were always sticky. Across from us, Tink had already abandoned her food and was busy reading a gossip magazine.

Gideon tugged on my ponytail. "What's wrong?"

"Math teachers are evil," I groaned. "And inhuman."

"Well, *that* one is," Tink agreed.

"If there's any justice in the world, he'll spend his next life as a toothbrush." Or a gym shoe. Or a stick of gum. Or maybe really old lettuce.

"I keep telling you to switch into my class," Tink said. She was basically a genius when it came to math, but she'd had an infamous altercation with Mr. Alvarez late last year and transferred into a section she liked to call Addition for Idiots. Now she spent her class time playing games on her calculator and writing lurid romances in the margins of her notebook.

"This is why I stopped after trig," Gideon said. He tugged at my ponytail again. "Come on, sit up. You're gonna get ketchup on your face, and you're already a disaster area."

I stayed where I was. "Maybe someone will mistake it for blood and they'll send me home."

"Or they'll assume you've been feasting on brains."

That made me lift my head. "What is with your zombie fixation today?"

Before Gideon could answer, Tink pulled my tray away and thumped her fist on the table. "I know what will cheer you up! Do a reading for me. I want to know if I should ask out Greg."

"I don't know why you want my input," I said. "Even if I tell you no, you'll do it anyway."

"Sure, but this way I'm prepared."

Tink was notorious for going through boyfriends. She had more of them in a year than most girls do throughout all of high school. I could predict without needing any sort of Knowing exactly how this next relationship of Tink's would go: a month of delirious giggling and nonstop chatter, followed by a shiftiness in her eyes, a tendency to pull her hand from his, a week of unreturned phone calls—and three days of me trying to assure the victim that it wasn't his fault and Tink still liked him as a friend.

But I did want to do a reading. I pulled out my cards and began to shuffle while Tink closed her eyes and leaned forward in her chair, drumming her fingers on the table. As I shuffled, I focused, studying her. Her fingernails were painted pearl, all except the pinkie finger on her left hand, which she had a habit of gnawing on. There was a smear of shimmer powder across her eyelids.

Once upon a time, Tink had been named Tina. Or, to be more accurate, Christina. But somewhere along the way, she had become Tink. The fact that she was blond, barely over five feet, pencil-thin, and pixie-haired made it seem as though her mother had given her the wrong name at birth, and Tink had simply been waiting for people to realize it. The sprinkling of glitter she always wore was just icing.

"I'm waiting," she said, opening one eye to peek at me.

"Quiet. The mysteries of the universe must not be rushed," I told her, but I finished my shuffling and began to deal.

The first card I dealt was number fifty. The Inverted Crescent. My readings always began with this card; it represented me and helped me to orient myself. I placed it in the center and drew the next card. Fourteen. The Mapmaker. In readings for Tink, this one represented her.

The rest of the reading was a jumble.

No reading was ever perfect. My Knowings weren't consistent, even with the cards. Proximity was a factor, as was my relationship to the subject; the bond of family was strongest, but friendship helped. Even then, Knowings came to me differently. Sometimes they came as images or impressions, sometimes in fragments and words—or just a sense, distant and indefinable. Gram told me consistency would come with experience, but so far, all I'd learned how to do was focus on a single subject, and I couldn't always do that. The cards helped. It wasn't like envisioning the future, or listening to thoughts. It was about becoming attuned to everything around me: motion, silence, the curve of a hand, scents in the air. My Nav cards adjusted my frequencies. And this reading was coming up static.

I bit my lip, frowning over the cards. This happened on occasion with Tink's readings—noise I couldn't sift through, little flashes in the dark, hints of almost-something that slid out of reach. Something secret. Something hidden. For someone so open and friendly, she could be annoyingly difficult to read.

This time, however, the problem wasn't Tink. The problem was around us.

It wasn't any specific person. There was no location I could pinpoint, no emotion I could name. It was broader than that. Friction in the air, tension I'd been too preoccupied to notice. For a second, my dream flashed before me—the city, a rush of color, the scent of blood—and then darkness. I shivered. I let my hands idle on my cards. I'd lost my concentration and couldn't get anything at all from Tink.

"That bad?" she asked, wrinkling her nose. "What, does he have too many toes?"

Gideon paused in the middle of chewing his hamburger. "Is that a deal breaker?"

"Depends on how many." She took a moment to consider this, then turned to me. "How many?"

I was no longer in the mood for the reading, but Tink was expecting *something*. I tucked my cards into my bag and shrugged. "Just the ten," I answered. "Unless some have fallen off. That's the problem—he's undead."

"That does seem to be going around," Gideon remarked.

Tink threw a fry at me. "You're hilarious."

"Even worse? He has a summer job as a rodeo clown."

Tink had a horror of rodeos. She refused to discuss it. She crossed her arms and glared at me. "Your cards told you he's an undead rodeo clown."

"With an unspecified number of toes," Gideon added, grinning.

"I need better friends," said Tink.

"You love us," I countered.

Tink responded by giving me the finger. "I'm still asking him out," she said. Then, with an exaggerated sigh, she went back to her magazine.

I turned away. My senses were still on alert. Taking a long breath, I tried to filter the chaos around me. The lunch room was loud, but the friction I'd felt was still there, beneath the noises. Here and there, I caught hints of it: murmurs, furtive glances. I twisted in my chair, scanning the room. There was definitely something going on. It was more than just the anxious, expectant air. Nearby, several students leaned in close across tables, speaking in hushed, excited voices. And—there. Clustered by the door, a group of freshman girls stood crying.

"Did something happen?" I asked, nudging Gideon with my elbow.

"Like what?" Tink looked up from her magazine, tilting her head as she surveyed the room. The chatter around us had increased in volume, and a small crowd was forming near the crying freshmen.

"If I knew, I wouldn't have asked."

"Hmm," Tink said, leaning forward on her elbow and staring directly at the throng.

I shook my head at her. "You're so subtle."

Tink was never one to be out of the loop. After a moment, she jumped up and announced, "I'll go find out." With remarkable ease, she pushed her way into the crowd, where a few of our friends stood whispering.

Once she left, Gideon asked quietly, "You all right?"

"I just have this uneasy feeling," I said. Though I told him about my Knowings on occasion, this wasn't one I could easily articulate.

"Something in your reading?"

"More like outside of it."

Gideon didn't press the issue. I picked at my food, waiting for Tink to return, but I didn't have much appetite. The disquiet wouldn't leave me. That was a problem with Knowing: sometimes I couldn't turn it off even when I wanted to.

By the time she returned to our table, Tink had lost her usual cheer. If I hadn't been alarmed before, I was now: she'd gone from sunny to somber in the space of a few moments. Her face was pale, her eyes lowered. She slid back into her seat, not speaking, and began fidgeting with her book bag.

Gideon and I exchanged a look.

"Tink?" I asked.

What happened then wasn't like Knowing. My senses didn't

clear; the fragments didn't align; the friction remained just at the edge of my focus, like sounds heard underwater. Instead, I felt a pinch of dread in my stomach at the look on Tink's face, the way her eyes wouldn't meet mine. She spoke softly, but her words sliced through me. I knew what she was about to say.

"It's Kelly Stevens. They found her."

Her body, Tink meant. They'd found her body.

Kelly had been in the grade behind us. I hadn't known her well—I'd spoken to her maybe twice, and for the life of me I couldn't recall what our conversations had entailed. But she'd been pretty and popular, and when she'd gone missing in July, all of the local news networks covered the story. She had disappeared somewhere in the stretch of half-light between seven and ten p.m. one hot summer night. A slender silver sandal was found near a park bench, straps twisted, scuffed with dirt. Nothing else.

They'd searched the entire metro area and the woods north of her home, checked nearby lakes and the river. The Cities united, holding candlelight vigils in the steamy blue twilights that lingered in late July; there'd been nothing like it since the string of murders the year before I was born. No trace had been found of Kelly. Rumors but no suspects. She had simply vanished, fallen into the blank haze of the relentless summer heat.

And now she'd been found.

"Where was she? Do they know what happened?" I wasn't sure I wanted to know, but something—some morbid curiosity, maybe—pressed me to ask. None of us had really believed they'd find her alive, not after all this time, but it was unsettling to have suspicion become fact.

Before Tink could answer, something else caught my attention. Another twinge of Knowing, brief but potent. A girl had paused by our table. I turned, and for a moment she met my gaze. She looked as though she might speak, and then her eyes flicked past me. She hurried away.

Iris St. Croix, the new girl in school. I wondered, briefly, if she'd known Kelly. I didn't think so. She'd only transferred to Whitman at the beginning of the year. But then again, maybe she had: the sense I'd gotten from her was vague, confused, but strikingly sad.

I watched her go. She was short, and her dark hair was so long it reached her hips, though not in a messy way. The sweater she wore was at odds with the unseasonable heat. But there was something else that made her stand out.

At her throat, she wore a necklace I hadn't seen before, but with a symbol I knew. A pendant with the triple knot. It was the sign of the Astral Circle, Gram had told me. I knew it for another reason.

It was the symbol printed on the back of each of my Nav cards.

A cop was standing at my front door when I got home from school.

I'd seen Detective Wyle before, and I recognized him even before he flashed his badge at me. He stood half hidden in the shadow of ivy that hung over the lattice, tapping his foot against the stone walkway. I studied him as I approached. His face was carefully blank, but there was a certain tension in his stance. Other details I'd noted before: the fading sunburn on his forehead, the worry lines around his eyes. He was maybe forty-five, a few years older than my mother; good-looking for an older guy. He had that dark and mysterious tortured-soul thing going for him, which normally would've made me think he might be a good match for my mom. She tended to date men who were terminally boring and thus unlikely to think her anything but quirky. It always ended badly. But Detective Wyle also wore a wedding band, so that was out.

Plus, the last time we'd seen him, he'd threatened to arrest her, which was probably a better indicator that they simply were not meant to be. Mom might not have the best taste in men, but she had a healthy sense of self-preservation.

"Hey, kid," he said when I reached him. "You live here, right?"

Since I'd dumped lemonade in his lap the last time he'd interrogated my mother, it seemed unlikely he'd forgotten me. I rolled my eyes, stepping past him to unlock the door.

"You gonna invite me in?"

I shrugged, turning on the light in the entryway. "You have a warrant?" Inside, the hall smelled like orange peels and socks, a sad case for a house built with the grand, imposing feel of a Victorian mansion. Mom must have been gone most of the day, and the house had been closed up, hot air thickening.

"It's not that kind of visit. I just need to speak with your mother."

"With or without handcuffs?" I turned back toward him. He'd gripped the side of the door, holding it open.

He gave me a bland, unamused smile.

I smiled back. "She's not here right now."

"When do you think she might be home?"

"Late," I said. Although, since she'd told me not to leave after school, there was every chance she'd pull into the driveway and prove me a liar at any moment.

"I can wait," Detective Wyle said.

I hesitated, wondering how difficult it would be to annoy him into leaving. I looked at him again. Wedding band—on. But he'd twisted it at least twice since we'd been standing there. He looked as though he'd skipped shaving this morning. His clothing was somewhat wrinkled, too, and he seemed tired, a little worn out.

"Don't want to go home, huh? What, did your wife kick you out?"

"You're a detective, too?" He scratched the stubble on his chin and gave me a hard glare, but I figured he was just trying to intimidate me.

I shrugged again. "Fortune-teller," I said. "I'll make you a deal. You can come in if you let me give you a reading."

I expected that to send him running for the hills, but I must have underestimated either his need to talk to my mother or his desire not to go home, because I found myself leading him into the house, past the stairway, and into the sitting room. I told him to have a seat on the sofa while I found him something to drink. The air-conditioning was broken—again—and the heat was heavy around us. That orange-peels-and-socks smell lingered.

Detective Wyle watched me suspiciously. "That's staying in the glass this time, right?"

I set the lemonade in front of him. "Only if you use a coaster. I'll get cranky if you ruin Gram's table." I dropped my book bag to the floor and knelt on the carpet across from him, reaching for my Nav cards. The news about Kelly had rattled me, and I

worried that I wouldn't be able to focus; but the motion of shuffling soothed me. I took slow breaths, feeling the texture of the
cards, the edges worn by long years of use. I glanced up at Detective
Wyle. I wasn't sure what exactly I hoped to see, but if he was planning to harass my mother, I wanted whatever advantage I could
get. Inconsistent though my Knowings were, a reading might give
me *something*.

Or fail miserably, as my reading for Tink had. I couldn't be
certain.

"How does this work?" Detective Wyle asked. "Is that a tarot
deck?"

"Nope. My own cards. Gram gave them to me. You just sit
there and daydream about sending bad guys to jail or something.
Or you can think of a question if you want."

He grunted.

"What's your first name, Detective? It helps."

He hesitated, his fingers tapping the table. He was a big man
—tall, broad-shouldered, fit—and he seemed out of place on the
dainty floral sofa. Like an action figure in a dollhouse.

"Mickey," he said.

I laughed. "Mickey. Really? Never mind—we're sticking with
Wyle."

He smiled, but he hadn't touched his drink. He probably
thought I'd poisoned him, or that drinking pink lemonade in a
room decorated with pastels and paintings of fruit might ruin his
tough-guy image.

"You gonna open a window?"

"This works better if you don't talk," I said, but I stopped shuffling to oblige him. I rose and tugged both of the far windows open, pausing at the sill to breathe. A cool wind pushed in, the sound of traffic, the rustle of birds taking flight.

Detective Wyle shifted slightly when I turned, though his expression didn't change. He'd been scanning the room, I realized. Working his way across the walls, the bookshelves. Nothing was wrong or out of place—no black pants or dark hoodies lying around, nothing that might hint of mysteries tucked behind the doors. But I shivered. He was searching.

I returned to my cards. "Okay, Wyle. I'm going to lay out ten cards, and they'll tell me all your secrets."

"I must not have many secrets," he said.

"I'm just that good."

I knelt, finished shuffling, and set down the first card. Fifty. Inverted Crescent. Good. I placed it in the center and laid out the rest of the cards.

I began at the top, taking another long breath and focusing. Card one, Compass. Card eight, The Witch. Card sixteen, The Beggar.

I frowned. In readings, the Compass card was always my mother. And this I got a sense of: the cooling twilight; a woman in black; a face in profile, the slope of her nose; light refracting off water. A single star shining. The Witch and The Beggar. Someone searched for and unseen.

Detective Wyle was after my mother, all right. He might not have proof of who she was—but he had his suspicions.

Still, I wasn't about to tell him that.

"You're getting a divorce," I said.

"I thought you'd already figured that one out. Not really fortune-telling."

"I'm getting there," I said. "Here. Card forty-nine. Inverted Anchor. You're feeling lost. You're probably one of those people who mostly has couple friends, and they've all taken her side. And she's getting the house, too, huh?"

He crossed his arms. "You didn't get that from the cards. You got that from looking at me. Are you planning a career in law enforcement?"

"Here, the cross cards. Forty-five, Sign of Brothers. Crossed by The Warrior and The Prisoner."

He leaned forward. "Meaning what?"

This part was easy, a Knowing so clear I didn't even need the cards. "You didn't start out wanting to be a cop. You followed in your father's footsteps. You probably wanted to be something totally ridiculous, like a football player. Or a rock star."

"Baseball player." His lips twitched.

"Another score for the fortune-teller."

"You've got good intuition, kid," he said. But he was giving me a look. A look that meant I was playing it a little too straight, and he was already suspicious of my mother, and he was well-armed with brains and his own common sense. It was probably not a good idea to give him more ammunition.

"Now the terminal cards," I said. "Sign of Lovers. Sign of Swords."

I bit my lip. That meant—

Well. I didn't really know what that meant.

The cards had been helping, up to this point. Sense and feeling coming into alignment, thoughts taking shape within me. My Knowing had formed an image of this man, Detective Mickey Wyle, who had spent his boyhood summers fly-fishing in Canada, whose eyes still saw past the dirt of city streets into the northern half-light of autumn, who went to bars with his cop buddies but rarely drank. But these two cards felt strange when I pressed my fingertips to them, and abruptly the world around us came into close focus. Details sharpened. I noticed the touch of gray at his temples. I saw the dust that floated in the light pushing in through the blinds. I breathed the deep, earthworm scent of soil that dwelled beneath the smell of the house—the smell of alleys at night, the smell of graveyards.

I wouldn't tell him that. I couldn't tell him there was something chasing him, something like a voice in the dark, or that I could see that he hadn't slept in three days and it had nothing to do with the wife he didn't want to go home to. That it was possible he wouldn't live very long.

I didn't know what it meant. I didn't know why he was really here, in this room, with his rumpled clothing and quiet stare. And suddenly I was a little frightened. I didn't know what it meant, but—

He *knew*.

About Mom. About us.

Some part of him knew.

I couldn't say that. So I went for the obvious answer. Lovers and Swords. Not a difficult leap, though an incorrect one. "You caught her cheating," I told him.

"Way off the mark," he said, but he was smiling a little. He ran a hand through his hair, leaning back against the cushions of the sofa.

"She was too successful. You're threatened by strong women."

He grinned at me. "Now you're just stabbing in the dark. But nice try, kid."

I was flustered, so I didn't say anything, just picked up my cards and began shuffling them idly.

"My turn," he said. "And I won't use any cards or fortune-telling."

"Somewhere you've got a file on my mom. It probably tells you everything you need to know about me."

"I don't need a file. You're easy to read."

I frowned, watching him warily, but kept my silence.

"You're close with your mom," he began.

"Wow. Impressive."

He ignored me. "Protective of her. It's just the two of you, so you think you need to look out for her. You worry that I mean her harm—but I don't. And I think you know exactly what I'm talking about when I say I believe your mother is a very gifted individual."

The front door eased open.

"Mom!" I called, jumping up and running to meet her, to warn her, before Detective Wyle caught her off guard. She tilted her head at me when she entered, frowning slightly. Mom was in the habit of dressing brightly during the day to contrast with her nightly attire, and today she wore old blue jeans with a rose-colored belt and a vivid pink tank top—but over it she wore her dark H&H Security coat. Very official looking. She yawned into her free hand as she glanced at me.

"We, uh, have a visitor," I said.

He was already at my side, leaning against the door frame and giving my mother a lazy smile.

"Entertaining kid you've got here, Mrs. Whitticomb. I'm thinking of recruiting her."

I could see the storm brewing behind Mom's eyes, and took a step backward.

"Miss. I never married," she corrected. "As I'm sure you know." She clenched a fist. "Audrey, how exactly have you been entertaining?"

"Um ... I gave Mickey a reading."

"I thought we were sticking with Wyle," he said.

"Mickey is less threatening," I told him. "My mom's a little vulnerable right now. She turns forty next month."

She sounded strangled. "Audrey. Room. Now."

Oh well. I already had a talk in store. I gave her a quick salute, then leaned in close to whisper. "Be careful, Mom. He's totally on to you."

Over the years, Mom had been interrogated by the police on a number of occasions. It was sort of inevitable, given her choice of careers. In the past, she'd always managed to explain away her activities with her connection to H&H Security. She even had a couple of friends on the force—or acquaintances, at any rate; Mom wasn't very big on friends. She tended to laugh off the idea that she'd be caught. Cops were far too pragmatic to believe in Morning Star, she told me. And maybe she was right. She'd never been arrested. She'd never been charged. Detective Wyle had been the first to even truly suspect her of anything.

"He's a pain in the ass," she'd told me, after the first time he'd questioned her. "But I can handle him."

Personally, I'd always thought that Mom rather liked being able to fool everyone. She didn't *have* to wear a costume, I'd argued once. It would be easier if she just saved the city in obscurity. Her response had been to tell me that Morning Star wasn't a costume, it was an identity. Part of who she was.

It hadn't begun that way. Not intentionally. It hadn't even been an outfit at first; it was just a bulky sweater with a star on it that some great-aunt had knitted for her one Christmas.

"I wore it ironically," Mom had told me. "And because I didn't care if I ruined it." She *had* ruined it, too. She'd thrown it away after it had become nothing more than a tattered, bloodstained rag; but by then, more than a few witnesses had seen a teenage vigilante running around wearing an eight-pointed star.

"And thus a legend was born," I'd joked.

That, apparently, had been the wrong thing to say. Mom had gone quiet and had never finished the story.

But that didn't mean she didn't enjoy playing with fire. I'd seen her snickering over newspaper articles that mentioned her alter ego a few too many times to think otherwise. I just hoped she was right and she could handle Detective Wyle. I felt a touch of apprehension. There had been no malice in him, but that didn't make him harmless.

An hour passed before he left. I slogged halfheartedly through my homework and watched the green numbers of my clock blink upward. Tink called to inform me that Greg, although not undead, was a terrible kisser, and she was gravely disappointed my reading had failed to reveal that.

I laughed, momentarily distracted. "Rejected him already? You work fast."

"What can I say? I know what I want."

"Too bad what you want changes by the hour."

"We can't all be Gideon, pining stupidly for the same girl for three years. That boy needs a good kick—"

I shushed her, listening to the movement below me. Downstairs, the hall door opened. Footsteps sounded in the entryway. I crossed to my window and shifted the blinds with my fingers. Outside, on the sidewalk, Detective Wyle shuffled toward the street. He turned, once, looking back at the house. Then he was gone.

Which meant—

"Audrey!" When my mother wanted to, she could really bellow. I supposed the superstrength extended to her lungs. "Down here, now!"

"Uh, I'll call you back. I have to go get yelled at," I told Tink, then hurried downstairs. Mom was in the sitting room, curled up on the sofa, drinking cocoa and appearing for all the world as though she couldn't actually rip both my arms off or dangle me upside down.

"You forgot a coaster," I said, when she set her mug on the table.

She rolled her eyes at me but dutifully slid one of the ceramic coasters beneath her cup. "We really should examine your priorities."

"Gram loved that table."

"Gram bought it at a garage sale for two dollars. Nice try distracting me, though. Since it didn't work, why don't you explain

41

to me why I just spent several minutes talking to Detective Wyle about my 'deeply intuitive' daughter."

"Deeply intuitive—without an ounce of common sense."

That was Leon.

I turned. I hadn't noticed him in the room—but then, it was possible he hadn't been there. He had this annoying habit of simply appearing, without bothering with nuisances like doors or asking permission. And though he was only three years older than me, he seemed to think being a Guardian meant he knew more about the world in general than I ever would.

I shot him a glare. He stood near the window, arms crossed, leaning back against the wall. Like Mom, Leon gave the illusion of being totally harmless. He was tall and broad-shouldered, but he was so skinny that most of his clothes just sort of hung on him. And he was tidy, clean-cut, the kind of guy you'd expect to see at some Ivy League college, taking eight classes a week and sucking up to professors, not smiting evildoers. He didn't like to go anywhere without a tie, and his white button-down shirts were always ironed. (I'd actually seen him iron them.) Sure, he looked good—I could admit that, just not to his face—but he didn't exactly look *dangerous*.

Of course, even if he'd wanted to appear moody and mysterious, the effect would've been ruined by the dusting of flour in his dark hair. Not to mention that he usually smelled like cake and frosting, and often appeared with cookies. You'd think that someone who had shown up in Minneapolis on a motorcycle with nothing but a backpack and half a cheese sandwich to his name might not want to criticize anyone else's life choices—but no. Leon was convinced he knew how to fix the world, starting with me. He didn't think I had any sense, common or otherwise. And since he appeared to be cookieless tonight, I wasn't feeling very forgiving.

I stepped toward him and gave him the sweetest smile I could manage. "We can't all be as perfect as you, Leon."

It took him a second. A little furrow appeared on his forehead —there was flour there, too—then he shrugged. "True. But that's no reason not to try."

"I hate doing things I'm not good at," I said. "Perfection will have to remain beyond my grasp. But, hey, lucky me, I've got you here to show me the error of my ways."

That actually seemed to annoy him. His frown settled into a glower. "You must have a brain in there somewhere. It's a shame you don't use it."

"God forbid I disagree with Almighty Leon."

Mom banged her mug on the table like a gavel. "As entertaining as it is listening to you two bicker, I'm still waiting on that explanation, Audrey."

I shrugged and turned back toward her. She'd forgotten the coaster again, but I decided to let it go, just this once. "That cop knows something," I said. "I wanted to see what I could find out."

"Did you get anything?"

"Um . . . he likes fly-fishing, and his favorite band is the Grateful Dead."

Mom sighed.

"And he knows about you. I'm not sure what he knows, or how—but I think he has some idea of your abilities."

"Another reason it was irresponsible of you to give him a reading," Leon interjected.

"I said he knows about *Mom*," I retorted. "You really think he's going to take a teenager telling fortunes seriously? How about this: if he calls asking for lottery numbers, I'll let you know."

"I'm more concerned about *you* not taking it seriously," Leon shot back. His eyes were fixed on me, and that disapproving slant to his mouth meant he wasn't done with whatever scolding he had in store. I decided to cut him off before he got the chance.

"How is this even any of your business? I hate to break it to you, Leon, but tagging along after Mom doesn't actually make you part of the family."

He went quiet for a moment. "I don't tag along."

I ought to have felt bad.

When it came down to it, we *were* pretty much the only family Leon had. He didn't talk much about his life before Minneapolis, but I knew his parents were dead, and so was the grandfather who had raised him. He didn't seem to have ties to anyone else in the Cities. Though he went to college, I don't think he had any friends. He took his life as Guardian so seriously, I doubted he had time for them.

He'd arrived three years ago, showing up at the house one summer evening in the blank heat of twilight. I remembered that clearly; it was only a few weeks after Gram had died. Mom and I had been sitting outside, eating Popsicles in the grass because the air-conditioning was broken and it was too hot to stay inside. And then Leon had appeared at the end of the drive, all puppy-eyed and starved-looking and earnest; and instead of returning him to whatever pound he'd surely escaped from, Mom had let him stay and be her sidekick. Or fellow Guardian. Or whatever.

At the time, I'd found it exciting—the way he'd appeared out of nowhere, on that night when the heat was so thick the moon was nothing but a smear in the sky above us. The way he'd walked slowly toward us, seeming nervous and confused and somehow vulnerable. How he'd introduced himself to my mother, his voice steady and strong, a confidence at odds with the wariness in his blue eyes. How he'd turned, then, and looked at me. He'd looked at me a long time, and there was a puzzled little smile on his face, an expression I didn't understand, but wanted to. And then he'd told us he knew our secrets. That he had secrets, too.

For the first few weeks, I'd idolized him. I'd followed him around, wanting to know everything about him—where he'd come from, why he'd come, how he'd known to find us. Back then, I actually thought he *was* perfect, with his dark hair that curled just slightly, that effortless way he moved. The gravity that never quite left his voice made everything seem important, even me. But before the month was out, he'd made it clear that he thought me nothing more than some bratty, clueless kid—and he'd been bossing his way around my life ever since.

So I didn't feel bad. Instead, I scowled and copied his stance.

Then my mother said, "Actually, Audrey, that's what I was meaning to talk to you about."

I was busy trying to outstare Leon, so it took a moment for that to sink in. I turned, giving her a blank look. "Huh?"

"We've been discussing it for some time now, and it really makes more sense for Leon to live here. With us."

"Funny," I said.

"I'm not joking. We have the room. And with everything going on—it's just safer this way." She broke off, turning toward the window. Leon straightened and lost his scowl. Outside, the drone of traffic and chatter of birds died away. The late sun flared through the panes, coloring the floor around us orange and red.

A sudden sharp awareness settled around me, not quite a Knowing. I glanced at them: my mother facing away, Leon silent and unreadable. Something unspoken had passed between them —one of those secret Guardian exchanges that never signaled anything good.

It's just safer this way.

I rubbed at my arms, feeling a sudden chill. "You two could not possibly be more ominous. What's going on?"

Mom gave me her standard answer: "Nothing you need to worry about."

An unsettling thought struck me. Strange that they'd brought this up today. It could be pure coincidence, but—"Does this have something to do with Kelly Stevens?"

Leon's gaze snapped toward me. "What do you know about that?"

"I know she's dead," I answered.

"This is about practicality," Mom cut in, giving Leon one of those quelling glances she usually reserved for me. "It just makes sense for Leon to be here when I'm out, so I don't have to worry about you being alone."

I didn't believe her for a second, but it was useless trying to pry information out of Mom when she was determined not to give it. She seemed to think that if she didn't tell me about the dangers she faced, I wouldn't notice the occasional bruise, or the dried blood on her clothing. She probably didn't realize I'd stocked every room in the house with first-aid kits.

Since she wasn't going to tell me anything, I tried a different tactic. "I'm a little past the age of needing a babysitter."

"As your conduct today clearly proves," Leon said.

I ignored him. "It'll be weird, Mom. As you two go to such pains to point out, keeping the secret is difficult enough without having a sidekick to explain away."

"A lot of people rent out rooms to college kids," Mom argued.

"But—"

She turned her quelling glance my way. "It's my decision, and I've made it."

My mind raced. Leon—*living with us*. How was I supposed to react to that? I didn't know. My thoughts wouldn't settle themselves, and I felt a strange, inexplicable surge of panic. Leon had turned away again, and I couldn't see his expression. He was one of the few people I'd never been able to read at all, not even with my Nav cards, and now I wondered what he was thinking.

I sighed. I felt scattered, out of sorts, but there didn't seem to be anything I could do. "When's he moving in?" I asked finally, trying to find out how much time I'd have to hide the really embarrassing things I'd left lying around the house, like romance novels and dirty laundry.

They exchanged a look.

"Pretty much now," Mom said.

I took a breath. "Right. How long did you say you were planning this?"

Another look.

"A while," Mom answered.

"And you waited until now to tell me."

"You won't even know I'm here," Leon said.

I almost laughed. "Right," I said. As though there was any possibility of *that* being true.

Mom and Leon took the early evening to move his belongings. Since Mom could probably carry everything in his apartment by herself, I didn't feel my presence was necessary. I went for a run.

I needed to clear my head. I kept thinking about Mom's words —*it's just safer this way*—and about what she wasn't telling me. Secrets. That hint of worry on her face that she struggled to hide. I thought back to my dream: the darkness of the city, the silence.

I thought about Kelly. Her twisted silver sandal. Her eyes closed, her face blue and marbled and dead.

And then I found myself at Gideon's.

It wasn't a surprise, really. Gideon only lived a mile or so away, and my legs were accustomed to taking me there. He opened the door before I could knock, giving me that lopsided grin of his.

"I had a feeling you'd show up," he said.

"What, now you're psychic too?"

"Say that a little louder."

I shrugged and followed him down the stairs to his room, then flopped onto his bed while he turned off his computer game. The two cats lounging on his pillows looked up at me irritably.

"How was your talk?" Gideon asked. A third cat began to slink out from under the bed, and he bent to catch it.

I groaned. "Sidekick Extraordinaire is moving in with us."

"Leon?"

"No, her other sidekick." I flipped over onto my stomach.

"And you're upset."

"Not...upset, exactly. Unnerved." It still wasn't anything I could put into words.

"Worried about having a man in the house?"

I rolled my eyes at that. "I wouldn't call Leon a man."

He grinned. "You are harsh on my gender today."

"So this is a male solidarity thing?"

"It won't be such a big deal," Gideon said. "Aren't you always complaining that he's there all the time anyway?"

"Exactly. He already treats me like the younger sister he never wanted—and if I wanted a brother, I'd hire you."

"What, do you really think he's going to tie your shoelaces together and put grasshoppers in your bed?"

"Okay, maybe I *wouldn't* hire you," I said, laughing. Gideon certainly had big-brother experience, though. His parents had been one of those couples that try for years to have a child, finally decide to adopt, and then promptly have three more children. As far as I could tell, all of his sisters worshipped him. I figured he was kidding about the grasshoppers. "But that doesn't make me any happier about this."

"Leon's not so bad."

Easy for him to say. For some reason I truly could not fathom, Gideon and Leon actually got along. "You just think he's cool because he can teleport."

"How is that *not* cool?"

Well, I had to give him that one. It wasn't as spectacular as, say, flying—but it did have a certain appeal.

I sighed. "At least he knows how to bake."

"What's really bothering you?"

"I don't know." I rolled to my side, dislodging one of the cats. Gideon's room was below ground level, but he had a window well, and the blue of twilight drifted in. "There's something going on," I said. "Mom won't talk about it, of course—but I think something's happening. I'm worried about her."

"Your mom knows how to take care of herself."

I knew that. She didn't need protecting. She was strong, and not just physically. She'd had to be strong.

But something was out there. Something I felt in more ways than just Knowing.

And it seemed, for just a moment, in the thready blue light that moved across the floor, that it was calling to me.

The night Gram had given me my Nav cards, she came into my room and sat on the floor, spreading the cards face up before her. The memory was always clear in my mind: it had been one of those dark midwinter nights when the frost on my window was so thick I couldn't see out and the wind was so loud it didn't rattle so much as roar. Gram loved nights like that. The best time for stories, she always said, and she lived to tell stories.

"Audrey, sweeting," she'd said, beckoning me toward her. "I have something for you."

I knew the cards. We'd used them before, when I was first learning about my Knowing. I hesitated, touching them lightly, feeling the smooth surfaces against my fingertips.

Gram smiled. "These are yours. They were given to me when I was a young girl, and now I'm giving them to you."

"You don't need them?"

"Not anymore. Not for many years. Someday, you won't, either. For now, they'll teach you. Your mother has no real talent for Knowing, and my gift isn't as strong as yours—they're meant for you. Now, listen. I'm going to tell you a secret." She gestured toward the cards. As I watched, she slowly flipped each of them over, so that only their backs were showing. All except one.

Card twenty-six. The Triple Knot. The knot image was larger on the front than the back, but otherwise the card might have simply been double-sided.

She lifted the card and placed it in my hands, closing her fingers over mine. "Remember this one," she said. "This is the Astral Circle."

I'd known about the Circle already. It was another one of Gram's stories, something she told me when we first moved to Minneapolis. She'd spoken to me of a power that dwelled unseen within the heart of the city. You will know it, she'd told me. You will feel it. It will call to you.

She was right.

I'd never been to Minneapolis before. Gram and Mom had lived here most of their lives, but they'd headed north before I was born, choosing a small, sleepy town dotted with lakes and evergreens. Until we moved, I'd never been farther south than St. Cloud—but I felt the difference as soon as we approached the Cities, even before the skyline appeared and the highways widened around us. A sudden warmth filled me—vibrant, pulsing, a sense so strong and sharp that for a moment, I couldn't draw breath.

But when we arrived in Minneapolis, I was disappointed.

"I don't see any circles," I'd complained.

Gram patted my hand gently. "That doesn't mean it's not here."

As Gram told it, the Astral Circle wasn't physical; it wasn't something we could hold or touch. It was visible only on rare occasions, appearing as a faint glow near the skyline, like the gleam of the northern lights. It couldn't be seen by everyone, she said—and for the past eight years, it hadn't been seen by *anyone*. Its light had gone out.

"There is energy within the Circle," Gram had explained. Not the type used to heat houses or turn on appliances, but energy all the same, urgent and wild. "But its power has diminished. It's been years now since the Circle went dark. Some even believe it to be dead."

It didn't feel dead to me. I sensed it like a hum against my skin, something whispered just out of hearing. "So, it's broken?"

"You might say that. Or sleeping, maybe." For a moment, she'd looked a little sad—but she continued her explanation. "The Circles are ancient and powerful, but very rare. There are only a few of them now, scattered across the world. One of them is here."

"Is that why we moved?" I'd asked. "The Circle?"

"Yes. Because it is a part of us. A part of you. And we have been away from it far too long."

So when she handed me the card, I didn't ask about the Circle. I knew. But I didn't understand what any of this had to do with the Triple Knot—and told her as much.

She gave a wheezy sort of laugh. "This is its symbol. It's about connection. Power woven around us. The same power that lives in you, that lives in your mother and all Guardians."

"There are other Guardians?" That was the first I'd heard of it. To hear Mom talk, the superhero club was extremely exclusive. She wouldn't even entertain thought of my following in her footsteps.

"Well, of course," Gram had answered. "But none quite like your mother."

Since that time, the only other Guardian I'd met was Leon, but I often wondered. I wondered where these other Guardians were—*who* they were. I wondered if they spent long nights and empty dark hours moving in silence through the streets, keeping the city safe. I wondered if they knew about us.

And I wondered about the triple knot worn by Iris St. Croix.

It could have been a coincidence. It probably was; that's what I told myself during school the rest of the week as I watched for her in the halls, trying to get another glimpse of the necklace at her throat. It likely meant nothing. It was just a symbol, after all, and not an uncommon one. She could've picked it up for five dollars at some junk-jewelry store. Except for that shiver of Knowing I'd had, I wouldn't have noticed it at all. And though I kept looking, I didn't catch sight of her.

The school was still reeling from the news of Kelly's death. It was all anyone wanted to talk about. We'd seen the television reports: the statement made by her parents, the pain haunting their eyes; the mayor offering his sympathies; promises that an investigation was ongoing, but no suspects could be named. Speculation was rampant. The police hadn't released the exact manner of her death, and the more ghoulish members of the student body spread rumors that Kelly had been mutilated in some terrible way. Teachers relaxed homework assignments for the week. The school set up counseling and memorials. A sheet was placed on the cafeteria wall for students to write out their condolences and sign their names. All of it took on an eerie familiarity. Kelly hadn't been the first student to die this year: a sophomore girl had been killed in a car crash the first week of school.

"It's a bad year for Whitman," Gideon remarked after we added our signatures to the wall.

"This is way too depressing," Tink said. "Let's talk about something else." That was Tink's style. According to her, the best way to deal with anything upsetting was to pretend it didn't exist. By the end of school on Friday, all she would talk about was our plan to meet at the Drought and Deluge. "Eight thirty," she told us. "Don't forget!"

At home that night, I ate leftover lasagna and sat on the couch watching the news. The anchor said our heat wave was nearly over, that repairs on some building were under way, and there was no progress in the Stevens case. Mom frowned at the television before she left for the evening, then told me not to stay out too late.

"Ditto," I called after her. "Superheroes need sleep too." She'd been busier than usual the past week, and she looked weary—but her only response was an exasperated sigh and a shake of the head.

I listened to the door shut, then headed to the kitchen to rinse my plate. Around me, the house sat silent and empty.

Despite his assertions to the contrary, I'd noticed Leon's presence in my home. Although he went out nights like my mother, he tended to leave later and come home earlier. He had an actual job and school to deal with, so he couldn't keep her hours. That meant he was around for dinner, and around for breakfast, and generally just *around*.

But that night I hadn't seen him.

I looked at the time. It was past seven thirty. Gideon was my ride, and I'd told him I'd be at his house at eight, which meant I should probably hurry.

I walked upstairs to my room and changed shirts. My hair—unruly even on the best of days—had begun to work loose from its ponytail and needed to be fixed. Whatever I did with my face, Tink was sure to change by pulling me into the bathroom and dragging out her makeup bag, so I didn't bother with anything more than a thin layer of lipstick. I looked pale. My summer tan had faded, leaving only a light dusting of freckles on the bridge of my nose. It couldn't be helped, I supposed. I tossed my phone into my bag and headed back downstairs.

I was almost out the door when, without warning, Leon appeared in front of me.

I dropped my bag. A startled scream lodged itself somewhere in my lungs and emerged as a gurgle. I clapped a hand to my chest, trying to gasp in breath.

"*God*, Leon! If you're going to do that in the house, could you at least say *BAMF!* or something? I'm too young for a heart attack."

My comic book reference was clearly lost on him. He just stood there, looking all innocent and confused. "Did I scare you?"

"Like you didn't do that on purpose." I resisted the urge to hit him. I'd tried that once; it hurt. He was a lot more solid than he looked. "And you say *I'm* immature."

His arm slid out in front of me as I tried to push past him, blocking my path to the door. He stood looking down, giving me his best surly-sidekick glower.

I wondered where he'd come from. Since he didn't feel the need to enter the house in a conventional manner, he could've returned without my knowing. He was dressed as he normally was: white shirt, dark slacks, tie, and he smelled like soap, not frosting, which meant he was once again lacking in baked goods. I glowered back up at him. "Did you need something?"

He didn't move. "Where are you going?"

"To plot your downfall," I snapped. I bent to retrieve my bag and ducked beneath his arm. It wasn't the most dignified exit, but it worked. I turned to face him once I reached the door. "Not that it's any of your business, but I'm meeting my friends at the Drought and Deluge. Mom knows."

"The Drought and Deluge," he repeated, frowning. "Lucy knows about this?"

Well. Sort of. She knew I was going out, at least. "Didn't I just say that?" When he didn't answer, I added, "I've been there before. They serve ginger ale and greasy mozzarella sticks. It's not exactly a den of sin." He went right on frowning. I might not have been able to get a sense of him with my Knowing, but that was easy to read: he was worried about *something*. "All right, now you're freaking me out. What's going on?"

"I just don't think you should go alone," he hedged.

"I'm not going alone," I said, turning as I reached for the door-knob. "I'm going with my friends. Problem solved."

"I think I should accompany you."

My mouth actually dropped open at that. I spun back around. "Shouldn't you be out with Mom? Patrolling or whatever it is you Guardians do?"

"Not tonight."

"Studying, maybe?" Not that I'd ever seen him open a text-book. He was probably one of those obnoxious people who just remembers everything. "Seriously, exciting as the prospect of having my very own sidekick is, don't you have some crime to fight? Homework to do? Pastries to bake?"

That annoyed him enough that he scowled at me. "This may astonish you, but, yes, I can think of any number of things I'd rather do than spend the night watching you and your friends grind to embarrassing music."

"Great," I gritted out. "Then go do them."

It was no use. Leon had gotten a particularly stubborn look on his face. Mom must have instructed him to play babysitter, and he was nothing if not dutiful. He took a step toward me and said, "I'll drive you."

I'd been on Leon's motorcycle before and had spent every moment of it fearing for my life, so I wasn't sure why he thought that was an incentive. "I'm not taking a ride on your deathmobile. That thing is beyond its last legs. Or wheels. Or whatever."

"I wouldn't let you ride with me if it wasn't safe," he said, looking a little wounded.

Well, that was probably true. He did have a safety fixation.

I stuck a hand on my hip. "Am I being punished for something?" I asked. Unfortunately, that only made him look *more* wounded. I sighed. He was going to use his Hungry Puppy eyes on me, I could tell. And that was definitely a losing battle. "Okay, you can come with me—but not dressed like that." I leaned forward, flipped up his collar, and loosened his tie. "This? This goes. And you are not wearing... any of this, actually. Go change." I paused, considering. "You do have other clothing, right?"

He furrowed his brow. "It's not a crime to dress well."

"It is at the Drought and Deluge," I replied. "You realize that you'll be hanging out with a bunch of high school students, right?"

"I'm not going to be *hanging out*."

"What are you going to do, lurk in a corner and scowl?" Actually, it was probably best not to give him any ideas. Before he could respond, I said, "Whatever you're doing, you're still not doing it dressed like that. Go change while I text Gideon. I promise not to run off before you get back."

Leon and I arrived late.

Friday evening traffic was a nightmare, and Leon appeared to have taken a page from the Book of Gideon and refused to drive any faster than five miles below the speed limit. Which was probably a good thing, considering his motorcycle had made several discouraging noises before he finally got it to start.

To my surprise, I enjoyed the ride. Leon was much easier to deal with when he wasn't talking. And I knew he was right: I could trust that he wouldn't let anything happen to me. After a while, I was able to just lean against him and watch the lights of the skyline rise above us. I breathed in, listening to the churn of the engine, the surge of traffic, the rush of cool air that billowed around me.

I just hoped Leon wouldn't mention how tightly I'd clung to him every time we turned a corner.

Once we parked, I slid off and handed him my helmet. "You could've just teleported us," I said, before he could get a word in. I took a cautious step forward; motorcycles made me a little wobbly.

"Into a parking ramp full of cars and cameras." He placed his hand on my shoulder, steadying me.

"To the Drought and Deluge," I suggested.

"A building full of people."

"Some place out of the way. Like . . . I don't know, the janitor closet."

He raised an eyebrow.

"Okay. Stupid idea. But you're paying for parking."

Gideon saw us as soon as we entered the club, and stood waving us toward the table where he sat with Tink. Tink was difficult to miss: she wore a bright red dress and appeared to have sprayed something sparkly over her entire body. Either that or she'd rolled in glitter. She glanced toward me, saw Leon, and even across the room I could see her eyebrows just about shoot up into her hair.

"You actually enjoy this place?" Leon asked. He'd clamped a hand on my shoulder again, which meant the odds of losing him in the throng weren't good.

"Not really your style?" I asked. Or rather shouted. We had to push our way through crowding bodies, and it was not a place for inside voices. "You could've stayed home."

"And missed this sweaty, hormone-infested experience?"

The Drought and Deluge was usually filled with groping teenage boys, and more often than not I had to be dragged to it by Tink's pestering—but I felt protective of it nonetheless. I made a face at Leon.

"What?" he asked.

I didn't answer. By that time, we'd reached the table, and Tink was giving me a displeased little frown. "Hello, Audrey...plus one," she said.

Officially, Leon was a *friend of the family*—at least, that was how we explained him whenever he encountered one of my friends. Unlike Gideon, Tink wasn't much of a fan. That surprised me, since Leon was reasonably attractive and male; but as far as I knew, she'd never even tried to make a conquest of him. Maybe it was those disapproving glares he liked to give.

"Leon's doing a study on high schoolers in social settings for one of his college classes," I said. "He's here to observe. Just ignore him. That's my plan."

Gideon, of course, gave another cheery wave and said, "Hey, Leon."

Leon didn't seem pleased by my explanation. He mumbled an excuse about how he'd actually planned to meet someone here, and disappeared into the crowd.

I turned my attention back to my friends. "It's just us?" Tink had invited a few others, but she'd really only perfected the art of bending Gideon and me to her will.

"Kit had plans and Erica ditched," Tink said, standing and tugging at my hand. "Okay, time to fix you up. Hold down the fort, Gideon, this may take a while."

And, predictably, I was hauled off to the ladies' room.

"This room is nasty tonight," Tink said, wetting a paper towel and wiping the counter before setting her bag down.

"It's always nasty."

"Nastier, then."

"You're in a strange mood," I remarked. "If you're angry about Leon, it's really not my fault."

"I'm not angry. I just don't like the crowd tonight."

The crowd didn't seem any different to me, but I shrugged.

Tink grabbed my chin, turning my face from side to side. When she was through with me, I supposed I'd have enough glitter on me that they'd be able to cut half the lights to save on electricity.

"Close your eyes. And quit moving around so much," she commanded. "What happened to your hair?"

"I had a helmet on," I responded, lifting a hand to tuck away a few stray curls. "It's not that bad. Are you almost done? If you make me look like a handmade Christmas ornament, I swear I'm never speaking to you again."

"Shush. I am making the world a better place—one pale, freckly girl at a time. Although I really should be teaching you. Give a man a fish, and all that." After a few minutes, she paused, turned me toward the mirror, and made a *ta-da* sort of noise. "All done!"

"I am transformed," I said. "I sparkle like a fairy princess."

In truth, it wasn't that bad. Tink knew what she was doing, even if she had a tendency to go overboard. Thankfully, the only dousing of shimmer powder had occurred on my neck and hair.

"A pretty, pretty princess," Tink agreed. "With helmet hair. That, alas, you will have to live with, for my talents lie elsewhere. And I do believe you're going to have to dance with me. Be my date, pretty princess?"

"You're such a romantic, Tink. I always wanted to get asked out in a bathroom."

She rolled her eyes at me, putting her fairy instruments back in their bag. "I'm serious. Two girls dancing. It's hot. Guys look."

"Which is clearly the main objective of our lives."

A wicked glint came into her eyes. "Easy for you to say. You brought your own."

It took me a second to catch her meaning. Then I snorted. "That's right. My very own tall, dark, and uptight babysitter."

"Still a guy."

Well, that part was undeniable. "But I didn't *bring* him—"

She grinned, grabbing my wrist and dragging me toward the door. "Perfect. So you're free to be my date, then!"

"That was sneaky," I complained, laughing. I didn't know what sort of guy Tink planned to meet here, since most of them just wanted to rub up against you on the dance floor, but her enthusiasm was difficult to resist. "All right, I'll dance with you. But you try to feel me up, and we're having a talk."

She paused, tapping a finger against her mouth. "I *think* I can restrain myself."

"Come on, then," I said, grinning back at her. "Let's go grind to embarrassing music."

"What?"

"Never mind."

I looped my arm in hers and we headed out the door.

On the dance floor, I did my best not to bump into anyone. The room was dim and crowded, a haze of blurred faces and flickering lights. Briefly, I caught Leon's gaze from the edge of the floor, but I turned away before I could see the critical stare he was certain to have fixed on me. Instead, I focused on the motion around me. Music and murmurs pulsed. Tink was so busy lifting her arms and tossing her head, I was afraid she'd get whiplash.

I might have felt bad about abandoning Gideon to his own devices, but as soon as Tink and I left the table, he'd found some girl eager to gain his attention. He was dancing with her not far from us—a tall girl in a dark blue dress. I felt sorry for her, and not just because Gideon was an even worse dancer than I was. Whoever she was, she'd be smiled at and maybe flirted with, then forgotten an hour later when his mind wandered back to Brooke Oliver.

"Can we be done yet?" I asked Tink, shouting to be heard

above the crowd. I was beginning to feel a little claustrophobic. My abilities weren't always a gift: with so many bodies around us, Knowing had begun to creep into my consciousness, and I was once again having difficulty blocking it. I felt off balance. My senses were skewed, my frequencies scrambled. I inched toward the back of the room, dropping a hand on Tink's shoulder to drag her with me. She shook her head, tossed me a grin, and turned toward the flow of the crowd. The light sparked along the glitter in her hair.

When the music slowed, I stepped away, pushing through the throng toward our table. Gideon had already retreated there. I took a sip of his ginger ale and sat, peering past the dance floor to the shadow of tables and bar. In corners, the light was thin and dusty. I wondered where Leon had disappeared to.

The girl Gideon had danced with was sitting at a table not far from us. Away from the whirl of the dance floor, I could see her clearly. Her hair was black and thick, and tumbled toward her slim hips. When she turned toward us, I saw her huge dark eyes pinned on Gideon. She looked like she'd stepped out of a movie.

I nodded to Gideon. "She's really pretty," I said.

He grinned, quirking an eyebrow. "Jealous?"

"Desperately." I leaned forward to drape myself across him. "You know how I yearn for you. I bet I could take her, though. That's the real reason I'm in martial arts—to scare away your potential girlfriends."

He laughed, prying himself loose, and nudged me back to

my seat. Then he tucked his hands behind his head and said, "I've always wanted girls fighting over me."

"Hey, I already fought Hannah Starkey for you. Remember? Second grade?" *I* remembered. Hannah had developed a crush on Gideon and had apparently never learned about boundaries. She'd pulled down his pants at recess.

I'd pushed her off the slide.

"Ah, yes. Your early life of crime. How could I forget?"

It had been something of an ordeal. The school had wanted to put me in counseling. Mom put me in martial arts, instead. To learn discipline and self-control, she said. I'd been in the classes—a mixture of judo, jujitsu, and kung fu—ever since, but though Gideon's parents had signed him up as well, he hadn't stuck with it.

Gram, of course, had found the Hannah incident hilarious.

"It worked, didn't it?" A little too well, even. Not only had Hannah never bothered Gideon again, for years she'd taken to running at the sight of us.

"Too bad you didn't get to her *before* she kissed me at the water fountain."

"Some battles, you have to fight yourself."

Gideon looked pained. "You wouldn't say that if you'd had to kiss her. She had terrible breath."

I laughed. Around us, the music picked up again, and we settled in to people-watch—which we were both much better at than dancing. Gideon's girl sent one final, longing look in his direction, then turned and got up to dance with someone else. Her dark hair made a glossy wave down her back. I decided not to pester him about it. Leave it to Gideon to find the most impossibly gorgeous girl in the room and then shrug her aside. I hoped he'd find the courage to ask Brooke out some time this century, but it seemed unlikely. Tink had once threatened to do it for him, and he'd stopped speaking to her for a week.

I leaned back in my chair, gazing out into the crowd. I didn't recognize most of the people around us, but a blond girl we'd met during our last visit to the Drought and Deluge stopped by the table to chat. Since I couldn't remember her name, I nodded along to her conversation and let Gideon occupy her. After a while, I began to tune them out, letting my eyes wander. On the dance floor, the low lights skimmed across faces and the movement of bodies, catching at colors, here and there a slight shimmer—

A sudden awareness rippled through me, an internal alarm that made my body snap. Something was wrong, in a way I hadn't felt since that foggy, unforgotten morning when I'd realized Gram had died.

Gideon and the nameless girl stopped talking and stared at me. "Audrey?"

My Knowings didn't often happen like this, but when they did, I paid attention. I paused. Focused. Listened. For just a second, the room around me went very still. I heard nothing, not even my own breath. Then, as the motion and noise and light rushed back, my frequencies abruptly cleared.

The knowledge was intense, visceral. Something about the way the light flickered. Something about that flash of color, that glimmer. I looked around the room dizzily. And then it struck me: where was Tink?

I knew it then. I should—

Go to her.

Find her.

Help her.

"Gideon—have you seen Tink?"

He shook his head. I heard him say my name, a question on his lips. I didn't answer. I hadn't noticed myself rise, but suddenly I was pushing through the crowd, searching. She couldn't be that difficult to find. Short or not, a blond pixie in a bright red dress would stand out.

Suddenly, everything was sharp and clear: the bar, where a waitress in a tight T-shirt was snapping her gum; bouncers looking bored and scowling; the dark corners where smuggled-in beer was being drunk from plastic cups. All of this registered, settling into my senses.

And there, through the crowd: a flash of red departing.

"Tink!"

She rounded a corner. I saw the edge of her dress, a glimpse of blond hair, the light catching—and she was gone.

"Tink!"

I pushed forward. She'd vanished at the other end of the building, and the jostling, laughing throng stood between us. I moved through an obstacle course of limbs and tables and chairs. The music pulsed, a song that kept a frantic beat with my unsteady nerves. Urgency hummed in my veins. I had to reach her.

I heard a voice calling my name, but I didn't stop. I stumbled against someone, muttered an apology, hurried onward. Dread clawed at me.

I rounded the corner where Tink had gone, and found nothing. Sudden stillness. An empty hallway arcing to the left. A light flickered overhead, across scuffed linoleum and faded green paint. Nearby, a janitor cart had been left unattended, mop handle jutting outward. There was a door marked EMPLOYEES ONLY, but I dismissed that. Beyond, a neon sign with an arrow said EXIT. Tink had gone into the alley.

I ran.

This part of the Drought and Deluge was new to me, darker and dirtier. It was colored differently, like I'd crossed a threshold into a separate world. My footsteps sounded unnaturally loud, and there was a faint smell of bleach in the air. I pressed my hands to the exit door and stepped out into the alley.

Cool air rushed toward me.

The world was blue, shadowed and dim with the fall of night. At first there were only walls and pavement, the dark brick of the buildings adjacent to the club, and, somewhere nearby, the clamor of downtown traffic.

Then I saw them.

A man bent toward the ground, crouching, half-turned from

me. I couldn't see his face. But I saw the object his hands moved over: one small, slender foot, the knot of an ankle, the curve of a leg. Red fabric in his hands. Tink.

He stood, pulling Tink up with him. Her legs dangled over his arm. In the light spilling out from the open door, I could see the blood that rolled down over her feet, dripping to the ground beneath her. It wasn't a lot of blood, but the sight of it sent a shock through me. I couldn't tell how badly she was hurt. With her face tucked against his shoulder, I couldn't see if she was conscious.

The man turned. I didn't recognize him. In my panicked state, I registered only disconnected features: tall frame, sandy hair, greenish eyes. I couldn't guess his age—maybe somewhere past twenty. His shirt bore the logo of the Drought and Deluge. A troubled frown creased his brow, but smoothed as he looked at me.

"Friend of yours?" he asked, with just the slightest trace of an accent. His voice was calm, easy, but I didn't trust it. Though a smile tugged at his lips, his eyes felt distant. "Or did the sweet night air draw you out here, as well?"

There was an edge to his words, a strange emphasis that I didn't understand. Warily, I glanced beyond him. Save for the three of us, the alley was deserted. I wondered if anyone would hear me if I screamed.

Somehow, I found my voice. It trembled, but it was loud, echoing out into the darkness. "Let her go."

He chuckled—a rich, low sound in the stillness around us.

"I'm afraid you've got the wrong idea." His arms twitched, drawing Tink closer to him. Her head rested loosely against his shoulder, but now I saw her face. Her eyes were closed, her lips slightly parted, her face ashen. Worry gnawed at me. She seemed so small there, thin and fragile, and the night was very dark.

"What did you do to her?" I gripped the edge of the door, trying to ignore the way my hands shook.

"I came out for a smoke," the man said. "She's terribly lucky I did."

Then Leon was at my side. "Audrey," he said, and touched my shoulder.

I'd never been so glad to hear his voice. "It's Tink," I whispered.

"Hey, I'm just here to help," the man said, shifting back as Leon took a step toward him. For a moment, they looked at each other without speaking. My lungs felt heavy, my breathing labored. Everything around me was gritty, but clear. I smelled garbage and blood and something acrid like burned plastic.

The man moved forward and transferred Tink into Leon's arms. I watched her slide between them as though she were weightless, her blood inking both of their shirts. Her head rolled back, but she was only unconscious. In the light from the Drought and Deluge, I saw the untroubled rise and fall of her chest.

"Is she all right?" I asked. I hadn't moved. Something about the alley felt off: a quality to the darkness, as though the night had grown edges.

The man gave me a long, measuring look, and a slow smile spread across his face. "Don't fret, angel," he said as he strode past me. "She seems ... mostly intact."

"Get out of here," Leon growled.

With a shrug, the man vanished into the corridor behind us.

Leon turned toward me, Tink cradled in his arms. I rushed forward, trying to remember what I'd been taught in martial arts about first aid. Airway, I thought. Airway came first. But she seemed to be breathing easily enough.

"I'll take care of her," Leon was saying. "Go back inside. Find Gideon. Have him take you directly home. Are you listening? Directly home."

I shook my head, hardly hearing him. "I'm staying. Or— should we go to the ER?"

"You're going home," he repeated, his voice quiet but unyielding. "Don't fight me on this."

Incredulous, I stared up at him. "Don't *fight* you? My friend is unconscious, bleeding in an alley, and you expect me to just abandon her?"

"Do you want to stand here arguing, or do you want me to help her?"

I balled my hands into fists. "I ..."

"She's going to be fine. I'm going to take care of her. But I need you to go. Home."

Anger warred with concern. I hated the idea of leaving her— but I didn't know how to help; I didn't know what to do. I felt shaken, dazed. My Knowing had faded. The urgency and alarm that had drawn me outside was now only an echo, but the apprehension remained, a touch of fear crawling up and down my skin, a quiet terror that Tink *wasn't* all right, that something horrible had happened to her—was *still* happening. I hesitated, looking down at the darkness that gathered beneath my feet.

"*Go,*" Leon said.

My resolve broke. With a final glance at Tink, I turned away and headed back into the club.

Gideon offered to stay with me until Leon arrived with news, but I wanted to be alone. I wanted to think. I'd tried to explain what had happened—my Knowing, the alley, the blood on Tink's ankles—but I wasn't even certain myself.

"You think someone hurt her?" Gideon asked, as his car idled in my driveway.

"I don't know," I admitted, remembering the strange man with the Drought and Deluge shirt. Something hadn't seemed quite right about him. "She wasn't gone very long."

"And you're sure you don't want me to hang out?"

"I'm sure. I'll call you later."

Inside, in the big emptiness of my house, I listened to the silence.

The experience had shaken me in a way I couldn't put into words. I still felt unease in my stomach, a flutter of nausea. I turned on the lights in the kitchen and stood in the yellow glare.

I didn't know what had happened.

Tink had been dancing with me, moving in the crowd, all energy and motion. And then she'd been gone.

Or rather: I'd left her.

I shook away the thought and sat, waiting for Leon. It was too early for my mother to come home, and I thought of her out there, in the blur of night and traffic and whatever lay beneath the swirl of city lights.

Once again, Leon didn't bother with the door. He just appeared in front of me in the kitchen, face somber, arms crossed. I blinked up at him. Though he assured me Tink was all right, my eyes drifted to the stain on his arm where her blood had dried on his shirt.

"Did she say what happened?" I asked, shifting my gaze. The sight of blood wasn't uncommon in my household, but that stain bothered me. Twin smears, small but vivid. I swallowed thickly.

Leon's words drew my attention back to him. "Nothing happened," he said. "She fainted." His tone was cool, clipped, and for a moment I simply looked at him, confused.

"She...fainted," I repeated.

"That's what she told me. She says she doesn't remember much."

"And what, she just spontaneously started bleeding?"

"There was broken glass in the alley. I think she cut herself when she fell."

Wounds on her ankles, I thought. A slash of red. A chill ran through me. "No," I answered, shaking my head. "Something happened out there. I felt—*something*."

He snorted. "Felt the need to run out into an alley at night without telling anyone where you were going."

Trust Leon to turn this around on me. "Tink was in trouble."

"Then you should've found me." He paused, and for the briefest of moments, something I couldn't name crossed his face. It might have been concern, or doubt, or maybe just weariness; I wasn't certain. Then it was gone. His eyes narrowed. "You don't go there. Ever again."

That got my hackles up. I knew I should just let it go. I should thank him for helping Tink, at the very least. I owed him that much. Instead, I met him glare for glare and demanded, "Don't you ever get tired of issuing commands?"

He didn't hesitate. "More than you know."

"Then maybe you should stop."

"And maybe you should start thinking. What if she *had* been in trouble? What could you have done?" I opened my mouth to protest, but he continued before I could speak. His expression was grim, his eyes dark and focused. "We don't always get to choose what happens to us, Audrey. Life isn't a game just because you treat it like one."

His tone sent a shiver down me. There was definitely more going on here than he would admit. "You told me she fainted," I pointed out. "You said nothing happened."

"That doesn't mean it couldn't have."

And with that, he vanished, leaving behind nothing but empty air.

I stared into the space where he'd been. When he didn't reappear, I let out a little growl of frustration and stalked out of the kitchen.

I considered hunting him down. He lived in our house now; he couldn't avoid me for long. But I didn't think he'd be any more forthcoming if I pressed the issue. Instead, I went up to my room and sat on my bed, my legs drawn up against me. I closed my eyes, going back over the evening in my mind, detail by detail. Tink pulling me into the ladies' restroom. The smell of the makeup she'd applied, the touch of the brush on my cheek. Laughing our way to the dance floor. And then the alley: her red dress and the cuts on her ankles.

I don't know when I fell asleep, but when I dreamed, I dreamed of Tink.

She stood on the dance floor, alone. It was hot, everything close and confining. She needed space, needed to clear her head. She would go, she told herself; just step outside. She would taste the sweet night air. She would only leave for a moment—

Someone in the darkness. Watching.

A sharp rush of wind. The flash of her dress as she turned. The curve of her throat in the moonlight. It had brought her out here. It had been waiting. It had—

It.

I woke panting, staring out into the half-dark of my room,

where starlight pushed through the blinds. I pulled the blankets tight against me and listened to traffic moving outside. My breath felt sticky, incapable of leaving my lungs. Because it hadn't just been Tink. In the last flickering colors and flashes of the dream, I had seen something else.

The pale, bloodless face of Kelly Stevens.

8

When I called Tink the following afternoon, she repeated what Leon had told me, insisting that she'd only fainted. It was probably the heat, she said. She'd felt crowded and dizzy and went outside for fresh air.

"I can't remember a whole lot about it," she said.

"What about your ankles?" I asked. "You fainted and just woke up with stigmata?"

"Yeah, you're hysterical. Thanks for the sympathy," she grumbled.

"I'm sympathetic! I'm just worried about you," I said. My dream had been troubling me, that sense of something waiting. Watching.

It could have meant nothing. It could have just been a nightmare, conjured up by my anxiety and the shock of the evening. But I didn't believe that. I hadn't forgotten Leon's words, or the frantic, frightening surge of Knowing that had sent me into the alley.

Tink sighed. "I think I landed on a beer bottle. I'm lucky I'm not still digging out glass."

Exactly as Leon had said. Somehow, that didn't reassure me. But I didn't know how to press the matter without explaining about my Knowing, and when I asked about the man who'd found her, she sounded genuinely confused.

"I thought *you* found me," she said. "Can we please stop talking about this? I'm traumatized enough, and what's worse, I'm *sick*. I feel terrible. I might even be dying."

As it turned out, she had the flu. Or possibly bronchitis—she wasn't certain. She stayed home from school the entire week and spent her days wrapped up in blankets, eating chicken soup and watching soap operas.

The next time I called, she could barely croak out her words.

"You really do sound like death," I told her.

She coughed into the phone. "I'm just bummed I have to miss the Halloween party at the Drought and Deluge."

"Maybe you could still come to Gideon's party," I suggested. "You won't even need a costume. Just start coughing and call yourself The Plague."

"I can't do that, either," she sighed. "Mom's still pretty upset about last Friday. She's not letting me out of the apartment. And before you ask me again, it was *really* nothing. I got light-headed, that's all."

I still wasn't reassured. Once Mom had heard about what happened, she'd forbidden me from ever returning to the Drought and Deluge. Which meant, whatever had happened to Tink, it wasn't as simple as fainting.

Not that anyone would tell me. Mom insisted I shouldn't worry, and Leon refused to talk about it. Whenever I tried to bring it up, he told me to let it go, and then conveniently found somewhere else to be.

But the thought wouldn't leave me.

"If Tink isn't upset about it, I'm not sure why you are," Gideon told me on Wednesday night. I'd once again invaded his home, since Mom and Leon had both left before dinner, and Gideon had offered me spaghetti. If there was one thing I appreciated about the Belmonte family, it was their food. I had no idea how Gideon was so thin.

"She wouldn't talk about it if it did upset her," I said. "You know how she is."

"Tink the turtle," he said, nodding.

"I think you mean ostrich."

"Turtle sounds better." He lowered his voice, even though we were in his room and all three Belmonte sisters were safely ensconced upstairs playing video games. "Is this something you know, or something you *Know*?"

"It's just a feeling," I hedged. I wasn't certain myself.

"You said your feelings aren't always right."

I didn't answer. Gram had always reminded me of that, too.

Knowings could be wrong, she said—or at least our interpretations of them. She would tell me to focus, to feel, to listen to what my senses were trying to teach me. It was all there, waiting, she'd say.

But I hadn't been able to sort out my senses. I was missing some piece.

My gaze drifted to the window well, where the edge of darkness crept in. The window was open, and the cool air brought with it the smell of rain and crushed leaves. I thought of Tink lying in the alley, the trail of blood that wound down her skin. Maybe it wasn't really a Knowing after all—just the memory of one. My mind playing tricks on me.

"You're right," I finally said, turning away from the window. "I should probably just forget it."

I didn't forget it.

It wasn't my fault. I tried to set my uneasiness aside. I concentrated on other things, like the test coming up in chemistry, and the fact that I'd scheduled my next driver's exam and I still couldn't corner back.

But at school, Tink's absence left a gap. Someone would mention her, and my thoughts would drift. I'd recall the scent of bleach, the silence in the alley, that tremor of fear in my lungs. So I didn't forget—I was just quieter about it.

Then, during precalc on Thursday, Mr. Alvarez asked me to stay after class.

I hadn't been paying attention. I'd been thinking about Gram, what she might have done in this situation. Her Knowing hadn't been as strong as mine, but she'd been able to focus it better.

Of course, she also didn't need to deal with irritable math teachers. I watched with dread as the rest of the class filed out.

"Torture by mathematics should be a felony," I grumbled to my friend Erica, who shot me a consoling look as she darted away from line of fire.

Apparently, Mr. Alvarez had heard me. Seated at his desk, he paused with his coffee cup raised halfway to his lips. "It would be a lot less painful if you just did your homework." He took a sip, then set his mug down on a stack of papers. "You're a smart girl. You simply lack patience. Not liking something doesn't mean you're not any good at it. But that's not what I wanted to talk to you about."

I waited. Talking too much tended to earn you extra quizzes with Mr. Alvarez, and even though class was over, I wasn't taking any chances. It was also best not to make eye contact. I kept my gaze fixed to the top of his head. There was chalk in his hair.

For a long moment, he didn't speak. He just sat there tapping his fingers against the desk. I risked meeting his eyes. He was watching me with an expression that wasn't quite a frown. Finally, he said, "How's Brewster doing?"

He meant Tink. Mr. Alvarez was one of those teachers who called everyone by their last name.

"She's fine," I said. "I mean, she's sick, but it's not a big deal." According to her, anyway. I wasn't sure why Mr. Alvarez cared, since Tink hadn't had class with him all year, and according to her, she never would again.

His eyebrows snapped together. "You're sure?"

I bit my lip. Tink's mom must have notified the school about her fainting episode. Tink couldn't be happy about that.

I watched Mr. Alvarez. He was difficult to read, but I sensed his concern was genuine—and strangely tinged with alarm. His eyes were troubled, and there was a grim, foreboding look on his face. I couldn't determine what it was, but he was worried about something. And given his history with Tink, it was probably something horrible. Like he thought she partied until dawn every night, and her weekends were filled with drugs, gangs, and orgies.

I hurried to dispel this notion. I found myself repeating Tink's words. "It's just the flu. She's really fine." Not that I believed that; I just hoped *he* would.

"Glad to hear it," he said, but now he looked downright ominous.

And then—as my mother so often accused me of doing—I said the first thing that popped into my head. "Fainting runs in her family. And, um, she's diabetic."

Tink was going to kill me.

At least that got a reaction. Mr. Alvarez interrupted his frown in order to blink at me. "She's not diabetic."

"I meant anemic."

Now he probably thought *I* was on drugs.

Instead of suggesting I take a trip to the nurse's office, however, he gave me a ghost of a smile and went back to tapping his fingers. "I'll let you go before you dig yourself any deeper."

I passed Brooke Oliver on my way out. "Careful," I warned. "He's scarier than usual today."

She looked at me like I was demented. I decided not to mention it to Gideon.

At lunch, Tink was still on my mind.

There was a reason my Knowing had flared up that evening at the Drought and Deluge—a reason I'd known I needed to help her. There was a reason I'd had that dream. Where most people saw coincidence, Gram had seen connection. Patterns, she would tell me. Patterns in the universe. Events that merged, ideas that overlapped.

I thought back to my conversation with Tink: her assurances that nothing was wrong, her cheerful tone when she talked about missing school. That catch I'd heard in her voice now and then. The things she wouldn't say. There was something else...

The Halloween party at the Drought and Deluge. Two were being held: one on Saturday, when the club would be its usual twenty-one plus, and one on Friday, for sixteen-and-up. The same crowd that had been there the previous week.

I closed my eyes, recalling the way my frequencies had suddenly cleared, the way my Knowing had screamed within me. Proximity was a factor with Knowing. Not the only one—but physical closeness helped. I couldn't properly focus on what had happened at the Drought and Deluge while sitting at home.

Gideon's plate clattered down beside mine at our table. "Save your nap for chemistry. We're watching a movie."

"I wasn't sleeping, I was thinking." I pushed my coleslaw around with my fork. "How upset would your mom be if I missed the Halloween party?"

Each year, the Belmonte family threw a big Halloween bash. Gideon's father transformed the yard into a haunted garden, complete with fake gravestones, electrical skeletons, and flickering lights. He decorated the house in orange and black, with cotton cobwebs that dangled from ceilings and door frames. And every Belmonte was expected to be in costume, including the various Belmonte pets.

Gideon frowned. "Bad idea, Audrey."

I crossed my arms and leaned back in my chair. Gideon might not have a Knowing, but he knew *me*, and I could tell from his tone of voice that he'd already guessed what I was up to.

"Something happened to Tink at the Drought and Deluge," I argued, keeping my voice low. No one at the nearby tables was paying attention to us, but I didn't want to chance starting more rumors. "I mean—something she's not saying."

"And so it makes perfect sense for you to go back there," Gideon retorted. "What are you going to do? If there's a problem, I'm sure your mom will look into it. Or tell the cops."

But aside from warning me away, my mother hadn't said anything. And she couldn't be everywhere at once. Minneapolis isn't a small city, and there was St. Paul to look after, too, and the suburbs.

"I'm going to find out," I told Gideon. "I think I can help."

I had to go with instinct on this one. And if there wasn't anything to it, if I was wrong, at least I'd know.

Gideon was less convinced. "Help how? You don't even know what happened."

"Hence *going to find out*."

He hesitated, leaning back in his chair and giving me a dubious frown. "You sure you're not just out to prove something?"

I matched his frown. "Like what?"

"I don't know, that you're a badass like your mom?"

He had me there. I would've liked nothing more than to have been parceled out a share of my mother's abilities, and Gideon knew it.

"Well, there's nothing like having a superhero in the family to make you feel inadequate," I admitted. "But that's not what this is about."

"You swear?"

"I swear. It's just—it's something I need to do."

Gideon sighed noisily, shaking his head. "Then I suppose I'd better go with you."

9

Fall announced its presence overnight. I woke Friday morning to the wind beating against my window and a dense cloud cover blotting out the sun. A cold rain began before Gideon arrived to pick me up in the morning, and by the time school was over, the streets and gutters were full of wet leaves. Thunder rumbled, low and ominous as night fell. The sky looked bruised. Suitable weather for Halloween, I thought.

By six that evening, I was beginning to wonder if it was some kind of sign. As a rule, I don't believe in omens, since nothing in life has taught me that nature is a better predictor of the future than my own intuition, but I began to feel a hint of unease. Still, it was only a storm. I wasn't about to change my plans because of a little water.

Mom had been complaining about the storm since I arrived home. Being a Guardian meant going out even when the weather was nasty, but—as my mother often told me—that didn't mean she had to like it. Fall and winter had the effect of making the Guardian lifestyle seem a lot less glamorous, even if the cold didn't affect her the way it did me.

At least the rain gave me a convenient excuse to have Gideon pick me up at my house, thereby avoiding questions from his various family members.

"Honey? Are you still getting ready? Gideon's here."

I jerked slightly. I'd been sitting on my bed, trying to come up with some sort of plan for the Drought and Deluge. Just because I was going there didn't necessarily mean I'd discover anything. Last time, I'd had trouble sensing anything in the crowd.

"Almost!" I called down the stairs, which was a complete lie. I darted across the hall to what had been Gram's room.

After Gram died, Mom and I had boxed up most of her things. I'd taken her books, and Mom kept some of her jewelry, but almost everything else had either been taken down to the basement or given away. Only a few of her belongings remained, tucked away in her room and quietly gathering dust. Though I hadn't been in her room for months, I remembered what it held. I pushed the door open and felt for the light switch.

"What's your costume?" my mother called up to me. She probably hadn't meant to shout, but her voice was strong. It was a good thing we had few close neighbors.

Gideon's words were quieter. "She's going as Teenage Angst," he said.

"A clever disguise," my mother remarked.

"I heard that!" I shouted to them, then turned my attention to Gram's room.

The air was dusty. One of the lightbulbs had burned out, and though the blinds were closed, I saw flashes of lightning outside. I moved slowly about the room, pausing at Gram's bed. It was neatly made, with the same quilt she'd always used. I trailed my fingers across it, feeling the patchwork. It seemed to me there was something unique about the spaces people used to occupy. Not just memory, but a quality to the air, a particular presence. Things left behind. In Gram's room, I smelled lavender beneath the dust. I could picture her sitting on the floor beside me, her hands moving across the Nav cards as she spoke.

She wouldn't approve of my sneaking out, but I thought she might understand.

I crossed the room and tugged her closet door open. Most of her clothes were gone, but the piece I wanted hung directly in front of me. I pulled it from the hanger, dusting it with my hands. A long, red, hooded cloak. It smelled of Gram's perfume.

I held the cloak against me, running my hands down the fabric. It wasn't the most original costume, but there was something comforting about the idea of wearing it. Gram would have enjoyed it. She had loved fairy tales.

She'd taught me all the classics: houses of candy and straw spun to gold and girls locked in towers. But she'd taught me her own tales as well, words that still haunted me. Stories that went beyond myth, stories that kindled within me and woke me in the dark, straining to hear voices in the wind. Stories of great battles, of villains and champions, of the Old Race, who dwelled in the Beneath, where red stars cast red shadows. Stories that told the source of our gifts, she said. A pinprick of light in a vast, cold darkness, where all hope began.

A shiver ran down my skin. Holding Gram's cloak, the fabric pooling in my hands, I could almost hear her. *Let me tell you about the dark,* she would say. *So that you don't need to be afraid.*

I left Gram's room and headed downstairs.

In the kitchen, Gideon stood with my mother and Leon, eating a sugar cookie in the shape of a pumpkin. Mom wasn't dressed to go out yet, which I supposed was because of the rain—even though Halloween was the one night of the year she could walk around as Morning Star and not be questioned. Last year, half a dozen little trick-or-treaters had come to Gideon's house with eight-pointed stars painted on the backs of their sweatshirts.

Leon was in his usual slacks and button-down shirt, his tie crisp and neat. I wasn't certain how he fought crime at all. With a cookie in his mouth and his wet hair sticking straight up, he looked about as menacing as a day-old puppy.

It was a shame I couldn't just stick him in a kennel.

Mom lifted an eyebrow when she saw me.

"What?" I said. "I'm Little Red Riding Hood. My costume is better than his." I hooked my thumb at Gideon, who was dressed up as some sort of video game character, or so he'd informed me.

From what I could tell, he'd just put on a bandana and drawn stubble on his chin with black marker.

It was a good thing neither of us embarrassed easily.

"Don't be out late," Mom told me.

Outside, I heard one last blow of thunder—and then the rain stopped.

Thanks to the Halloween party, the Drought and Deluge was even busier than it was most Fridays. Gideon and I stood outside as the line was gradually ushered inside. In the aftermath of the storm, the sky was clean and bright, though the lights of downtown Minneapolis drowned out the stars.

"You realize this is a stupid idea, right?" Gideon said, adjusting his bandana as the line pushed forward. "And your mother will murder me if she finds out I helped."

"So why *are* you helping? You're not scared of her?"

He grinned at me. "I'm more scared of you."

"As you should be," I said, nodding in approval.

Within the Drought and Deluge, it was difficult to sense anything. Though the air outside had cooled, the heat inside became increasingly unbearable. Wearing a heavy cloak among so many bodies was probably a bad idea, especially since most of the other girls were dressed in sleek outfits with cat-ear or devil-horn headbands.

"What's next?" Gideon asked after we made it to the refreshments table. The watery punch and bowls of chips set out for partygoers hardly seemed worth what we'd paid to get in, but since it had been my idea to attend, I wasn't going to complain.

"We wander," I suggested. I turned, searching the crowd. For what, I wasn't certain—something out of place, a particular shift of light, some hint I would recognize. The lights were low, everything shaded. I recognized a few faces, but no one I'd spoken to before.

Gideon and I wove through the throng until we found a free table tucked into a corner on the second floor, where a boy dressed as a vampire was doing some serious sucking on a bunny girl's neck. We didn't have much of a view of the dance floor, so I let my mind drift, listening to the sounds that flowed around me. The air was warm, thick, and beneath the music I heard glasses clinking on tables, footsteps and the rustle of cloth, voices, whispers, someone's happy laughter floating up from below.

I considered trying to find the man from the alley. He'd been wearing a Drought and Deluge shirt, so I figured he must be an employee, but I hadn't seen him when we entered the club. He'd been rather unsettling, and the thought of encountering him again made me nervous. But if he hadn't hurt Tink, maybe he was telling the truth; maybe he *had* been there to help. Either way, he must know something. It was possible I could get a sense from him—provided he was present at the club.

Closing my eyes, I tried to focus on him. I hadn't seen him clearly, so I concentrated on what I'd felt: the shiver in his voice, that smile that didn't reach his eyes. In the back of my mind, some nagging voice whispered that perhaps I shouldn't try to speak with him, or find him, or read him, that perhaps he was dangerous, but I dismissed it. I wouldn't confront him alone, and if he meant me harm, I'd be able to sense it.

Except, as it turned out, I couldn't sense anything. No images or impressions, no fleeting emotion, no hint of Knowing. If the man was there, he wasn't close enough for me to get anything from him. So much for that idea.

Beside me, Gideon let out a long sigh and said, "Well. This is exciting."

Distracted from my musings, I opened my eyes and turned toward him. From the look on his face, I knew he was about to remind me we could be back at his house, which might not be the most fashionable scene in the Twin Cities, but at least had chairs that didn't stick to the floor.

I decided to strike first. "You'd really rather be at home watching your grandma scare trick-or-treaters?" That was another Belmonte tradition. It wasn't Halloween until some poor kid ran screaming into the street. I loved Granny Belmonte, but she didn't need a costume to look undead.

Not to mention, I knew how those parties went. Last year, his mother actually made us bob for apples.

Gideon gave me a grumpy look and crossed his arms.

"You have to admit your family is weird," I said.

"Pot. Kettle."

"Say what you will, but I guarantee you my mother has never

bobbed for apples." I glanced away. An awkward combination of spooky music and some dance remix played overhead. The heat made me a little light-headed. I wished again I'd thought of a more practical costume.

Then a thought struck me. What was it Tink had said? She'd gone into the alley because she needed air.

"I'm going to the ladies' room," I said, leaving Gideon at the table and heading for the stairs. I had a sense of—something. A certain pull. I trailed my hand down the railing. I pictured Tink, the swirl of her dress, her footsteps fading, the way her hair caught the light. In my mind, I followed her path: the dance floor, where suddenly everything was too bright and confined, the overbearing smell of cologne and sweat and grease; the hall, where a door swung open to the alley and the cool gleaming night; and then outside, the wind brisk against her skin.

The night air, I thought.

The sweet night air.

The crowd was thicker on the first floor, a tangle of limbs and costumes and voices. I stepped near the dance floor and skimmed my eyes over the throng. There was an energy here, a rush of pulses, something communal that ran through my blood. I felt what Tink must have—the flicker of panic beneath my ribs, the need for space. The urgency. Turning, I headed for the ladies' room.

A jolt of Knowing surged through me.

It wasn't a sound, precisely, but I heard it. Like a whisper, a voice beckoning, frightened, far away.

Then I saw her. I knew her by the fall of her hair. The long dark sway of it, near her hips, curled just slightly. Iris St. Croix. The girl who wore the triple knot. I caught only a glimpse: sleeve and shoe and black hair disappearing down the same hall Tink had taken.

Coincidence, the rational part of me said.

Connection, my Knowing screamed.

And I thought—*It's happening again.*

I should have stopped. I should have turned and gone back and alerted someone, anyone. I should have found Gideon. But I didn't. I could only move forward, slowly at first, my hand touching the wall as I followed Iris around the corner. It was exactly the same: the smell of bleach, the closing door. The corridor was empty. Iris had gone into the alley.

I hurried the last steps, not sure what I would find. My breath came fast as I shoved the door open and rushed out into the night.

Outside, the street had grown cold. I saw my breath in the air before me. The alley was empty. There was nothing but brick and trash cans and the gray siding of the nearby buildings. A handful of feathers, blown up by the wind, swayed downward onto my cloak. No trace of Iris.

I called to her. My voice sounded harsh and loud. A strange dread seized me. I thought of Kelly Stevens disappearing into a hazy twilight. That could have been Tink's fate. Perhaps the night itself would have swallowed her, seizing her, taking her— *somewhere.* I imagined a hole opening in the world, shadows spreading across her ankles, dragging her down into it.

It struck me, then, that I was alone in the alley. I hadn't moved far from the door, but as I turned, the distance between the building and my body seemed endless. Panic surged in my chest. My pulse slammed in my ears.

"Stop it," I said aloud, startling myself. "You're fine. Just go back inside."

I took a long, steadying breath and stepped forward. The door was there, near, only a heartbeat away. I would return to the club and find Gideon and stop scaring myself. I was mistaken. I'd been seeing things. No voice called me out here. Iris St. Croix was fine, safe, wherever she was.

All at once, the lights of Minneapolis flickered and vanished.

I stopped where I stood, half-turned toward the door. Above, the stars were full and bright, no longer obscured by the glitter of traffic and streetlamps and office buildings, but all other light had died. The city stood silent, the buildings dark. Everything was still and empty. I heard nothing. I sensed nothing. The night air was thick and suffocating and anything but sweet.

A wind rushed up. Gram's cloak billowed around me. From the corner of my eye, I saw something move.

I spun around. Nothing there.

I tried to calm myself, to focus. I wasn't helpless. Instinct kicked in; I took a low stance, raising my hands in front of me, ready to block. But nothing in my training had prepared me for this.

It was something I sensed more than saw. An idea that formed an image. A flash of silver. The barest glimpse of skin that rippled. Eyes that blinked and then stared. Movement.

Someone.

Some*thing*.

Something human and not human.

Something with talons and teeth.

I had known fear before. Small, irrational fears—of spiders, of falling, of dark water. The looming, uncertain fear of death that sometimes strayed into my thoughts. But I'd never felt fear like this.

This was bone-deep. It filled my body, closing my throat. I couldn't move. I couldn't speak. I wanted to call out for my mother, but my voice wouldn't obey me. It was as though the universe had stopped.

Then.

The flash of silver blurred past me. Something sliced across my ankles. My legs buckled. I tumbled forward.

I seemed to fall forever. Suspended in time, the wind around me, I remembered my dream. Fire that burned at my fingertips, Minneapolis dark and quiet and dead. I remembered Gram, the movement of her hands, the blue line of veins beneath her skin. In the silence, I heard her whisper, telling me not to be afraid.

But I couldn't listen to what she wanted me to hear. I couldn't cry out. I couldn't find my balance, or sink into my center as I'd been trained to. I could only fall, and keep falling—

Someone caught me before I hit the ground.

Strong arms whipped around me. Headfirst in his chest, I didn't know who held me upright—but I understood that he didn't mean me harm. My senses returned, and my Knowing, jarring and sudden, told me I was safe. I gasped for air. My breath had been knocked from me, and my thoughts wouldn't organize themselves. Everything felt out of focus, as though some disconnect existed between my body and the world. I caught small, disjointed details: the smell of leather and blood; the pain that snaked across my ankles; the rapid, birdlike beating of my heart.

A voice intruded. "Might want to reconsider this rush-headlong-into-danger bit of yours, angel. You're not quite the bright shining star your mum is. Your light's a touch shy, yet, isn't it?"

In a daze, I struggled to make sense of that. The voice was familiar, the trace of an accent, the hint of amusement—

Somewhere nearby, another man spoke. "This is the second time in two weeks."

The man holding me answered. "I run a popular establishment." An icy silence. "What would you like me to say? I can't control them any more than you can. I rang you as soon as I saw her—terribly sorry if I ruined your night. I thought there might be a... problem."

A short laugh came from the other man. "A problem. You keep rescuing Kin girls, your friends will give you plenty of those."

"I can't resist a damsel in distress. Especially one as eager for trouble as our little dark star here."

I felt as though I were swimming upward through a fog, groping toward an unreachable surface. Nothing I saw made sense.

There were only fragments: the dirty pavement, the angle of the man's shoulder, a dark slash of night. I struggled to arrange them. Voices, I thought. Familiar voices—both of them.

I jerked away, or tried to, but my body wasn't working. The man who had caught me eased his grip and took a step backward, and for the first time, I saw him plainly.

Wordless, bewildered, I gaped at him. I knew his face. I knew his sandy hair and dark green eyes. I'd seen him once before, when Tink dangled helpless in his arms. The man with the Drought and Deluge shirt.

"You," was all I managed to choke out.

"So it would seem," he agreed.

But before that information could sink in, I was in for a bigger shock. A hand came down on my shoulder, and I whirled, wobbling, until a second hand steadied me. I looked upward, directly into the unsmiling eyes of Mr. Alvarez. And if he wasn't the last person on earth I ever expected to come to my aid, he was certainly in the top ten.

"Can you stand on your own?" he asked. I gave him a slow, numb nod, the best I could manage, and he turned toward the other man. "You know who she is. You didn't call her mother?"

The man looked down at his hands. "I thought I'd let you handle this mess. I've grown rather fond of living."

"I doubt she'd kill you. She hasn't yet."

"Maybe not, but I also prefer my limbs attached."

The world had definitely flipped upside down. I stared at Mr.

Alvarez, struggling for rational thought. I'd never seen him outside of school before, and it suddenly struck me as absurd that he was wearing raggedy jeans and a leather jacket. Not to mention that his hair was spiked straight up. I felt a bubble of laughter rise in my throat even as I swayed on my feet.

He steadied me again. "We need to get you home."

I moved automatically, letting him guide me. I thought I might pass out; there was darkness behind my eyes, and nausea waved through me. My throat felt thick and dry.

It wasn't the pain. That was fading. I felt as though something were missing, like I was a glass of water and half of me had been poured out. It took a long moment for me to realize that I was no longer in the alley, that the lights of downtown had returned and the roar in my ears was the Friday night traffic outside the Drought and Deluge. Mr. Alvarez had brought me to a car.

From the chaos of my thoughts, panic flared. "Gideon," I croaked out. I wasn't certain how much time had passed, but he must have noticed my absence by now.

Mr. Alvarez didn't seem to register my words. He pulled open the car door and set me inside. I said it again, and this time he bent toward me to ask, "He was with you?"

I managed to nod.

He stepped back from the car, hesitated a moment, then said, "Sit tight. I'll take care of it."

Inside, the car was warm. A deep chill had spread through my body, and I leaned back against the seat. I took long, slow breaths.

Mr. Alvarez's car smelled like french fries and mechanical heat. Curling my legs up against me, I closed my eyes and listened to the hum of the motor.

I was dreaming.

I had to be dreaming.

I was only dreaming.

And repeating this to myself, I fell asleep.

The sound of the car door slamming woke me. Confusion returned. I hadn't slept long, or deeply, and I remembered that I was in a car, but I still couldn't make sense of what had happened. Gram's cloak was wrapped around me, but I had somehow lost my shoes. Through the windshield, I saw familiar objects: the mailboxes down my street, damp and gleaming from the storm; the curve of the road, full of leaves; evergreens stretching skyward. And my own sidewalk, partially obscured by hedges and the hint of ivy.

Mr. Alvarez had walked around to my side of the car. He opened the door and bent to remove me, but stepped back in surprise when I blinked up at him.

"Oh—you're awake. Can you walk? Do you need me to help you out?"

Although my world was still fuzzy around the edges, I felt more lucid. And I wasn't about to go anywhere without an explanation.

"You need to tell me what's going on," I said, hunkering down in the seat. Even with Gram's cloak and the heat from the car, I was cold all over. I couldn't stop shivering.

Mr. Alvarez ran a hand through his spiked-up hair. "Your mother should be here soon."

My mother. I hadn't considered until now what she'd say to me. Or do to me.

"She's going to kill me," I whimpered. But then another thought struck. It was still early in the evening. Mom and Leon would be out in the dark of the city, where things I'd never before imagined hunted in the streets. Things that seemed human, but weren't.

My mind caught there.

Not human.

"Whitticomb?" Mr. Alvarez asked. When that didn't get a response, he added, "Audrey?"

"I'm not moving," I said. "I'm not going anywhere." I heard the edge of hysteria in my words, but I didn't care. I wasn't going out there, out into the open, empty street, where darkness beckoned and the wind shifted the trees and anything could be waiting, silent and watchful, ready to spring. I couldn't do that. I couldn't move, I couldn't think. I could barely breathe. I could only sit paralyzed, searching for motion along the street.

I don't know how long I stayed there. It could have been minutes, an hour, forever; it could have been only a second. Time seemed to freeze. Distantly, I was aware of Mr. Alvarez speaking, but I didn't answer. I sat clutching my cloak around me and thinking of all the stories Gram had whispered and all the things she hadn't said.

And then, suddenly, there was a shape before me. A tall form in a thin jacket, bending into the car. I caught the curl of dark hair, a searching glance, blue eyes shadowed with concern.

Leon.

"Let's go," he said. He slid one of his arms across my back, the other under my knees, and lifted me out of the car.

He set me on my feet and I sank against him. I tucked my head into his shoulder, gripping his shirt. I held tight. In that instant, I didn't care how angry he could make me. I didn't care about whatever lecture he had in store. He was familiar—that scent of vanilla and soap, the worry that creased his face, the sound of his voice repeating my name. He was steady, solid. Safe. His arms circled me. His hands were warm. For a moment, I just stood there, leaning against him, breathing, shutting out the world.

Then his arms fell away. Slowly, gently, he reached for my hands. His fingers closed over mine, detaching me from his jacket. He took a step back. His gaze dipped downward to my bare feet in the grass and the blood that had dried on my skin.

I took a shaky breath. His eyes met mine. Neither of us moved. I looked across the darkness at him and recalled another night we'd stood here at the end of the drive. That night he'd first appeared, a strange boy with a backpack and a motorcycle and a secret we shared. I remembered him stepping through the grass toward us, that crooked little smile he wore.

He wasn't smiling now. Something I couldn't name flickered in his eyes—and then fury blazed across his face.

He grabbed me by the shoulders, his fingers digging in almost painfully. "What is the *matter* with you?"

The anger in his voice sent a shock through me. It managed to do what neither the fear that gripped me nor the pain in my ankles had been able to: I started to cry.

I said his name, pleading, my voice trembling, but he wasn't done yelling at me.

"What were you thinking, Audrey? Why would you go back there? You think nothing can hurt you? Do you know what your mother faces every night? It's worse than you met. Worse than you can imagine."

A shudder ran through me. I felt that flash again—blank eyes I'd almost seen, an impression of movement, something sharp against my skin. Tears scalded down my face, and I began to feel hot, crowded, unable to breathe.

"Back off, Farkas. You're scaring the poor kid."

That was Mr. Alvarez again. It had never occurred to me before that I'd be grateful for his presence, and now he'd come to my rescue twice in one night.

Leon didn't release his grip. "She *should* be scared!"

"No," Mr. Alvarez said. "She should be educated. She froze up tonight. Fear can be crippling if it's not overcome."

My mother's voice cut in, her tone an echo of Leon's as she asked, *"What the hell happened?"*

I tore free of Leon's grasp, twisting toward my mother. In the darkness of the street, my eyes met hers. She was dressed for work, blending into the night in her black hoodie. Her hair was pulled back, and in the moonlight her face was pale and grim.

I would have gone to her. I wanted nothing more in that moment than to hug my mother, to huddle against her and shut my eyes and forget that anything else existed. But Mr. Alvarez's next words stopped me.

"It seems that your daughter has met her first demon."

The words bolted through me.

Suddenly, it was all too much: the strangling fear; the image of those eyes that weren't eyes and skin that wasn't skin. The smells of the night—bleach and blood and leather and something rank, like decay. My senses were on overload.

I didn't go to my mother.

Instead, I turned, stumbling over Gram's cloak, ran to the hedge, and threw up.

Behind me, the voices stopped. My whole body felt hot, and the edges of my vision darkened briefly, but I didn't pass out. Tears burned down my cheeks. Dimly, I was aware of someone steering me into the house, a cool washcloth wiping my face, a glass of water being pressed into my hand.

"Sit," my mother commanded.

I sat.

"You're okay." She leaned forward and kissed the top of my head, smoothing my hair with her hand. "You're okay."

I nodded, because she seemed to expect it. I didn't tell her I was afraid I'd left some important part of me at the Drought and Deluge—like maybe my brain—or that I was beginning to feel a little unhinged, and sitting in the parlor with my superhero mother, her sidekick, and my precalculus teacher was not very good for my sanity. And that was without adding *demons* into the mix.

My skin felt hot again.

"You're okay," she said a third time. Then, assured that the shock I'd suffered was not life-threatening, she whirled, stalked toward Mr. Alvarez, and began arguing. "You know I don't like that word."

Demon, I presumed. I didn't like it, either.

"It has its purposes," Mr. Alvarez answered. "It's evocative." He and Mom stood near the doorway, facing each other, both with stern looks and crossed arms. Morning Star versus Math Teacher. Another irrational bubble of laughter rose.

"You used it to force my hand," Mom said.

"She was attacked," he retorted. "Your hand was already forced. How long did you really expect to keep her ignorant? What did you think to gain? She needs to know where she comes from."

"She's my daughter, Ryan. You have no authority in this. You pull rank, I pull off your arms."

It was too much effort to try to make sense of this. Turning away, I gulped down water to clear my throat.

Leon had vanished as soon as we entered the house, only to reappear a moment later with the gauze from at least three first-aid kits. Now he pushed Gram's garage-sale table aside and knelt in front of me, bandaging my ankles.

I was too numb to protest. I just sniffled weakly, staring down at my feet, and said, "You're making me look like a mummy."

Without speaking, he pulled a tissue out of nearby box and handed it up to me. He kept his eyes lowered. He wouldn't look at my face, and I couldn't look at his. I felt all knotted up inside.

The night had separated into fragments: my mother in her Morning Star hoodie; the alley with its smell of bleach; the air thickening around me; the vanishing lights. Demons.

Demons.

My mind shied away from that thought. I concentrated on little details, trying to orient myself. I focused on the air. The windows were open, and the cool autumn wind pushed in, smelling of rain. I watched Leon's hands. His hands were really too big for the rest of him. A long, slender scar snaked down the back of one, forming a hook at his wrist.

Mom and Mr. Alvarez went right on arguing.

"We're not having this conversation here," Mom was saying. She flicked a glance toward me, like she'd suddenly remembered I had ears.

"Secret's out, Luce. Hiding things now will only make it worse," Mr. Alvarez said.

"Let's try this again: *my* daughter, *my* business."

"You know I'm right. She's a target because of who she is, and you can't change that. She deserves the care and protection of the Kin."

Kin.

He'd said that earlier, in the alley.

It was a word I'd heard before, but not in the way he said it. His tone, the emphasis he gave it, resonated within me. It had a homey feeling, a sense of something safe and old. I thought again of Gram's stories. She'd never spoken of any sort of kin, but I could almost hear her say it, and with the word came a sensation of history. It held an image of cool rivers deepened with rain, of tree roots stretching far below the earth, of the dark, secret spaces of memory. Kin. It knew me, that word. And I knew it.

Leon's voice, low and rough, broke into my thoughts. "We can protect Audrey."

"Tonight you didn't."

I sucked in a breath. Leon went very still beside me; he seemed about to respond, then vanished instead. It was Mom who spoke.

"If you're trying to get me to kick your ass," she told Mr. Alvarez, "this is the way to do it." Looking at her, I didn't doubt it. She'd pulled back her hood, and her hair had come free from its bun, floating wildly about her head—but she looked every inch Morning Star.

Mr. Alvarez held his hands up in front of him. "Just bring her to Esther, that's all I'm saying. Right now we have bigger problems. This makes eight confirmed attacks, and they're accelerating. We were lucky with these last two—"

Mom gave him a look of disbelief. "Lucky."

"Two injured girls instead of two dead ones. *We were lucky.* You can thank Shane for that, by the way."

She snorted. "Yeah, I'll do that." Pausing, she tapped her fingers against her arms. "Did you happen to get a look at the Harrower?"

"Only a glimpse. It went Beneath before I could reach it. But it wasn't Tigue, if that's what you're asking."

Tigue. The name stirred a brief memory in me, then slipped away.

Mom frowned. "Maybe I'm wrong about him. I still can't link him to anything—but at this point, we don't have many other choices. Unless someone out there is taking great pains not to be seen."

"It wouldn't be the first time."

Mom's voice was soft. "No. It wouldn't." After a moment, she shook herself, rubbing her face with her hands. "We won't figure this out tonight. And if I'm here, you should be out on the streets."

"Already gone," he said, spinning around and heading out of the room.

"And, Ryan," Mom called after him. "Thank you."

He lifted a hand to wave, but didn't turn. "Anytime."

As soon as Mr. Alvarez left, my mother sent me up to bed. "It seems we're going to have to talk," she said. "But not tonight. You need sleep."

Warily, I moved toward the stairs, not meeting her eyes. "You're not mad?"

"Trust me," she said. "I am far beyond mad."

A sound at my window woke me.

I couldn't remember climbing the stairs or crawling into my own bed, but the covers were tugged up around me. I hadn't dreamed; I hadn't seen the flash of silver, or Tink's red dress, or Kelly Stevens lying dead—there had only been silence and safety. Until that sound, sharp and repeated, intruded.

I jerked upward, my heart slamming against my ribs.

It was still dark. Moonlight pushed through my blinds, tossing shadows along the walls. The sound came again, and this time I recognized it.

Shivering, I wrapped a blanket around me and slid off the bed. I tugged the window open and peered out into the yard.

Gideon was standing below, getting ready to launch another rock. I ducked backward to avoid his aim, but he'd seen me, and lowered his arm.

"I tried calling!" he yelled, cupping his hands around his mouth.

"Mom is gonna kill you if you break my window again!" I called back.

114

I sensed him smiling down there in the darkness. "I just wanted to make sure you were okay," he said. "You *are* okay, aren't you?"

I hesitated. I wasn't okay—but I didn't know how to say it. I didn't know how to explain what I'd seen, how the wind had rushed up, and time had frozen, and for a second I'd been certain I would die. There weren't words for that.

"I'm fine," I lied. "I'll tell you about it tomorrow."

I closed the window and crawled back into bed, dragging the covers over my head. Weariness swam over me. I didn't want to think of anything or remember anything or feel anything. I just wanted to sleep, dreamless and dark.

I didn't get out of bed for a week.

Saturday morning, I woke with a sore, swollen throat and aching joints. I coughed so hard I was surprised the city didn't put me under quarantine. It was an aftereffect, my mother said, the body's response to being cut by a demon. The same thing had happened to Tink. The effect was like the chicken pox, Mom said: you could only get it once. But when she tried to explain more than that, I covered my face with my blankets until she went away.

She returned later, and I rolled to my side as she placed a cool hand on my forehead. I didn't want to talk to her. I didn't want her to say whatever it was she was waiting to tell me. And I didn't want to go back out into a world where words like *demon* had moved from fiction into reality. I would rather stay in bed, where all I had to worry about was how gross my cough syrup tasted.

After her first attempt to talk to me failed, Mom seemed to

give up. Except to take my temperature and bring me chicken soup, she left me alone. She didn't even yell or tell me I was grounded; she just said we could talk whenever I was ready, brushed her hand over my cheek, and looked concerned.

She did, however, give me a warning.

"This isn't something you tell Gideon," she said.

"Right," I croaked out, keeping my back to her. "I'm going to run straight to him and tell him what a fun time I'm having with demons." How would I even begin that conversation? *Hey, Gideon, you know all those monsters that you used to be afraid lived in your closet? The ones your mom assured you didn't exist? Guess what!*

"I'm serious about this, Audrey. Some things can't be shared. Okay? You don't have to look at me, just nod if you understand."

I nodded.

Leon checked in on me now and then, and though I expected another lecture—or at least some very disapproving frowns—he only asked how I was feeling. I told him I was fine, and pulled the sheets back up over my head.

Gideon came to see me on Sunday.

"You haven't been answering your phone," he admonished, sitting at the foot of my bed. "And you look terrible."

"Thanks," I said, making a face at him. "Just what every girl wants to hear." I punctuated this with a cough.

"You doing okay?"

I was a little relieved Mom had told me not to tell him. I didn't want to talk about what really happened. Not yet. Not for a few decades, at least. I told him I thought the punch had been spiked. And that I'd fallen.

He didn't believe me, but—unlike me—Gideon wasn't one to press. He just shook his head and said, "I hope you're not planning to come to school looking like that."

"I'm not even planning to leave my *bed*," I answered.

By Tuesday I was beginning to feel better, but I still kept trips outside my room to a minimum. I ignored everything except my TV, my computer, and the romance novels I'd made Mom pick up from the library. Tink tried calling a few times and sent me strange, indecipherable texts, but I didn't respond. I wasn't ready to talk to her. I was afraid I would ask her what she'd felt, what she'd seen. If something had drawn her out there into the night, and she'd turned to a sound, a motion, to find herself alone and not alone. If she'd felt that flicker in the darkness and then that sudden, knifing horror as the light died around her. If she'd known what she was facing.

We shared this now, and I didn't want to share it. I wanted to stay hidden, safe in my room, where I could huddle under my covers and ignore the rest of the world.

But I didn't feel safe. I wondered if I ever would again.

"Don't you think this has gone on long enough?"

I looked up from my book. Leon was standing in the doorway, leaning against the frame.

It was Thursday night, and although my sickness—or aftereffect—was gone, I still refused to rejoin the land of the living. The closest I planned to get to outside was my window. I'd left it open. The air felt cool and wet and smelled of rain, which was enough to convince me I was better off indoors.

"You're interrupting my reading." I regarded Leon suspiciously. He hadn't spent any time yelling at me since Friday, but that didn't mean he wasn't about to start again.

"Get up," he said. "We're going out."

"I'm not going out," I protested, faking a cough. "I'm sick."

"You're better." He stepped toward me. He was as well-dressed as always, but there was a slight nick on the left side of his jaw where he'd cut himself shaving.

"It's going to rain. Or snow. Or *both*. You never know with Minnesota. We could wander right into a blizzard."

He shook his head, advancing another step. "Not tonight."

I scooted backward in my bed, pulling my knees against me and dragging the covers to my chin. "Anyway, I thought you were mad at me. And I'm not in the mood for lectures."

He sighed. "I'm not mad at you."

"Fine, but I'm still not going anywhere. It's the middle of the night."

"It's *eight*."

"I'm in my pajamas."

That gave him pause. "Do you smell?"

"What? No! I showered an hour ago." I pointed to my damp hair.

He shrugged. "I don't see a problem, then."

I felt it coming before it happened. I could never read Leon very well—or, okay, at all—but there were certain warning signs I recognized. The way his eyebrows lifted slightly. The wrinkle in his brow. The tilt to his head. Then—

He turned his Hungry Puppy eyes at me.

There was no defense against Hungry Puppy.

"Damn it, Leon! Fine, I'll go," I said, kicking away the sheets and climbing out of bed. "I *hate* it when you do that."

Leon was all innocence. He'd reverted to normal, but I wasn't about to protest again, not when he could go back on attack at any moment. I didn't think I could handle the Hungry Puppy twice in one night.

"You are so completely manipulative," I sniffed.

He ignored that. Seeing that he'd won his battle, he hustled me downstairs, pausing by the front closet to wrap me in a coat, and steered me out the door.

"We're riding?" I asked. "Not taking Air Leon?"

"A drive will be good for you. You could use the fresh air."

He was right about the weather. Clouds were thick and low in the sky and the air was damp, but it wasn't even sprinkling, and the night was still too warm for snow. I didn't ask where we were going, but hopped up behind him on his motorcycle and leaned forward.

We headed north, onto the freeway, west across the river and out of Minneapolis. Past the city, we took sleepy back roads where the traffic was quiet and the lanes empty, save for a few late commuters headed back to the suburbs. The drive *was* soothing, but it didn't take long. Less than half an hour passed before Leon slowed and I heard the crunch of gravel beneath us.

I slid off the bike and looked around. He'd brought us to a lake. Considering there were about a billion of them in the state, I wasn't certain which one. The area where we stood wasn't large, just a circle of red picnic tables with peeling paint, a few grills jutting up out of the grass, and a thin path of packed dirt that led toward the water. In the distance, the surface of the lake glittered with stars. The clouds above us had scattered.

I didn't like it. It felt empty, exposed. I turned to Leon. "We're here... why exactly?"

"I come out here to think sometimes." He turned, his hands in his pockets, and stared skyward. A sliver of moon rose small and distant between the clouds. After a moment, he shrugged and faced me. "And I thought we should get you out of the house before you grew roots."

I hunched my shoulders. The chill in the air had deepened. Around me, everything was very still. "If this is an intervention, could we please do it someplace less... open?"

"It's all right for you to be scared," Leon said. He hopped up onto one of the picnic tables and sat with his elbows on his knees, leaning forward, looking at me. In the meager light, his eyes were dark and unreadable—but his voice was kind.

"Great," I answered, turning away from him. Somehow, his sympathy bothered me more than his disapproval. "Glad I have your permission. Can we go home now?"

He snorted. "So you can get to work boarding up the windows?"

I spun about. "What do you want from me? Yes, I'm scared! I'm terrified! Happy?"

"Audrey."

"Let's get this over with," I muttered. "Now that I'm your captive audience, go ahead—lecture away."

He was silent a moment. I watched him warily. With a quick, graceful movement, he jumped down from the picnic table and bent, crouching in the grass. His hand curled around a rock, which he flung into the darkness. It skipped across the path and disappeared. Finally, he stood, looking at me as he said, "I'm sorry I yelled at you."

I didn't speak. I stared at him, confused, wondering what alternate universe I'd stepped into.

He wasn't finished. "But what you did was still stupid."

That was more like it.

"You didn't have to drag me out here to tell me that," I grumbled. "I am well aware of your views on my intelligence."

"I said what you *did* was stupid," he said, giving me a look that was stuck somewhere between irritation and impatience. "There's a difference."

Yet another episode of *Leon Knows Best*. I was more than a little sick of it. My hands tightened into fists.

"What did you expect?" I demanded. "That I wouldn't be curious? That I wouldn't be worried? I knew something had happened. Good job, lying to a psychic."

A muscle in his jaw twitched. Silence. I had him there. But I wasn't one for quitting while I was ahead. "It wasn't just some feeling," I said. "It was something I Knew. I couldn't ignore what it was telling me. And maybe it was a stupid idea, but I had to trust it since no one else would tell me the truth."

Leon moved forward, closing the distance between us. "So you sensed danger and your first impulse was to run directly into it. Again. That's really not the sort of instinct you want to trust."

"Right—because you're clearly the poster boy for cautious living. Or do you think I've forgotten how you just showed up out of nowhere and decided to play superhero?"

"I didn't have any choice in the matter, and believe me: I don't play." I tried to turn away, but Leon took hold of my shoulders, fixing me where I stood. His voice was quiet, intent. "Did it never occur to you that there might be a reason we weren't telling you things? That there was a reason we told you to stay away from the Drought and Deluge?"

"Well, maybe if you'd said, 'Stay away from the Drought and Deluge, *it's overrun by demons*,' I'd have paid more attention!" I snapped.

"There are plenty of things out there that can hurt you, and most of them have nothing to do with demons." Abruptly, he stepped back, releasing me, and let out a strangled sort of sigh. "I didn't bring you out here to argue."

"Why *did* you bring me out here, then?"

He didn't answer. A crisp wind rose around us, tugging at my coat sleeves and ruffling his hair. Then, for the second time that night, Leon surprised me. He gave me a rueful smile and said, "I was trying to make you feel better."

I gaped at him. He looked so sheepish, I couldn't help it: I burst out laughing. "This is your idea of a *pep talk*?"

"I could've handled it differently," he admitted. He tucked his hands into his pockets again, looked down, and kicked at the grass. A pebble bounced toward the picnic tables, followed by a clump of dirt. "But you need to understand—"

There was no way that sentence could end well. I grabbed his arm to get his attention. "You should probably stop talking."

He frowned, but obeyed.

I turned toward the lake. The night was hushed, save for the gentle lap of water. City traffic was distant, a low hum at the edge of my hearing. Now and then a lone car rolled past us, headlights slicing through the darkness. Nothing moved—that I could see.

"I *am* scared," I began. "Of course I'm scared. And maybe I did think it was a game. I thought you guys were just fighting crime or something. All this time, I thought you were out there making the Cities safe from—I don't know. Muggers and murderers, I guess."

Leon's voice was gentle. "I know you did."

I stared down at my feet. The grass beneath them was dead and brown. It wouldn't be long before the first snowfall.

"I don't know if I can handle this," I said.

"You can handle it." Leon stepped close to me, but I kept my eyes focused downward. "Most Kin kids grow up with this knowledge. It's just the way of life. They adapt to it. So will you."

I knew he meant it to be reassuring, but I didn't feel reassured. I didn't want to adapt. I kept looking at our feet: my old, scuffed softball tennies and the edge of his black shoes, smudged with dirt. "You're saying I should just—get up every day and pretend I don't know what's out there?"

"No. But remember that we're out there too."

We. Guardians, he meant. Him. And Mom. And apparently Mr. Alvarez. And others—I supposed he meant others, as well. Other Guardians, out in the streets, watching, fighting, keeping the city safe.

I shifted my gaze upward, but I didn't meet his eyes. I looked at his hands. I saw the scar that twisted down his left hand—a slender, jagged line, a cut that could have come from anything, but served as a vivid reminder that Guardians are made of flesh, that they hurt and bruise and bleed. I'd seen the wounds on my mother too many times to pretend nothing could harm her.

And Leon's words came back to me. What my mother faced. Worse than I'd met, he'd told me.

Worse than I could imagine.

I was imagining now. Not imagining what I'd seen in the alley, or almost seen—that blur of eyes and rippling skin, the sense of something waiting. Not those dreams of Kelly and Tink, flashes of red and then darkness. Not a threat against myself. I was imagining my mother. Dead.

Leon must've seen it on my face.

"Lucy's tough," he said. "You don't need to worry about her."

"I always worry about her," I said. "But now I'll worry *more*."

"You'll adapt," he repeated. "That comes with the territory. It's part of being a Guardian's kid."

Something in his tone sparked a thought within me. My eyes snapped to his face. It wasn't a Knowing—only a guess. "Your parents were Guardians?" I asked. "That's how they died?"

Leon's gaze was steady on mine, his voice calm. "That was different. Not something you need to worry about."

He didn't speak of his parents often. He'd told me, once, that he didn't really think of them; he'd been barely two years old when they died, and his memories were few. But now, for the first time since we'd met, I got a sense from him: a vague almost-Knowing—only a flash. An image of a small boy, waiting with huge hopeful eyes. An echo of laughter, abruptly ceasing. And then a tall man bending down, reaching for the boy's hand.

"What happened to them?" I asked.

Leon frowned, and I thought for a moment he wouldn't answer. Something else he didn't want to tell me. Then his eyes flicked away and he said, "We call it a Harrowing."

Harrowing. A charged word, like Kin. But different. It didn't make me think of home, or safety, or spaces of rest. It was bitter, filled with anguish and anger.

"A war," I said.

Leon's voice was soft. "Your mother ended it."

I didn't speak. I waited, taking deep, steadying breaths. A bird trilled somewhere above us, long and mournful. The air here was cool, clean, soothing. But it didn't soothe me.

A Harrowing, I thought. Leon's parents had died because of it. My mother had fought a war before I was born.

And somehow he thought this would comfort me. I almost laughed again. "All of this was supposed to make me feel *better*?"

I gazed across the darkness at him. In the slice of moonlight, his blue eyes were black, his dark hair tipped with stars.

His hand grazed my arm, then fell to his side. "Audrey—"

"I'm not okay," I said. "You can't—you can't just bring me out here and give me a talk and act all nice and expect me to be okay."

"Of course you're not. I've lived with this knowledge a long time, and I'm not okay with it. You don't need to be. But you do need to keep going."

He looked so stern and serious that, this time, I did laugh. "No offense, Leon, but you suck at this."

His smile returned—a crooked, apologetic sort of smile that warmed his entire face and made me smile back. "Come on, then," he said, jerking one of his shoulders toward his motorcycle.

"We're going home?"

"Not yet," Leon said as I climbed up behind him on the bike. "This was only step one. There's someone you need to meet."

Once again, Leon didn't tell me where we were headed. Our route skirted Minneapolis and brought us into St. Paul, past the lights and looming buildings of downtown, past lakes and drowsy neighborhoods. Leon parked at the end of a circular driveway. I slid down from his motorcycle, pulling off my helmet, and attempted to tame my tousled hair. The neighborhood was quiet. The soft yellow glow of streetlamps did little to brighten our surroundings, instead tossing stark shadows up and down the sidewalks. I looked forward, past the drive. An iron gate barred the way. Beyond, I could see the tall, sprawling shape of a house.

My home was large, but this building was massive. It was dark and sharply angled, like something out of a horror film. I half expected lightning to shoot out of the sky around it, or to hear ominous music cue up behind me.

"They're not going to let us in there," I said. Whoever owned this house, it seemed unlikely they would open their gates for a skinny college student and a girl in cow-print pajamas.

Unconcerned, Leon put a hand on my shoulder, dragging me to him. "You'll be fine," he said. "Just . . . try not to be a smartass." Then he pulled us through the air, into nothing.

I blinked. One moment we were outside, the driveway beneath us, the wind in my hair, and the next we were standing in a well-lit room with floral wallpaper. Leon had teleported me before, but it wasn't easy to grow accustomed to. Disoriented and off balance, I clutched at him.

"A little *warning* would've been nice," I complained. "I really hate it when you—"

I broke off. We weren't alone in the room.

"Well, Mr. Farkas. You do like to make an entrance."

The woman who stood before me was tall and thin, dressed in a tidy peach-colored business suit. She was older, in her late sixties maybe, though she hadn't quite gone to gray. Her long hair had a dark luster to it, thick and curling, and her eyes were a color somewhere between brown and gold. A string of pearls circled her neck. She smiled tightly as she watched us.

"This is the girl? You may leave her here."

Before I could protest, Leon gave a short nod and vanished.

I looked down at my ratty old coat and faded pajamas, feeling out of place next to this elegant woman, in this clean room furnished with chairs of dark wood and antique tables. I didn't recognize the paintings on the walls, but I assumed they were expensive.

The woman continued to watch me. I clasped my hands and stood straight.

She cleared her throat. "Your mother lied about your age. Ryan was right. I should have made an effort to meet you sooner."

I couldn't think of anything else to say, so I blurted out, "Who are you?"

A faint smile crossed her face. "I'm Esther St. Croix, leader of the Kin. And I'm your grandmother."

Esther. Like my first name. I was too bewildered to think clearly. An image of Gram flashed before me: the wrinkles that mapped her face, the broad smile she always wore, sunlight upon her as she bent in the garden. "My grandmother is dead," I answered.

"Angela Whitticomb is dead. I am your father's mother. Have a seat."

I did as she instructed, mostly because I felt awkward standing. I moved to the closest chair and sank into it, watching Esther St. Croix with narrowed eyes. She took the seat across from me, folding her hands in her lap.

My mother had never told me much about my father. He'd left, and she didn't want to talk about him. When I first began asking questions, Gram had been the one to answer. *Don't go to your mother,* she'd said. *Come to me, I will tell you what I can.* Eventually, I'd stopped asking. I didn't know that I ever wanted to meet the man who had injured my mother so deeply that she still felt the wound.

I had never thought to ask about his family.

"Your mother never told you about me, I see," Esther said, still watching me with those strange eyes. "We have that in common. Lucy always did want to have things her own way."

I kept my silence.

"Your mother tells me you're afraid."

"I think I have a right to be," I said.

Esther dismissed this with a shrug. "So you met a demon. It happens."

My mind withdrew from the word. I closed my eyes. "Things like that—they're not supposed to exist. They're just stories."

"Like Morning Star is a story, a myth some reporter thought up. And the Kin too, no doubt?"

"I don't even know what this Kin is."

"I see. You thought you were special. You thought you had these abilities, these gifts, and no one else did."

I didn't answer. She was too close to the truth. Peripherally, I'd known there were other Guardians, but I had never met them. Until this week, I'd thought of them in simple, comic book terms. My mother was a superhero, and Leon was her sidekick.

"Well, you are special," Esther continued. "You're Kin. But you're not the only one."

"I don't know what that means," I said helplessly.

"Another issue I'll be taking up with your mother," Esther said. "Let's do a reading, shall we?"

Without waiting for my response, she stood and moved across the room, pulling one of the tables toward us. She set it between our chairs, then opened a drawer and withdrew a deck of cards.

Nav cards.

I looked up, startled.

Esther's lips curved in a smile. "You have Angela's deck, I think, but there are others. Here. I'll deal."

I watched her shuffle, her long fingers moving deftly. I didn't speak. I tried to focus. I was able to get a sense of Esther easily: an image of long halls, of curtains fluttering, the smell of cotton. I saw her as a younger woman bending to lift a child into her arms. I saw her grim and stern, speaking to a young man whose face was turned away. She had called herself a leader, and I believed her.

She placed the first card on the table.

Seventeen. The Archer.

"I don't do readings often, but this is me," she said, and placed it in the center. "This, I presume, is you."

And sure enough, there was card fifty. Inverted Crescent.

She placed the next two. The Child. The Untilled Earth.

"Your mother thought to protect you," Esther said. "She didn't want you to grow up Kin."

I caught an image of my mother, fleeting and distant. She was young, her belly round, swelling against her hands.

Esther paused then, looking up at me, her fingers idling upon the cards. "Before we go any further, I want to be certain you understand something. What I am about to tell you is to be kept within the Kin. It's not to be repeated. Not to your classmates, not to your boyfriend."

"I don't have a boyfriend."

"Very good. You'll want to date other Kin. There are several eligible boys your age."

"Uh, thanks, but I'll pass on the whole arranged-marriage thing."

Esther favored me with a peevish frown.

Belatedly, I remembered Leon telling me not to be a smartass. "Sorry," I said.

Turning her eyes heavenward, she muttered something beneath her breath. Then she returned her attention to me. "Let's continue."

She dealt three more cards. The Garden. The Desert. The Triple Knot.

"This is the Kin," she said. "This is what you need to know. Are you ready? I'm going to tell you."

When I was little, there was one story Gram loved to tell more than all others: the story of the Old Race.

In the beginning, she said, before the time of words and wheels and flint to make fire, there was the Old Race. They didn't live on Earth as humans did, but inhabited the Beneath. They lived in the space between sun and shadow, the space between seconds and breaths, between thought and voice. They began with time and remembered the first burst of light in the vast swell of darkness. They were powerful, indestructible, without love or malice.

When humans first appeared on Earth, the Old Race took no notice. But as humanity evolved, the Old Race became fascinated with them: their ingenuity, the way they experienced the world around them, the way they lived and died. And suddenly, the Old

Race was not content. They no longer wanted to live in seconds and spaces. They wanted the physical world as well.

So the Old Race crossed over. They built bridges into our world, paths made of light and energy, of spiderweb and sinew, of sound and silence. They left the emptiness behind and came to live among humans, letting their powers sleep.

I imagined great beings with wings moving down from the heavens with a warm golden glow. "Like angels?" I asked, curled up beside Gram on the porch swing.

"Not at all," she answered. "They became human, just like you and me."

But, she told me, not *all* of the Old Race crossed over.

Some stayed. Some were left behind in the void. The paths closed, and those on the other side learned, without knowing hope or love, what it was to grieve.

And to hate.

"Those who crossed over took the light with them, you see," she explained. "The very last pinprick of light. And the world they left behind grew very dark, indeed."

"What happened to the ones left behind?" I asked.

"Nothing," Gram said. "Nothing happened to them. It's just a story, sweeting."

It was the same story Esther told, but she told it differently. The Old Race crossed over, she said—and became the Kin.

"We have been here since time before memory," she said,

watching me as she spoke. She leaned forward, her hands lingering over the Nav cards. "Though there are few of us now. We are secret, hidden across the world. We live where the Astral Circles lend their light."

Histories woven into fairy tale, I thought. My skin prickled; I'd heard all this before. But those had been stories, nothing more. I shifted in my seat, swallowing. "You expect me to believe I'm some kind of—mythical being?"

Esther's gaze narrowed. "I don't *expect* you to believe anything. Either you'll understand who you are, or you won't. Belief has nothing to do with it." She turned another card. Sign of Brothers. "We *are* human, but we're something more as well. I said you were special, didn't I? There is power that lives in our blood, the mark of our ancestry. Energy. The ability to do things most humans cannot."

Like teleport, I supposed. Or pull the door off a car. Or—

"Knowing," I said, sliding a hand forward to touch the Nav cards.

"A valuable gift, though gifts vary. Different bloodlines trend toward different abilities. Seeing. Healing. Fighting. We use them in service to others. The Kin live to protect," Esther said. "It is our duty and our burden."

"Guardians."

"Yes," she said. "All Guardians are Kin, though not all Kin are Guardians."

I pictured my mother disappearing into the dusk, her hair pulled back, her face shadowed. I knew the way she moved, agile and deliberate. I saw the dark circles beneath her eyes, the way she occasionally fell silent and stared into the distance. A duty and a burden.

I'd always been proud of her, of her secret: my mother, Morning Star; the living, breathing myth; the superhero; the savior. But that pride had been mixed with a certain jealousy. Not just of her strength, but of her courage, her will, her very identity. When teachers asked me what I wanted to be when I grew up, I told them a doctor or a lawyer or maybe the president. I never told them the truth: I wanted to be a Guardian, like my mother.

Now I wasn't so sure.

Now I knew just what it was she was guarding us against.

"Tell me..." I swallowed, clenching my hands into fists. I lifted my gaze to Esther. "I want to know about demons."

In the yellow light, her strange eyes glittered. "They have no true name. They are known by many names. Demons. The Unseen. Here, we call them Harrowers."

Harrowers. Harrowing.

Mom might not like the word *demon*, but this one felt worse. "What are they?"

Esther's hands stilled. She'd flipped the final card over. The Beast. "They were a part of us, once."

"The Kin?"

"The Old Race. Or so the story goes," she said, giving me a delicate shrug. "So much is myth now, but I'll tell you what I know of it. Our ancestors were a dying people. They saw humanity as their salvation. That is why they crossed over. And the Harrowers—they are those who remained behind. Over time, their realm deteriorated. The Harrowers became corrupted, twisted, until there was nothing left of them but their hate. Now most tread the emptiness Beneath, tortured by endless envy and rage. Some are able to breach the barriers, inhabit our world, but they cannot truly escape. The Beneath lives in them, calls to them. And so they are never content, never at ease. There is no joy within them, no peace. They abhor the light, and roam in darkness. They cannot feel as we do—but they hunger to."

I gazed at Esther, almost believing, not wanting to believe.

Seeing my hesitation, she shrugged again. "You have doubts? Perhaps some of it is only myth. Yet we are connected to them, and they are driven by their hatred for us. I'm certain you've felt it." She leaned forward, peering intently at me. "You met one, after all."

"But what I saw—" I shook my head. "I didn't see it. I sensed it, I think. But it felt . . . almost human."

A slow nod this time. "Yes, it would have. They have abilities, just as we do. When they are not Beneath, they take both human shape and name. You sensed its true form, what it is when it doesn't wear our skin."

I'd had only flashes, nothing concrete. I was suddenly very

glad I hadn't seen it. "Just when I thought this couldn't get any more disturbing." I leaned back, drawing my knees up against me. "What do they want?"

Her gaze didn't waver. "Death. Pain. Power. The more vicious ones hunt humans for sport, but we are their true targets. They revile the Kin, and yearn to be what we are. They want *us*."

"So, what, they just go around luring girls into alleys and slicing their ankles?"

"Ah, you mean, what did the one who attacked *you* want? There is something particular it craves. They're searching for something, you see. And they're bleeding Kin children to find it."

"Bleeding," I repeated. Pain slashing through me. Red in the street. I hugged my knees tighter.

"There is power in our blood," Esther continued. "And ankles are easy. They're two of the five sacred spots. They bleed, but not enough to kill. Not immediately. First the Harrowers test you, test your blood. They cannot risk destroying the very thing they seek."

I took a shaky breath. "What is it they seek?"

Our eyes met across the table. Esther reached forward and placed one cool, wrinkled hand against my cheek.

"A Remnant," she murmured. She sat back, folding her hands in her lap. "Something left behind in our bloodline. A piece of the past, best forgotten."

Before I could ask what she meant, the door was thrown open, and a whirlwind of black hair rushed in.

I recognized the girl immediately. I'd last seen her in the Drought and Deluge, her eyes pinned on Gideon, her dark blue dress catching the light. Now she wore checkered boxer shorts and a faded T-shirt. There was facial cream on her forehead, but she looked just as gorgeous as she had in the glow of the dance floor. Looking from her to Esther, I could see the family resemblance. Though the girl's skin was darker, both she and Esther were tall and slender, both had long black hair that tumbled wildly down their backs. The shape of their eyes was similar, and the curve of their jaws.

The girl, running into the room, went directly for me. Before I could react, she'd grabbed me by the hand, pulled me upward, and hugged the breath from me.

"I've been waiting to meet you!" Whether or not she meant to shout, her voice was loud in my ear. "I heard you were getting a Kin lesson. I'm your cousin. Elspeth."

"Um—hi," I said, submitting to her hug. Then I glanced up, and surprise stopped the breath in my lungs. Beyond us, in the doorway, stood the girl with the triple knot.

Iris St. Croix. I could see the resemblance in her, as well, though she was shorter than Elspeth and lacked her stunning beauty. Her dark hair was pulled back from her face, and she was smiling shyly. As I looked at her, I felt a hint of uncertainty. I hadn't given her much thought since that night at the Drought and Deluge when I'd seen her step into the alley and vanish as though she were nothing but shadow and smoke.

Or maybe I'd imagined it. Maybe she'd never been there. Now she was here.

"I know you," I told her. Then, as Elspeth released her death grip, I added, "Both of you."

"Oh, I know. I've seen you before," Elspeth said, giving me a sunny smile. "You're Gideon's friend."

I laughed. Gideon's friend, of course. "Only because his mother pays me to hang out with him."

"Can she pay me?" Elspeth asked.

Iris, moving into the room, rolled her eyes at her sister. "You should try to ignore Elspeth. Everyone does." She stepped before me, and though she didn't try to give me a hug, she continued smiling. "I had a feeling about you. Kin are drawn to Kin."

Esther tapped her fingers against the table. "Girls, it's a school night."

Elspeth didn't spare her a glance. "I won't stay up late, I promise." To me, she said, "Your mother told us on Monday. I can't believe you've been here all along and we didn't know you!"

Iris shook her head. "Settle down, before she decides she doesn't want to know *us*."

Elspeth only gave me another grin. "You'll be spending time with us now, right? You're a St. Croix, after all."

"Mondays and Wednesdays after school," Esther cut in, turning toward me. "I've arranged it with your mother."

I wasn't certain what that meant, but I *was* certain I didn't like my mom signing away my afternoons without consulting me, especially since I already had martial arts on Tuesday evenings. But before I could object, Esther waved her hand in the air and spoke again.

"We'll finish our conversation later. It's time you were getting home."

Which reminded me . . . "What did you do with Leon?"

As if on cue, he appeared before us. Elspeth gave him a little wave, pulled me into another hug, and departed, followed by Iris. "Monday, five o'clock," Esther told me—and then, without a word, Leon put his hand on my shoulder and brought us back to the driveway.

The night was colder now, the moon distant and blurred by clouds. I shivered as Leon started his motorcycle.

"You okay?" he asked, handing me my helmet.

There was no way I could answer that question. I couldn't articulate what I felt. Words moved through my head, but none of them seemed right. I had closed my eyes for a moment and woken in a world that was unsafe. But it was a world that was suddenly larger, too. I was something else. I was Audrey Whitticomb, and I was Kin.

I climbed up behind Leon on the motorcycle and set my hands on his waist, leaning into his back. I breathed against him. We sat idling in the driveway, exhaust rising around us.

"Audrey? Are you okay?"

"I don't know," I sighed. "It's a lot to process. I feel . . . different."

"You're still the same person."

I laughed. Trust Leon to take that literally. "I didn't say I *was* different. Just that I felt it." I glanced back at the house, where the curtains were drawn against the dark. "I don't think I like her."

He shrugged. "You'll get over it. Esther has that effect on people. You have to get used to her."

"Kind of like you?" I teased.

Leon went abruptly still, his shoulders straight and tense. I knew I'd said something wrong, but before I could take it back, he told me, "Being Kin—being a Guardian—is a privilege and a duty. It's important. It's not about being liked."

"Hey," I said, reaching upward to touch his shoulder. "I wasn't being serious."

His words were soft. "That's the problem."

Subtly, indefinably, something had altered. I wanted to speak, but I didn't know what to say. I settled on his name, but he didn't seem to hear me. His voice was gruff as he called back, "Just hold on."

We rode off into the night.

14

Friday night, Tink decided she'd had enough of my ignoring her, and barged into my room with a backpack, a bottle of hair dye, and a bag of chips.

"I'm sleeping over," she declared. "And I'm going brunette."

She got this impulse once every few months but never actually went through with it, so I just rolled my eyes at her. Predictably, she lost her nerve as soon as we opened the package, and we spent the evening turning my brown hair browner.

"This looks . . . exactly the same," I said, peering at myself in the mirror.

"Could be worse. Remember that time we turned Gideon's hair purple?"

"That wasn't purple," I said. "It was a brand-new color, all its own."

Tink only shrugged. "It washed out."

"Two weeks later."

"If he didn't want to suffer, he wouldn't hang out with us. He has other friends." Turning away, Tink went digging in my closet for a skirt she swore I'd borrowed. Like I'd fit into anything she owned.

But the real reason she'd appeared was to talk about the Kin. Or rather, to make sure we *didn't* talk about the Kin. Ever.

"It's not a part of my life," she said, after she'd abandoned her search. "And I'd like to keep it that way."

"But you *are* Kin?" I'd given up trying to notice a difference in my hair color and sat in my desk chair, eating Tink's potato chips.

"That's what they tell me." She sighed, flopped down on my bed, and began paging through the book I'd left on my nightstand. "I'm not a Guardian, I don't have any powers, and I'm only half-blooded anyway. My mom isn't Kin."

"But—you really don't want to be a part of it?" I asked. I understood being afraid, but I recalled the feelings the word *Kin* had first sparked within me, that impression of home, like some missing piece had slid into place.

Tink had another take on it.

"A creepy cult where all anyone wants to do is talk about demons and fighting and special powers that I don't have? Yeah, I *think* I can live without that."

Well, when she put it that way...

Another thought struck. "Is that what your fight with Mr. Alvarez was about?"

"Did you really think we were arguing about logarithms?" She wrinkled her nose. "He's some kind of Guardian leader, so he thinks he knows what's best for everyone. He kept trying to tell me it was my heritage. I told him it was none of his business. I hear that enough at home."

"He knew about—what happened," I said, then looked down. Neither of us wanted to mention the attacks.

She waved my words away. "He said it was more reason I should accept the Kin. Thanks for telling him I'm a diabetic with anemia and a family history of fainting, though."

I grimaced. "Heard about that, did you?" When Tink just raised her eyebrows, I shrugged. "I can't believe you didn't tell me any of this."

"I'd rather not *know* any of it. So if you go all Kin-crazy, please, please, please keep it to yourself."

Which was as much as Tink was willing to say on the subject. When I tried to bring it up again, she pretended to be engrossed in my book. I decided to let it go for the time being.

By Sunday night, I had other things to worry about. My week of illness and rest had only been a reprieve, and Mom hadn't forgotten that I'd lied to her and gone to the Drought and Deluge.

"You broke my trust," she said. "And like it or not, now you have to deal with the consequences."

Part of this, Esther had already told me: every Monday and

Wednesday for the foreseeable future, I would head to St. Paul directly after school.

The other part involved being grounded for a month. That meant no after-school activities, no friends coming over, and no sneaking out to clubs frequented by demons, even if there was a free-appetizer night.

I thought my sentence was a little unfair, but Mom wouldn't hear any arguments on the subject. Instead, she repeated her warning. "I meant what I said earlier: you're not to talk about any of this."

I assumed she meant *to Gideon.* "Yeah, I know. Keep it in the Kin. Esther said the same thing."

"For a reason. This isn't about my secret. It's not about self-preservation, or protecting *you.* It's about protecting the people we care about. Humans who get mixed up with Harrowers have a tendency to end up dead."

On other subjects, Mom remained annoyingly silent. Whatever reason she had for keeping *me* in the dark about the Kin, she wasn't willing to share it. When I asked, she simply told me it was her decision, and she stood by it.

"But don't you think I should be, you know, prepared?" I asked, following her out into the approaching twilight. She zipped up her hoodie and turned to face me.

"Esther will tell you about the Kin," she answered. "She knows everything there is to know about our history. Trust me, she'll be the better teacher."

"I'm not talking about the Kin."

In the blue shadows along the porch, Mom's eyes met mine. "I never wanted you to have to face that," she said.

"But I did. And I completely froze up. I don't want that to happen again." Much as I never wanted to meet another demon, if I *did*, I wanted to know how to handle it. How to escape. If necessary, how to fight.

"You could try listening when I tell you something."

"Mom."

She reached a hand toward me, her fingers feather-light on my shoulder. With that touch came a glimmer of memory, fleeting impressions of the day we arrived in Minneapolis. I felt her anxiety, knots of fear in her stomach—not for her safety, but for mine. Now, her voice hushed and worried, she gave a slight nod and said: "Esther will teach you about the Kin. I'll teach you about Harrowers."

I was behind on schoolwork, but thanks to Gideon dropping off some of my assignments the previous week, it wasn't as bad as it could've been. I had a book report due in English and I'd missed a chemistry test, but mostly I had to catch up on reading.

It was strange being back in school. I felt altered, as though I'd been gone for months. Though I was still frightened, there was excitement in me, too. Suddenly, I was part of something secret and a little thrilling, something larger than the mysteries my mother kept hidden. It wasn't just superheroes in dark outfits, the hushed rumor of Morning Star. It was an entire world. A history of folklore and fairy tales, and the truth beneath them. *You are special,* Esther had told me. *You're Kin.*

Unfortunately, not everyone agreed on that count.

"Whitticomb," Mr. Alvarez said, stopping me after precalc. "When it comes to this class, you're a student first and Kin second. Whatever else you have going on, I expect you to have your homework in on time." But then he got a worried little frown, asked how I was doing, and told me not to push myself. I nodded and dashed away. I knew I owed him my gratitude, but I had difficulty reconciling the strict, no-nonsense math teacher with the leather-wearing rebel Guardian who had stood in my house and argued with my mother. It was unfathomable.

True to her word, Tink stayed silent about the Kin, even when we were alone. I realized it must be something she was accustomed to, just as I'd grown up with Morning Star and all of Gram's whispered secrets—and I remembered that Tink wasn't nearly as open as she seemed. I recalled those flashes that slipped away during her readings, hints of what she kept hidden. She'd probably been given the same guidelines about secrecy that I had. Still, I found it difficult to believe she'd kept so much from me for so long. Tink couldn't go ten minutes without finding something to gossip about.

At the same time, I understood. And even though I didn't like hiding things from Gideon, I did as Mom and Esther had instructed and didn't tell him about the Kin.

But there were other things I couldn't keep from him. Monday afternoon, Iris appeared and sat by us at lunch.

"I promise not to be an obnoxious relative," she said, giving me a slight smile as she set her tray down beside mine, "but it's not every day I get a cousin." Then she looked directly at Gideon. "You're the one my sister likes. I'll tell her you said hello."

That took a bit of explaining. But at least long-lost cousins were a safer topic than demons lurking in the city streets—and though the addition of Iris had been unexpected, I was curious about my new family. Tink, who must have known Iris was Kin, looked annoyed, but said nothing.

Gideon managed to take it in stride. "Next time you tell me my family is strange," he told me later, "I'm reminding you of this moment." And he didn't question me further.

After school, Mom drove me to the St. Croix household. I stood outside, surveying the property. A circular drive spread outward from the house. A tall fence curved down toward the street. The lawn was still green and looked carefully tended, with trimmed hedges and a small pond off to one side, where smooth gray rocks surrounded a garden. The house itself was so tall it seemed to blot out the sun. Dark windows stared down at me.

The door opened.

"I hope you're not mad about lunch."

Iris stood in the entryway, smiling softly. She took a step back, gesturing for me to enter.

"I don't know that many people at school yet," she continued. "And I can't pass up an opportunity to embarrass Elspeth. Even when she's not there."

I decided I was glad she was my cousin and not my sister. But I grinned at her. "No, you should sit with us," I said. "At least until the novelty wears off and we start hating each other."

"I give it a week, at least," she said, and turned to lead me into the house. "It would be a shame, though. You're the only cousin I've got."

She led me out of the entryway, down a long, narrow hall, and into a parlor with soft blue furnishings and the clinging scent of roses. Crossing the room, Iris moved to each of the windows and tugged them open one by one.

"I never had cousins before, either," I said, though I couldn't say I'd really felt the lack. But there was something both strange and familiar about Iris, as though we'd shared secrets long ago. For the briefest of moments, I could see what it might have been like if we'd known each other as children: the two of us with our heads bent in the garden, whispering, turning to flee the long shadow cast by an adult. I saw our hands cupping butterflies in fields overgrown with wildflowers. An almost-history, a what-if that lay between us. Then it was gone, replaced with the image of Iris as she was, her dark hair falling down her back. There was a sadness in the way she held herself.

But her smile warmed her face. "It *is* nice we're at the same school," she said. "Though I guess the odds were good.

Grandmother wouldn't let me transfer unless I went to another Kin school."

"Kin school?" I repeated.

"Most Kin students attend one of a few schools around the Cities. Whitman is one of them."

I supposed that explained Mr. Alvarez's teaching there. "Where were you before?"

"Private school. It—wasn't my thing. Elspeth loves it, though. She threw such a fit when she found out I was transferring. She's a bit of a baby sometimes." Iris laughed lightly, shaking her head. I looked at her, assessing. Iris was short and thin, fine-boned as a bird. She wasn't beautiful like Elspeth, but there was an elegance about her that I envied.

In the cool evening light that poured in through the windows, I saw again the triple knot on the chain at her neck. The silver pendant dangled at the hollow of her throat, just above her collarbone. Watching my gaze, she lifted her hands behind her head and unclasped it.

"It was a present from my boyfriend," she said, handing the necklace to me. "You can look at it."

"The symbol of the Astral Circle," I said, taking it in my palm. The triple knot was light and cool against my skin. It wasn't silver, as I'd first thought, but some other metal I didn't recognize. I handed it back. "It's beautiful. I guess you're dating one of those eligible Kin boys Esther was telling me about?"

Iris continued smiling at me. "Is she already starting with that?

Don't let her bother you. Just pretend you're letting her manage you, and then do as you please." She paused, closing her hand around the triple knot.

I turned away and moved to the windows. A low breeze pushed at the open curtains.

"You live with Esther?" I asked.

"My parents passed away two years ago. Elspeth and I have lived here since. And our brother, when he's home from school."

A sense came to me then. A sudden, clear image, as though it had been drawn on the windowpane in front of me. Iris dressed in black, her hands folded, grass beneath her feet and the long sad length of a graveyard; her eyes were lowered, and when she looked up—there was something broken and haunted within them, a grief so sharp and sudden I had a physical reaction to it. I stepped back from the window to take a long breath.

"I'm so sorry," I said, and hoped she knew I meant it.

I turned, and Iris caught my left hand, folding it neatly in hers. "Audrey, I owe you an apology," she said. Her eyes, the same gold-brown color as Esther's, were wide and worried. "I was at the Drought and Deluge the night you were attacked. I was in the alley, but I got scared. I panicked, and I ran. I'm sorry. I should never have left you there."

The sudden wind, I thought. Iris's long hair disappearing down the dark hall.

At least I knew I hadn't been imagining things. I couldn't blame her for panicking, not after I'd spent the past week hiding in my bedroom and trying to pretend the rest of the world didn't exist.

"I'm fine," I said. "You don't have to worry."

She smiled and released my hand. "All right. I'll leave you to Grandmother, then. I have plans tonight, but I'll see you at school tomorrow. We'll talk."

According to Esther, my grandfather Charles was overseas on business and wouldn't return until December. I had another cousin— Iris and Elspeth's brother—and somewhere in California I had an uncle. Eventually, I would be given an introduction to the rest of the Kin. I would then be expected to take my place as an active member of the community, or so Esther informed me.

"But what about my father?" I asked, an uneasy knot forming in my stomach. "Where is he?"

Esther's mouth tightened into a thin line. "New York," she said, and would say no more, no matter how I pressed. When I asked what he was doing there, she said, "Business." When I asked if he ever visited, she said, "Rarely."

Instead, she told me about the Kin.

There were many of us once, she said, when our ancestors first crossed over from the Beneath to live as humans, letting their powers sleep. Our gifts were echoes from the past, a force running through our blood, binding us together, making us Kin. But as time passed, our people fragmented, wandered, scattered across the earth. The bloodlines thinned.

"And then," she said, "the Harrowings began."

The first of the Harrowers crossed over, and they were no longer like the Old Race, gentle beings of wisdom and peace. They were hungry, vengeful, distorted by their hate. They hunted the Kin. And the casualties were staggering.

"But we were not defenseless. Among some of our people, the sleeping powers woke, creating Guardians. Those who were called gained strength, speed, resilience—and the power to fight our enemy. We survived. We prevailed. And we were no longer scattered. Now, we band together where the Circles lie, protecting them as they protect us."

"The Circles," I repeated.

"You will have sensed ours, no doubt."

I nodded hesitantly; it wasn't constant, but it was something I felt now and then, at the edge of my Knowing. A quiet presence.

Esther's voice grew solemn. "You won't have seen it, however," she said. "The Circles' energy manifests as glimmers of light . . . and ours has been dark for some time."

I nodded again. Gram had mentioned that, as well. "But what exactly are they?"

"The Circles are shields. Barriers. When the Old Race crossed over, the fabric that separates our world from the Beneath was weakened. Our ancestors could not seal their points of passage, you see, and in the areas surrounding their crossings, the fabric had grown thin. So they created the Circles, to hold back the dark. To bar the way as best they could."

"Like a force field."

Esther blinked at me. "In a sense."

"Gram said—" I thought back. *The power that lives in you.* "Gram said the Astral Circle was a part of us."

"More of Angela's stories? I suppose she did try to prepare you, in her own way." Esther inclined her head. "Our remaining knowledge of the Old Race is limited. We don't know precisely how they created the Circles, but we suspect it was connected, in some way, to their blood. We know the power that runs through the Circles is the same power that courses through our veins. And that is why we sense them. Blood calls to blood."

I considered this, remembering the way I had first felt the Circle, the hum in my skin, the warmth pulsing through me. "That's a little creepy. But neat. I think."

Esther gave me a stern look. "It's of considerably greater significance than that. When the Astral Circle's power is full, only the strongest of Harrowers are able to move through it. It keeps the threat contained, keeps our people safe."

"And our Circle is broken."

"Not broken, precisely. Diminished. It was severely damaged during the Harrowing seventeen years ago. Its energy is nearly spent. Far too many Harrowers are able to push through it, and their numbers have grown at an alarming rate."

"So, it's a force field that's running low on batteries." I chewed my lip. "And if it *were* destroyed?"

Esther wasn't one to sugarcoat things. "The Harrowers would pass through unchecked."

Not a thought I wanted to entertain. I shuddered.

"But," she told me, "that's why there are Guardians. We protect what the Circle cannot."

Guardian, she explained, was both a specific and a general term. Most Kin who were called as Guardians weren't meant to protect any one thing, but used their powers to fight—and to shield anyone in need. It was an act of devotion, a bond between Guardian and the world. Some Guardians were called with a particular purpose, though it was rarer. Only when the need was great, she said. Or the danger.

And then there was my mother.

"There's never been anyone else quite like Lucy," she said. "Her power was like nothing we'd seen before. She was a herald of change, a symbol of hope. And of fear. We knew when she was called that there would be a Harrowing, and that she would be the one to end it. It's what she was born to do. No matter how she fought against it."

That part took me by surprise. We'd lived away from the Cities for years, but it had never occurred to me that my mother hadn't wanted to be a Guardian.

That once, perhaps, she had wanted to be something other than Morning Star.

"The key to defending yourself against a Harrower is to make yourself an unlikely target. If you fight back hard enough, they usually give up. Go for the throat, always." Mom lifted two fingers to her neck and pressed against the notch above her collarbone. I nodded, following her movement.

It had taken a few days of pestering, but after school on Thursday, Mom brought me to the room in the basement that doubled as her office and training area. I wasn't allowed here often, and since Mom usually kept the door locked, I'd taken to calling it Bluebeard's Chamber. I was always a little disappointed to discover it mostly held exercise equipment and spare hoodies, no hidden cache of weapons or severed heads. A desk and a filing cabinet sat at the far end, and a few folders with the H&H Security logo were arranged nearby. Closer to the door were Mom's punching bag and treadmill, and a blue exercise mat lay beneath us.

"The goal is to disable," she said. "That's all you need to do—disable and run. Are you following?"

"Disable and run," I repeated, giving her a little salute from my position on the floor. "But...doesn't that leave them a little too alive?"

"I'm teaching you to defend yourself, not go on a killing spree."

"Dead Harrowers are less likely to hurt me," I pointed out. "And I already know self-defense."

"You know self-defense against humans," she said. "Harrowers are different. They're more powerful than you. They're faster, they're stronger, and they heal quickly. Your best chance is to land a blow here"—she tapped her throat again—"and get the hell out of there."

"It still seems like a better idea to kill them."

"Remember to stay focused," Mom continued, ignoring my remark. "Harrowers rely on your fear of them, and fear can be hypnotic. Don't let them distract you. Stay in control."

I sighed, pulling my knees up against me. "Isn't there some way to...I don't know, repel them?"

Mom gave me a curious look. "What did you have in mind?"

"Sunlight? Garlic? Silver bullets? Salt? Or, you know, *a gun*?"

"I'm not letting you near firearms."

"Why not?"

"Do I need a reason to not want my teenage daughter running around with a concealed weapon? The point of this exercise is to put you in *less* danger." She paused, frowning. "Generally, guns aren't much use against Harrowers. You'd have to be incredibly quick, and you'd need perfect aim."

"So…that's a no?"

"And this is why *I'm* not teaching her," Leon said from somewhere behind us.

I jerked in surprise. "You know it's creepy when you just appear without announcing yourself, right?"

"I took the stairs. Not my fault you didn't hear me," he said, walking into the room. He'd been quieter than usual the past week. We'd barely spoken since the night he'd taken me to meet Esther, and I hadn't seen him around the house. If not for the half-eaten bowls of cereal he left in the sink, I might have assumed he'd moved out.

He handed Mom her phone. She glanced at it briefly and said, "Well, hell. I've gotta go. Could you finish up here?"

I turned to Leon. Neither of us spoke as Mom hurried up the stairs. He wasn't quite looking at me, and a knot had worked its way into his forehead. Above us, the front door slammed shut. "It's okay," I said, standing. "I can wait until Mom has more time."

Leon sighed. He walked over to Mom's desk and tapped his fingers against it. "She's not going to have more time. Let's just get on with this."

"Not if you're going to be grumpy about it."

"I'm not grumpy."

"You do an impressive imitation, then." The corners of his

mouth twitched upward, which I took as a good sign. "Does this mean you're planning to be helpful?"

He folded his arms, leaning back against the desk, and tilted his head as he looked at me. "Lucy covered the basics. What more do you want to know?"

How to stop being scared, I thought.

"How do we kill them?" I asked.

Leon shrugged. "How do you kill anything? Cut off its head. Stab it through the heart. Break its neck. Bleed it to death."

I blinked. "Well. That's . . . um, gruesome."

"You asked. What did you expect me to say?"

"With kindness?"

Apparently, that was the wrong response. Leon's eyebrows snapped together. "I'm glad you've overcome your fear enough to make light of the situation," he said, suddenly stern. He kept his arms crossed, his eyes narrowed, doing his best to look grim and foreboding. "You really want to know how to kill? Have you ever killed anything that isn't an insect?"

"Like what, small fuzzy animals? No, because I'm *not* actually a serial killer in training." I'd hit a deer with Mom's car last spring, but I didn't think that counted, especially since I'd cried for an hour afterward. But a demon? That would be different. "And you can't tell me you go around cutting off heads. You're just trying to freak me out. Also, *ew*." I gave him a critical look. His shirt was white and crisp, freshly ironed. I'd seen blood on his clothing before, but only when he'd been injured, himself. "How do *you* kill them?"

The frown disappeared. His expression was carefully blank. "Guardians have resources. We always have our best weapon with us. Our powers nullify theirs. And—Lucy would prefer to keep you out of Guardian business."

Which meant he wasn't going to tell me anything. Good-little-sidekick Leon would never dream of disobeying.

"So, that's it. Being a Guardian is some sort of special club, and I don't know the secret handshake?" I groaned in frustration. "But what if I'm called? Shouldn't I be ready?" That had been bothering me since my last session with Esther, when she'd told me how Guardians were called. Until then, I'd always believed Mom and Leon had simply been born with their powers, the way I'd been born with my Knowing. Now...

Now, Leon wasn't even looking at me. "You won't be called," he said, facing the wall.

"I could be," I argued. "Esther says it doesn't usually happen until the late teens. And Mom was called, and she's only half-blooded." Esther had told me that, too: Mom's father, Jacky, hadn't been Kin.

"It's not determined by your parentage," Leon said. "It just happens."

"Exactly." According to Esther, no one knew what triggered the calling, only that it seemed to be a sort of biological response to the Harrower threat. "You can't say I won't be called—unless

162

you understand the grand scheme of the universe." In which case, I really would have to start calling him Almighty Leon.

He turned to stare at me. "You want to be a Guardian." Not a question. Pure disbelief.

"I don't know," I admitted. A few weeks ago, I wouldn't have hesitated—but that was when I thought it meant being a hero, saving the city, helping the helpless. Now I wasn't certain what to feel. On the one hand, it meant power and excitement and purpose. On the other hand: demons. Fighting them. Killing them. Despite my bravado, I wasn't at all certain I could handle that.

I looked at Leon again, studying him. He had a particular way of standing, an ease and confidence in the way he moved. I wondered if that was a Guardian thing, or just him. "Did you want to?"

Instead of answering my question, he said, "A week ago you wouldn't leave your bedroom, and now you want to face demons."

"I don't *want* to face them," I said, heat creeping up my cheeks. I wasn't about to tell him how frightened I still was. "But they're out there, and I want to be prepared. I'm Kin, so I'm a target; isn't that how it goes? I may as well fight. I'm not helpless. I've been in martial arts since I was eight."

"To defend yourself," Leon said.

"Which I failed at, in case you forgot. It was horrible, and I don't want it to happen again."

"It won't happen again." His voice was soft.

"No?" My hands clenched into fists. I hated how easily he could dismiss my words. "I'm not *actually* stupid, Leon. I know something is going on, something big. It's why you moved in, right? Why Mom is so cryptic and moody and the two of you go silent whenever I enter the room. I don't want to be kept in the dark anymore. I want to be taught. I want to be trained."

A look of alarm, brief and anxious, flickered across his face. "It's not that simple," he said. "Physically, most humans—even Kin—are no match for Harrowers. Guardians are stronger. We're meant to fight, and it's still not easy for us. It's not fun, and it's not safe. People get hurt. People die."

People like his parents.

Leon had a right to his concern, but considering how much effort he'd expended trying to reassure me only a week ago, his words rang a little hollow. "Aren't you the one who told me not to worry? That I don't need to be scared? *We're out there*, you said. So it's all right for you, but not for me? You go out and fight while I sit around hoping I don't get attacked?"

"That's what Guardians do. We protect the rest of the Kin."

"Just because I haven't been called doesn't mean I can't fight."

"That's *exactly* what it means." Before I could blink, he was standing before me, so close it was uncomfortable. I threw a hand up to push him away, and he caught my wrist. His eyes burned down on me. "Wanting to be a Guardian doesn't make you one. It's not all about training, or skill. It's about strength, and speed, and endurance. Humans are fragile. Harrowers aren't."

His attitude provoked me. Even if I wasn't a Guardian, I wasn't defenseless. I'd taken down bigger adversaries than him. I decided to show him just how fragile I wasn't.

I circled my wrist under, breaking his grip. It would be immensely satisfying to send him to the floor, I thought. I took hold of his arms, turning him for the throw as I did a foot sweep.

Leon reacted faster than I anticipated.

He lifted one of his feet, hooking it around mine, and grabbed my shoulders, dragging me down with him. I tried to twist away, to keep myself from falling, but his grip was firm. When he hit the floor, I landed directly on top of him.

My eyes met his. For a split second, neither of us moved. His expression held a fleeting hint of surprise.

"Not bad," he said.

I pushed away and jumped to my feet. Leon was quick to follow.

Hoping to catch him off guard, I went on the offensive. I didn't plan to hurt him—just bruise his ego a little. Knowing he'd have no choice but to block it, I aimed a blow high, intending to follow up with a punch to his stomach. Knocking the wind out of him would be a suitable lesson.

Again he was ready for it. He didn't block my fist; he caught it, moving backward to dodge my second punch. Before I could pull out of his grip, he jerked me forward and spun me, putting me into a hold with my back tucked against him.

"But not *nearly* good enough," he whispered into my ear.

I wasn't about to concede defeat. I dropped my weight, ducking out of his arms. On one knee, I spun around and lunged for his leg, pulling it out from beneath him. So much for his boasts of Guardians and their abilities. Down he went.

Or rather, down he *started*. He didn't hit the ground. He didn't hit anything. He was just—gone.

It took me only a second to realize what had happened. The little cheater had teleported himself away, presumably to land someplace comfortable. Like his bed.

With a growl of outrage, I hopped to my feet and headed for the door, intending to tell him exactly what I thought of such a maneuver.

I'd only taken half a step when my arm was jerked behind me. I didn't have time to fight back before I found myself lowered face-first to the floor, with a close-up view of the exercise mat—and Leon's shoes.

Seething, I pushed myself upward with my hands and glared at him. "You don't fight fair."

His voice was cool, quiet. "No, I don't fight fair," he said. "What makes you think a demon will?"

And then, before I could answer, he was gone.

During the next few weeks I settled into routine. School was busier than usual, but since it was my only opportunity to see my friends, I didn't complain. Not that I was particularly happy with them. Some of Gideon's friends from the baseball team began invading our lunch table—even though it was several months before practice started—and they refused to talk about anything that didn't involve sports. Tink had a new boyfriend, an exchange student from Brazil she kept pretending to not understand. She started ditching us to make out with him in the orchestra hall.

"I don't get how you have so much success with boys," I told her during Chemistry, one of the few times I managed to see her.

"You don't let them talk," she said. "If they start, you just kiss them until they shut up." Unless, of course, they were terrible kissers. Poor Greg.

"You are truly the most dysfunctional person I've ever met," Gideon said.

She retaliated by dumping shimmer powder on him.

My sessions with Esther continued. She taught me about the Kin, about abilities and social structure, about communications with Kin in other areas. There weren't many of us, so connection was important. She spoke of duty and the hidden role the Kin played in the management of cities.

Elspeth sat in on some of the sessions, though she spent most of the time interrupting her grandmother, or dozing off in an armchair whenever the talk grew too dull. She was a Guardian, I'd learned, and something of a prodigy: she'd been called a year ago, and though she was still a few months shy of sixteen, she was active in Kin policy whenever she could be. But despite Esther's talk about the burden of being a Guardian, the weight they carried, Elspeth was anything but serious and subdued; she was everything sweet and sunny. If my ability to detect auras had extended beyond Gideon, I was certain hers would be bubblegum pink.

Iris was different.

Because they were so close in age—born only sixteen months apart—I'd expected Iris and Elspeth to be best friends. But, while it was apparent they cared for one another, they didn't spend much time together. I guessed it had to do with the differences in their personalities. Where Elspeth was outgoing (and admittedly rather loud), involved in a variety of school activities, and enthusiastic about the Kin, Iris was much more reserved, keeping mostly to herself. Not to mention, Elspeth was a Guardian and Iris wasn't. It couldn't be easy having your younger sister constantly in the spotlight. I didn't question them about it.

There were other matters troubling me.

Three weeks after my attack at the Drought and Deluge, another girl went missing.

The missing girl's name was Tricia Morrow.

The TV stations flashed her school photo, and her warm smile beamed out in black and white on the front page of every paper. Her mother was shown teary-eyed, pleading. Tricia loved ballet, she said. She dreamed of being a veterinarian. She was only sixteen.

The details on Tricia's disappearance were few. Like Kelly Stevens, she'd vanished at dusk, without word or witness. There was no blood trail, no sign to follow, no hint of where she'd gone; she'd simply been swallowed up into the cooling night. But, unlike when Kelly disappeared, the news didn't spread immediately. Tricia had reportedly been unhappy at home. The police had thought her just another runaway, until her coat was found discarded in an alley, dirty and torn, two weeks later.

Though the police had yet to establish a definitive link, the similarities between Tricia and Kelly were enough to cause whispers and concern. At school, teachers cautioned us not to go out alone at night, to keep our phones with us, to keep our friends close.

Since Mom was unwilling to discuss Guardian matters with me, I asked Esther about it during our session that Monday.

"She's dead," she said flatly, taking her customary seat, appearing entirely serene. "If they bled her, she's dead."

Her matter-of-fact declaration rattled me, but I tried not to show it. Instead, I said, "I'm alive. They bled me." I felt a burn at the back of my ankles.

She gave me a cool glance. "You were lucky. Others have not been so fortunate."

Aside from her certainty that Tricia Morrow was dead, she wasn't willing to spend much time on the subject. "The Guardians are doing all they can," she assured me, giving me another calm, even look. "We must trust in their abilities. Presently, I'm more concerned with your education. You are here to further your knowledge of the Kin, and we have a great deal left to cover."

I decided to ask Elspeth instead.

Elspeth's favorite subject was the Kin, and she was never hesitant to discuss it with me. She was the one who told me the sort of everyday things that Esther didn't deem important—like the fact that the Kin ran H&H, the security company my mother worked for, and that, when he wasn't busy torturing high school students, Ryan Alvarez led the Cities' Guardians.

"Tricia went to my school," Elspeth said, seated at the edge of her bed. It was the first time I'd seen her frown, and she did it with her entire face, turning that sweet, cheerful demeanor solemn. "We didn't know she was Kin—it must not be a close connection."

"When I first asked about it, Esther said the bleedings are happening for a reason," I said. I sat on the floor, in the small space of carpet not buried by Elspeth's belongings. "That the Harrowers are searching for something. A . . . Remnant, I think. She called it a piece of our past."

Elspeth shook her head. "It's not something, it's some*one*. The Remnant is Kin—someone born with the abilities of the Old Race."

That only confused me more. "I thought all our abilities came from the Old Race."

"This is something specific," she said. Then she was silent a moment, chewing her lower lip. "Look—you know about the Circles, right? The Old Race left them behind as shields, spread across the original passages, where the fabric is thin. But Harrowers can still pass through in places where the barriers are weakest, and they can't cross over anywhere else."

Esther had mentioned this already; Harrowers couldn't travel up from Beneath just anywhere. That was also the reason Kin stayed near the Circles: to protect them and keep the Harrower threat contained.

I nodded, waiting for Elspeth to continue.

"A Remnant is born with the power to—Grandmother calls it *the ability to manipulate the fabric between realms.* They can open

171

more passages, just like the Old Race could. Anywhere. Everywhere. In places not shielded by the Circles."

"No wonder the demons want it," I said. My tone was light, but my insides had gone very cold. I sat back, hugging my arms.

"Some think it might be even worse than we know. They think a really powerful Remnant could open the Beneath entirely—across the entire world. Forever. Maybe even create a passage through time. I don't think that's possible, but if Harrowers could cross anywhere they wanted . . . we couldn't fight that." Elspeth wasn't paying attention to me. Though she sat facing me, her eyes were distant and vague. "That's why the last Harrowing happened. This demon—Verrick—he'd Seen that something was about to happen. The birth of *a Kin-blooded girl who carries the powers of old.* Or something like that. The Harrowing ended when Verrick was killed, but I guess other demons are still after this Remnant. They don't know who she is or exactly when she was born, so they're searching. They'll know when they find her. And if they do, they'll use her to open more passages."

"Which could mean another Harrowing," I said, swallowing tightly.

"Not just any Harrowing," Elspeth whispered. The fear in her eyes chilled me. "The worst we've ever seen."

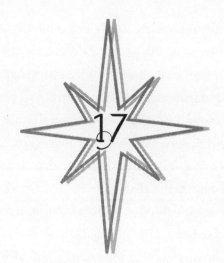

"Are you sure you know what you're doing?" I looked at the assortment of bowls and baking products Leon had set out on the table. There didn't seem to be any order or particular arrangement to them, and there wasn't a recipe in sight.

"If you don't want to help, stay out of the kitchen." Leon hooked a thumb over his shoulder and pointed at the door. I remained where I was.

I wasn't feeling very charitable toward him. I was still angry about his behavior during my demon-defense lesson, and for the past couple of weeks I'd done my best to avoid him—especially since he didn't appear inclined to apologize to me. When I did see him, he'd been polite but unrepentant. That only served to aggravate me more. Tonight I'd called an informal truce between us for the occasion of my mother's birthday; not that he seemed to notice, or care.

"It's not really *me* baking her a cake if *you* do all the work," I said, opening the lid of the frosting I'd bought and dipping my finger into it. I might be useless when it came to baking, but frosting, at least, I understood.

In addition to Mom's fortieth birthday, the end of November had brought with it cooler days, longer nights, and the year's first major snowfall. It was only 10 p.m., but I could already see the lace edge of ice creeping up the kitchen window. I hoped my mom had remembered to wear one of her fleece-lined hoodies, even if the cold didn't bother her.

Mom had insisted we not throw her a party. Since she hated surprises and didn't exactly have any friends, I'd agreed not to. But I did plan on celebrating, regardless of demons, bleedings, potential annihilation, and whatever else was going on out in the Cities. Barring any catastrophes—human, Harrower, or otherwise— Mom had promised to stop home around midnight. Which meant Leon and I had two hours to bake the cake and finish decorating.

"You're doing this without a recipe?" I asked.

Leon ignored me and set to work, measuring out flour and dumping it into one of the mixing bowls. His sleeves were rolled up, but he'd declined to wear the heart-dappled apron I'd made in eighth grade. "Watching doesn't actually qualify as helping," he said, reaching for the baking soda. "In case you were wondering."

"I'm supervising." I took my frosting and retreated to the counter, where I continued to watch him.

"I already made icing. I told you not to buy any."

"Oops," I said, taking another scoop. "Looks like I messed up again. Guess I'll have to eat this."

He glanced toward me, giving a pointed look to the containers I had set beside me. I'd bought two flavors. Pink and vanilla. "All of it?" he asked.

"Maybe if you're nice, I'll share." I leaned back against the counter, disturbing the paper streamers I'd taped to the cupboards. Leon worked in silence, his hands moving between bags and mixing bowls. I glowered at him. "But considering you've already met your niceness quota for the year, I wouldn't bet on it. And you can't have any sprinkles."

"There goes my reason for living."

"I thought that was to make me miserable," I muttered, giving him a sour look.

"Still nursing that grudge, I see."

I left my position at the counter, padding across the linoleum to the table. "You don't think I might deserve an apology?"

He snorted. "You deserve *something*."

"For being curious? For wanting to know how to defend myself?" Leon opened his mouth to respond, but I waved a hand and rushed on. "Maybe you're right. Maybe I can't fight demons. I'm not some big badass Guardian with amazing superpowers. But that doesn't mean I should be kept in the dark about everything. There's a lot more going on than you guys are saying."

Leon was silent a long moment. He'd paused in his work, his hands on the mixing bowl, but he wasn't looking at me. Finally he said, "That's not my call."

"Does that mean you don't agree with Mom?" I asked, with a touch of surprise.

"It means that whether I agree or not is irrelevant."

I sighed. "This is why you're only the sidekick, you know." When that didn't get a reaction, I added, "And you're still a dirty cheater."

He glanced up long enough to give me his very best condescending look. "You tried to prove something. You failed. Get over it."

And then he went back to measuring things.

I narrowed my eyes, watching him. There was that ease of motion again, that quiet confidence. He was always so sure of himself. And so tidy, with his nice, crisp, white shirt.

Entirely too tidy.

My gaze flicked to the table. Moving leisurely forward, I dragged my fingers across the tablecloth and reached for the bag of flour. "Again, you are absolutely right," I announced. Then I grabbed a handful of flour, pressed it into a ball with my fist, and flung it straight at him.

Most of it disintegrated before it hit him, but when he looked at me, he had a nice layer of white dusting him.

His frown made a floury wrinkle on his forehead. "Uh, what are you doing?"

"Getting over it." I gave him a bright smile and aimed another handful at him.

He saw this one coming, and managed to teleport away before it hit him. Half a second later, he returned, looking at me with a mixture of confusion and annoyance. "Are you throwing a tantrum?"

"I'm expressing my feelings." I flung a third handful of flour at him. "With cake mix."

This time, when he teleported, he grabbed the bag of flour and took it with him. He reappeared behind me and poured it directly over my head.

I gasped, seeing white. Through the sudden haze in my vision, I saw Leon back on the other side of the table. He only had that thin layer of flour on him. I was covered in it.

Hiding my face with one hand, I cringed sideways. Toward the sugar. "Did you have to get my *eyes*?"

He was instantly contrite. "I'm sorry—"

I grabbed the bag of sugar and flung its contents toward him.

He was quick, but not quick enough. Sugar hit him in the shoulder, sliding down his shirt, and when he teleported behind me to make a grab for the bag, I wriggled away from him and dashed across the kitchen.

Unfortunately, Leon had decided to fight back in earnest. When I blinked, he was in front of me. I turned to flee, but not before he dumped half a box of baking soda on my head.

Worried he might launch another attack, I ducked beneath

the table, taking the remaining flour with me. I moved quickly, dropping both hands into the bag, then I rose and lobbed the flour at him. One handful landed on his collar; the other caught the side of his head. I darted away, searching for more ammo.

"This is *not* how you make a birthday cake," Leon complained as a stream of salt caught him in the chest. "What exactly are you trying to express here? Lunacy?"

We faced each other across the room, the table between us. His blue eyes were dark and intent. He watched my movements, his gaze wary, like he stood in a war zone, not a brightly lit kitchen with peeling floral wallpaper and too many fridge magnets. I almost laughed. Only Leon could manage to look serious while covered in baking ingredients.

"Did I ruin your nice clean outfit?" I taunted, my hands closing around the nearly empty bag of flour. "Bet you wish you'd worn that apron."

He snorted again. "You're right. Knowing your temper, I should've predicted this outcome."

Like he was really one to talk about tempers. That earned him another handful of flour. "I forgot. Saint Leon never loses his cool."

"Admit it," he said, tossing more baking soda in my direction. "You're just pissed that I kicked your ass."

I rolled my eyes, grabbing a mixing bowl and holding it in front of me as a shield. "I wouldn't call your cheating an ass-kicking. If you hadn't teleported, I'd have won."

"You keep telling yourself that." He leaned forward, pulled the bowl out of my hands, spun it once on his finger, then let it slide to the table.

"I don't have to," I replied, my hand groping toward the nearest bag. "I was *there.*"

He didn't even bother to dodge the flour I tossed at him. It caught his jaw, giving him a white dusting of stubble. With a smile, he said, "I was going easy on you."

"Really? Was that before or after I knocked you off your feet?"

"I don't seem to recall going down alone."

"Yeah, but as you keep telling me, *you're a Guardian.* I'm just some kid who knows a few tricks."

"If you really want a rematch," he said, "you know where I live." Then he sent the rest of the sugar onto my blouse.

I searched about frantically for any sort of ammunition. The kitchen was a mess, and most of the baking ingredients were scattered about the room. The cake pans had somehow ended up on the floor. There was very little left to throw. My hand shot toward the vanilla. I unscrewed the cap and aimed it toward him.

He ended up with a streak down his shirt and a frown on his face. But I wasn't done yet. I'd spotted the big guns.

"This *is* the rematch," I said. "And I'm about to win." I made a dash for the counter, where I'd left the frosting. Both containers: pink, vanilla, and all of the sprinkles. I'd nearly reached them when Leon once again teleported behind me.

Just as I'd anticipated.

I dug into the frosting, grabbing handfuls of both flavors, and whirled around—catching him square in the chest.

I sighed happily. "Sweet, sweet victory," I said, smearing the frosting down his shirt. "Literally."

He glanced down at the mess I'd made of him, gobs of frosting leaving a pink-and-white trail along his ribs. Then he looked at me, raising a single eyebrow. "Feel better?"

I nodded, not bothering to hide my grin. "That was pretty satisfying, I've gotta admit."

He didn't retaliate. He didn't scold. He didn't even try to Hungry Puppy me. Instead, he let out a little sigh and said, "Are we even now, or are you planning to stick me in the oven next?"

It wasn't *I'm sorry,* but it wasn't bad, as far as apologies went.

"We're even," I said. "Almost." And then I reached up to drag frosting through that dark curly hair of his.

He caught me by the wrists.

"All right." He laughed. "We're moving into cruel-and-unusual territory, here."

I tried to pull free, but he held fast. With my back to the counter, I had nowhere to retreat. He had me trapped. I flattened my palms, doing my best to appear repentant. "Okay. Truce time. I surrender."

"I believe you." He didn't release me.

I looked up at him. He didn't look tidy any longer. He was a mess. Flour streaked his hair and face, dusting the ends of his eyelashes, the bridge of his nose. I'd somehow managed to get frosting on his chin. He kept fighting a smile that tugged at his lips.

My heart did a funny little flip.

From the hall came the sound of the front door opening.

Leon dropped my wrists. We turned toward the door, then back to each other. We didn't move. We probably should have. Even if we couldn't clean the kitchen in the time it would take my mother to reach us, we could have at least fled the scene. Instead we just stared at each other in horror as the sound of footsteps grew louder. Which is exactly how my mother found us a moment later.

But, as it turned out, we had bigger problems.

Mom wasn't alone. Beside her, in the slant of light that cut through the doorway, stood Detective Wyle.

It took my mother a moment to register the state of the kitchen. She'd been speaking to Detective Wyle as she entered, then broke off mid-sentence. She looked around at the damage: flour and sugar scattered across the linoleum, bags and bowls overturned on the table, pans on the floor, frosting on the counter.

"What the hell happened in here?" She didn't even sound angry. Just really, really confused.

That made two of us. Her clothing wasn't necessarily incriminating—she had her H&H Security coat on—but she'd left that night to patrol as Morning Star, and here she was, home early…with a police officer. One she wasn't on the best of terms with. That didn't bode well.

"Baking?" I suggested.

Detective Wyle cleared his throat. Mom continued to stare.

Leon just looked sheepish. "Sorry, Lucy," he said. Then he made a dash for the door.

The traitor.

I looked back at Mom and shrugged. "We were making you a cake. We, um, missed."

Detective Wyle chuckled. He looked tired and even scruffier than the last time I'd seen him. He certainly knew how to play the brooding antihero, all rough edges and stubble and dark rumpled hair.

Except for his clothing, anyway. He was dressed plainly, in old jeans and a raggedy black sweatshirt with a hole in the collar—but considering I was two eggs and a stick of butter short of being walking cake batter, I couldn't say anything.

"Hi, Mickey," I said, giving him a jaunty smile.

He scrutinized me closely and chose not to comment on the flour in my hair or the frosting on my hands; instead he said, "Hey, kid. You doing all right?"

"Except for being a powdered doughnut."

That got a smile. "Feel like any more fortune-telling?"

I glanced at my mother. Her expression was stormy. Even without a Knowing I'd be able to sense the trouble brewing. I could almost see little thunderclouds gathering around her. Her forehead was creased, her lips a thin line, and from the glare she was aiming at Detective Wyle, I guessed it hadn't been *her* idea for him to follow her home.

Maybe he'd threatened to arrest her again.

"I predict you're about two seconds from getting tossed out of here," I told him. Literally, I suspected, if Mom could figure out a way to do it without raising more questions.

His smile turned wry. "I see your opinion of me hasn't improved."

He was wrong. Looking at him, his way of standing, the tilt of his head, how the light caught that hint of gray in his hair—I Knew I could trust him. He was easy to read, and I had this sense about him: he didn't mean my mother any harm. There was no malice in him, no desire to injure. He wanted to help.

Of course, I also saw suspicion in his eyes. Not of Mom's motives, but of her actions.

"I hope you're not here for the party," I said, stepping between him and my mother. "Because I didn't finish putting up streamers, and our cake exploded. And it doesn't look like you brought a gift. Did you at least say happy birthday?"

He shoved his hands in his pockets and muttered under his breath.

Mom walked farther into the kitchen. Though her face was flushed, her eyes were focused and alert. She looked nothing like the sleepy, disheveled working mom she liked to portray in the outside world. I doubted it had escaped the detective's notice.

She must have had the same thought, because she reached back and pulled her hair free, shaking it messily onto her shoulders. She pulled off her coat, revealing a rose-colored tank top with a bunny on it. I was pretty sure she'd found that in the kid's department at Target.

Then I noticed a smear of red on her left arm.

"You're bleeding!" I cried, moving to her side.

"It's just a scratch," Mom said in dismissal, covering the wound with her hand. "Someone tried to mug me on the way home tonight. Luckily, Detective Wyle was on hand. He scared the man away."

He grunted, crossing his arms. "*Luckily.* You seemed capable of handling the situation."

Mom walked to the sink, widening the distance between them. "It's part of my job. And anyway, I grew up learning the value of self-defense," she said. "My father was a cop."

The corners of his mouth quirked up. "Yeah, I know. My old man's been giving me shit for hassling Jacky Whitticomb's little girl. I don't think I'll ever hear the end of it."

A frown flashed across her face. "Your father is Hank Wyle. Your parents came to my father's funeral."

There was a note of sadness in her tone. It was slight, something I Knew more than heard. A catch in the syllables of *funeral*, like the word didn't want to leave her throat. I'd heard the same thing in Gram's voice countless times. My grandfather had died when Mom was only fifteen, and though there were photographs of him around the house, though Mom and Gram spoke of him often, there was always a small silence between breaths. An ache that lingered.

"He was a good man," Mickey said, his voice gentle. "I wonder what he would think of vigilantism."

Mom turned away, grabbing a dishrag from the sink and slowly wiping down the counter. She shrugged. "I don't think the topic ever came up. Not really the sort of thing we talked about. He didn't like to bring his work home. He always said he couldn't be a good husband or father if he let it hang over him." She glanced over her shoulder at Mickey, and if he couldn't see the focus of her gaze, I could: the bare space of skin where his wedding ring had been.

I was about eighty-six percent certain that what she'd said was a lie, and she was just being mean. They'd clearly forgotten my presence at this point, so I sidled backward, toward the door.

"We met before, you know. As kids," Mickey said, ignoring her jab. He'd moved across the kitchen and stood looming over her. I couldn't tell if he was trying to intimidate or charm her. Maybe both.

Regardless of his intent, Mom was immune. She lifted a hand to wave away his remark. "I'm sure we did."

"Precinct picnics," Mickey added, continuing to crowd her.

"I don't really remember," Mom said. She stepped away from him, giving up ground. But she didn't seem nervous, just annoyed. "Was there something you wanted?"

"You never did say what you were doing lurking around the streets of Edina at ten at night."

She yawned into her hand. "I was visiting one of my boyfriends."

I couldn't help it. I giggled.

Mom, reminded of my existence, sent a silencing glare my way.

"Patrick Tigue?" Mickey asked, a perplexed look crossing his face. I couldn't tell if his tone meant disbelief or disgust.

"His gardener," Mom deadpanned. Then she gripped Mickey's arm and started leading him toward the doorway. "I'd like you to leave now, detective. It's late. And you're upsetting my daughter."

"Uh, he's not, really." I probably should have played along, but I was as curious as he was. Tigue—I'd heard the name recently. Mr. Alvarez had mentioned it the night I was attacked.

Which might mean it was connected to the bleedings.

Mickey was raising his eyebrows at me. "You're on my side now?"

I shrugged, trying to ignore the look my mother was giving me. "She grounded me. I have to get even somehow."

He put a hand on his chin, rubbing the trace of stubble there. A thin, jagged scar ran along his jaw, close to his mouth. "Tell you what," he said. "Why don't you go clean yourself up? I'll take care of this mess while I chat with your mom."

She appeared about to protest, but kept her mouth shut. I gave the detective a grin. Even if it was an obvious ploy to get rid of me, I decided I definitely liked Mickey Wyle.

18

I showered quickly. My clothing had taken most of the damage, but my hair was sticky with sugar. I scrubbed myself and shampooed and stood in the steam, letting the heat fog around me. I decided to toss my clothing in the wash before I went to bed —but first I wanted to hear what Mom and Detective Wyle were discussing. And I was not above spying.

After toweling myself dry and pulling on my pajamas, I slipped down the hall to the top of the stairs. They were still in the kitchen, their voices muffled. Cautiously, I crept downward, skipping the steps that creaked.

Through the door, I saw my mother's back, the light catching in her hair. Her voice came to me clearly.

"—if what you're suggesting is true, why hasn't there been an investigation? Or am I wrong in assuming you've taken the initiative here?"

"The first deaths were staged, made to look like accidents. The connection is subtle."

"Cuts," my mother said.

I Knew what that meant before Mickey said it. A shiver ran through me.

His tone was all seriousness, calm, intent. "On the backs of their ankles, just below the calf. Razor-thin," he said. "Five girls with it, and those are just the ones I was able to verify. The deaths are related. An individual—or a group of individuals—is responsible."

Mom moved, leaning back into the doorway, her arms crossed in front of her. "We've had this discussion before. Why are you here now?"

"We found another dead kid. A sixteen-year-old girl over in Eden Prairie."

Not Tricia Morrow, I thought. Someone else. More bleedings.

"That's horrible," my mother said. "But I don't see what it has to do with me. I know you've been following me. Unless you have police business, I think that counts as stalking. What is this about?"

"A month after the Stevens girl went missing, I was called to the scene of an accident. Two girls in a car had been involved in a hit and run. Both dead at the scene."

Mom was silent. She held herself very still, her body tense. Whatever Mickey was about to say, she knew it was coming.

"The thing is, they didn't know each other. They weren't friends. They lived in different cities, went to different schools. They didn't share the same hangouts or work together. There was no reason for both of them to be in that car when it crashed. In fact, the only connection between the two girls . . . is you. You were at both of their houses the night they died. Which is why I don't think it will surprise you when I tell you the crash was staged. The girls were already dead."

"If you know that much, I'm sure you also know that both their families contacted my firm, H&H Security. What are you accusing me of, detective?" Her voice was soft.

Mickey stepped into view. His hand hovered beneath my mother's elbow, almost touching. "I'm not accusing you. Maybe I should be—but I'm not. I'm asking for your *help*. You know something I don't, and you're holding out on me. And while you're holding out, kids are dying."

Mom's tone was deathly cool. "Believe me, detective, if I knew anything that would save lives, I'd share it. I can't help you."

He sighed deeply, moving away. "Two girls were attacked outside a club downtown recently. I heard one of them was yours."

"My daughter is fine," Mom told him. "You just saw her."

"Why is she grounded?"

"I caught her with weed."

I was rather offended by that, but thought it better to keep my mouth shut.

"What were you really doing in Edina tonight?"

"I work security in the area. The details are confidential. Contact my boss if you want confirmation. It's all legal."

Mickey's voice went low, quiet. "Look, we both know there's something here you're not telling me—but that's not what I'm after. These attacks are escalating. More kids are going to wind up dead if this isn't stopped, and soon. All I want is information. I won't ask how you came by it."

"That's generous of you."

He sighed again. "All right, we'll play it your way a while longer. When you're ready to talk, you have my number."

I shrank back against the steps as they left the kitchen. Mom was quick on Mickey's heels, as though she thought he might start snooping if she didn't get him safely outside.

He paused at the front door, turning back to face my mother. "The funny thing? Three of the dead kids are linked to Patrick Tigue. They volunteered at one of his charities. I wasn't staking you out tonight. I was watching him. Same as you. Good night, Miss Whitticomb. Happy birthday."

I sat on the staircase after Mickey had gone, trying to sort through what I'd heard. My hair was drying in clumps against my shoulders, and I teased my fingers through it absently, watching water pearl and drip at the ends. There was a slight chill in the air, blown in from outside, but I barely felt it.

Slashes on the ankle, I thought. Cuts, to test the blood. This was bigger than I'd realized. Five deaths, Mickey had said. Or was it six now? Or seven? Was he counting Tricia Morrow?

The scars above my heels itched.

"If you were trying to be sneaky, you really should've gone back upstairs."

I hadn't heard Mom approach. Startled, I let out a little yelp and tried to jump to my feet, only to lose traction on the slick bit of staircase where my hair had been dripping. I sat back down with a thump, sliding down the remaining three steps until I came to a halt on the floor.

"Ow."

"Oh, *Audrey*," Mom sighed, reaching out an arm to help me back up.

Leon stood behind her. The expression on his face told me he was trying very, very hard not to laugh. Not that he presented the most dignified appearance himself. His hair had been washed clean of flour but had dried strangely, bits sticking up on one side and curling around his ear on the other.

Unlike me, he hadn't changed into pajamas. He'd put on a clean shirt and pants, and stood holding his coat.

"I thought you weren't going out tonight," I told him.

"I was out. I'm back now."

"I needed him to take care of something for me while Detective Wyle was here," Mom said. She'd pulled her hair back into its bun and put her hoodie on. The night was still young; the streets needed watching. She'd leave again soon. But instead of heading out the door, she took a step back, looked at me, and said, "Let's go into the kitchen."

True to his word, Mickey had taken care of the mess. Part of it, anyway. The floor needed mopping, and bits of sugar were stuck to the walls, but the table had been wiped clean, and the mixing bowls were set neatly in the sink.

Mom motioned for me to sit. She stood across from me, near the counter, keeping her arms folded. I wondered if her injury had already healed. "Gonna try to pretend you weren't spying on me?" she asked.

I bit my lip. "Um..."

"You don't want to answer that." She sighed. Closing her eyes, she lifted a hand to her forehead. "I assume you heard most of it."

"I was in the shower part of the time," I said.

Her eyes flicked back open. She gave me an unamused look.

"Points for honesty?" I suggested.

Mom just sighed again. "I'd really rather keep you out of this," she said. "But it seems you're bent on working it out. So, we'll talk. But I need some assurances from you. I need you to understand how dangerous this is. The threat is very real, and anyone involved could get hurt. That includes you. I want you to promise me, from now on, you'll think before you act. You won't do anything like you did at that club."

"Once was enough for me," I said. I darted a glance toward Leon, who stood silent near the door. His face was unreadable.

A little worry knot appeared in Mom's forehead. "I'm serious."

"I promise," I said. "Does this mean you're going to answer my questions?"

"That depends on the question."

"I've already figured out some of it." When Mom lifted her eyebrows at me, I shrugged and said, "The Harrowers are searching for a Remnant. And they've been bleeding girls my age to find it, right? Killing them. That's what Mickey was talking about."

"What *Detective Wyle* was talking about," she corrected.

"And they're making the deaths look like accidents? I didn't know Harrowers did that."

Mom leaned back against the counter. She folded her arms, cupping her elbows with her hands. "No. They don't, usually. Most Harrowers don't bother with that sort of cunning. They like to kill, and they like to flaunt it. Their activity is easy to detect. But this—this is different, subtle. Well-hidden. And deliberate."

"They don't want us to know what they're up to," I guessed.

She nodded. "It began a little over a year ago, and it took us far too long to make the connection. It wasn't until the fourth death that we realized the girls were being bled." Pausing, she rubbed her face with her hand. "We should've used subtlety ourselves. Now that they know we're aware of their goal, they've increased the attacks."

"How many have there been?"

"You were the eighth," Leon said, his mouth tightening. Mr. Alvarez had said that as well; I'd forgotten.

Mom turned toward the window and tapped her fingers

against the counter. "We might have known about it sooner if the girls had been associated with the Kin, but most of them didn't have a close connection, just a trace of Kin blood. We still don't know how the Harrowers are finding them."

"They're—detecting them somehow?" I swallowed. That wasn't a comforting thought, but I did want to know.

"Somehow," Mom agreed. "On some level, Harrowers can always sense Kin, but this is stronger than that. More specific, more sophisticated. And we never know who they'll target next."

I heard the frustration in her tone. My mother was powerful. She was strong, fast; she knew how to fight and how to protect. She wasn't accustomed to being helpless. An image flashed through me: my mother, crouched near a hedge, the moonlight skimming off her hair. In the distance, a man hunkered low in a parked car. A shadow moved toward him.

She'd been watching someone. Waiting.

"Is that what you were doing tonight? Looking for one of their targets? You weren't mugged."

Mom looked offended at the suggestion anyone could possibly have mugged her, but it was Leon who spoke.

"We think Patrick Tigue has something to do with it."

I turned toward him. His voice was low and controlled, his blue eyes focused. There was no hint of playfulness now, or even of the stubborn, argumentative sidekick. This was Leon the Guardian.

I frowned. Patrick Tigue again. I closed my eyes, thinking. I knew of him, peripherally. He'd moved to the Twin Cities a few years ago, among rumors that he would be financing a new stadium or trying to buy one of our sports teams. The papers had been full of tidbits about him: his wealth, his life in Los Angeles, his exploits in Europe, the time he'd dated a princess. I'd never been able to figure out why anyone who had spent time sailing islands in the Pacific would want to move to a state where it snowed half the year—but, then, I'd never been able to figure out why the rest of us stayed, either.

Patrick Tigue, a young playboy, rich and idle and apparently up to no good. But what would a human be doing with Harrowers?

A jolt ran through me. I remembered something Esther had said in one of our sessions, about how demons took the shape of humans. Took human names.

"He's a Harrower," I said.

"He's old," Leon answered. "And very powerful."

"If you think he's behind it, why don't you just twist him into a pretzel?"

Mom shook her head. A lock of hair had come loose from her bun, curling near her jaw. "That's not how it works. We suspect Tigue is involved, but we aren't certain. He's not doing the bleedings himself, so we can't prove it."

"But... he's a demon. Isn't that sort of the main category of Things to Smite?"

"Some Harrowers live as humans and coexist peacefully," Leon said. "Until now, Tigue's done his best to fit in with society. He's a philanthropist. A model citizen."

That was news to me. No one had bothered to mention that aspect of demons.

"And he's high profile," Mom said. "That lends him some protection. He's lived as a human for a long time. He's known. If I'm going to wind up charged with his murder, I'd rather not do it until I have concrete evidence."

I made a *pffft* sort of sound. Mom had been running around as Morning Star most of her adult life, and she hadn't been caught yet.

"But that's not the main problem," she was saying. "If he is involved, he's not working alone. There's someone else connected to this, someone with power, helping to organize other Harrowers. That's why I've been watching him. I need to find his accomplice before I make my move, or the bleedings won't stop." She closed her eyes, letting out a long breath. "Unfortunately, he's good. He's got his own security—the human variety—and I always lose him when he goes Beneath."

I looked between Mom and Leon. Their faces were somber, their bodies tense.

"What can we do?" I asked.

"Continue to watch. Wait for him to make a move, which is what I was doing tonight when Detective Wyle interrupted me." Her tone was just a little bit sour.

I recalled her explanation. A mugging. And that image I'd had: the street dark and quiet, sudden motion in the stillness. "Detective Wyle saw you attacked?"

Mom snorted. "The Harrower went after *him*. I intervened and caught its attention." She paused, growing thoughtful. "I'm not sure if the attack was a ploy to get rid of me, or if Wyle's getting too close."

"He doesn't mean any harm," I said. "I get a sense from him. He means well. He's been after this a while."

"I didn't lie for my own self-preservation. We keep the Kin secret because we have to. He can't be involved, for his own protection."

She'd told me this before. It was the same reason she'd kept me in the dark. The same reason she insisted I never tell Gideon.

"But some humans must know," I objected. "What about your father? He wasn't Kin. Did he know?"

Mom hesitated, looking down at her hands. "My father was like Detective Wyle," she began. "He was a good man with an earnest desire to help."

She lifted her eyes to mine. For one fleeting moment, I felt in her something I'd never felt before: the buoyant, unburdened girl she'd been before Morning Star—and the sudden, staggering weight of grief.

"Yes," she said. "He knew. That's why he died."

19

Tricia Morrow was found the first week of December. Or rather, her body was found, somewhere in a park not far from downtown, just off 94 East, where an early morning snowfall glazed the metal swing sets and the empty branches of maple trees. There was no mention of cuts on her ankles, but I knew. The Harrowers had taken her, tested her, and when they discovered she wasn't the one, they'd let her bleed.

That night, before Mom left for the evening, she paused by the front door to tell me not to worry. It wasn't her usual frowning evasiveness: she was trying to reassure me. She would stop the bleedings, she told me.

But I wasn't reassured. She still hadn't been able to find who was working with Tigue.

The following week arrived with a blizzard, eighteen inches

of snow hurtling down upon the Twin Cities, closing schools and turning the roads into elaborate obstacle courses of snowplows and slush. The forecast had claimed the storm would miss us and head east into Wisconsin, but I woke to a world gone abruptly white, wind blowing drifts into the yard and burying cars along the avenue. Since my grounding had ended the previous week, I dug my winter boots out of the closet and trudged across the arctic waste to Gideon's house. He and Tink were throwing me a belated prison-release party, and even though their idea of a party tended to include bad action movies and microwave egg rolls, I welcomed the distraction.

"Someone wake me up when it's spring," Tink whined when I arrived. She'd come down with a cold and was using it as an excuse to hog Gideon's bed. She sat huddled in the middle with all the blankets, a small blond lump with a pink nose.

"Not happening," I told her. "I need someone to share my misery."

"Oh, come on. Winter's not *that* bad," Gideon said.

I made a face at him. "You bike in the snow and wear shorts when it's twenty degrees out. Your opinion is invalid."

He just grinned. "Minnesota born and raised, baby!"

"So am I," I retorted. "Guess I just missed out on that extra dose of crazy."

Tink sniffed.

Gideon shook his head in disgust. His entire family thought

the snowstorm was fantastic. His sisters were stringing Christmas lights, his grandmother was searching online for eggnog recipes, and his father was actually out on the porch barbecuing.

I asked if this meant that something new was on the menu.

"You like egg rolls," Gideon replied.

That was undeniable. It was really the microwave part I objected to. "I like them better without soggy middles and freezer burn," I said.

"We could maybe make an exception." He paused to turn and give me a stern look. "But not if you keep trying to set me up with your cousin."

Gideon wasn't a big fan of my St. Croix relatives. I'd dragged him Christmas shopping with my cousins recently, and at the end of it, he'd declared that Iris was creepy and Elspeth insane. He seemed to think this meant I was once again winning—or perhaps losing—the weird-family competition. I decided not to mention that his father was, at this moment, cooking steaks in a blizzard. Instead, I asked, "What's wrong with Elspeth?"

"She's just so . . . cheerful," he said. "She makes Tink look like a pessimist."

"Hey," Tink said, then paused, as though uncertain whether or not this was meant as an insult. She settled for blowing her nose.

I looked at Gideon. "You're just worried that going out with someone would ruin your ability to pine tragically."

Brooke Oliver: the one subject guaranteed to make Gideon bring out his grumpy face. Or the closest thing to a grumpy face he could manage, which usually involved squinting. This time he threw in an insulted stare. "Remind me again why I put up with you?"

"'Cause you sold me your soul for five bucks, and now you must submit to my will?" I still had the sheet of paper, written in his untidy fifth-grade scrawl. *Gideon David Belmonte. One soul.*

The rest of our conversation was put on hold by Tink's insistence that we start the movie already.

I tried to relax and focus on the film. Tink had picked it out, which meant lots of hot guys, explosions, and hot guys dramatically walking away from explosions—plus a few half-naked girls for Gideon—but I couldn't seem to follow the plot, if it even had one. My mind was too busy.

Gideon noticed my distraction and looked wounded that I wasn't enjoying my party, but I assured him I was having a fabulous time, I was just a little tired. At least, I thought I assured him. Later that night, Tink called to inform me otherwise.

"We have a problem," she said. "Actually, *you* have a problem." She had to repeat her words twice; she'd called me from work and was whispering into the phone while hidden in the employee bathroom.

"Aren't you sick?" I asked. She worked at the Caribou Coffee a few blocks from her apartment, and though a snowstorm wasn't likely to deter the truly devoted coffee drinkers, I couldn't imagine *anyone* wanting to see a barista with a runny nose.

"Sick and miserable," she affirmed. "But I like money. And

that's not what I called you about." Someone knocked on the bathroom door, and she yelled at them to give her a minute. She lowered her voice even more, so that she was almost hissing into the phone. "Gideon asked if I thought something was going on with you. I think he's smarter than we give him credit for."

I took a breath. "What did you tell him?" I asked.

"I said it was probably PMS. That shut him up pretty fast."

I figured I deserved that one, after the anemia incident.

I hesitated. Tink didn't like to talk about Kin matters—but she was the one who had brought it up. "Do you know much about what's going on? The attacks, I mean?"

She let out an angry sigh. "No, and I don't *want* to know. That's the point of this conversation. You need to stop thinking about it."

"Because, clearly, that will make it all just go away."

"Worrying about it isn't doing you any good, either." She made a little noise—possibly of annoyance, possibly of frustration— then told me she would say no more.

After she hung up, I sat on my bed, considering her words. It wasn't as though I wanted to worry, but I didn't see how ignoring the problem would help.

Not that anything else I'd done had helped. Mom was finally being more open with me, but there was little I could do with the information. Earlier that week, I'd suggested I use my Knowing— maybe I could get some idea of who Tigue's accomplice was, or definitively connect him to the bleedings. It hadn't gone over well. Mom had given me a look of such severity, I was afraid she'd re-ground me purely on principle. I hadn't brought it up again. And even if she'd agreed to my suggestion, I didn't know where I'd start. I'd never met Tigue; I couldn't do a reading on him. I told myself to take Tink's advice, to just forget about it.

But that night I lay awake thinking of girls lured out into the sweet night air, the darkness that awaited them, vanishing lights and a rising wind. Tricia and Kelly and those other nameless girls, bound to me by a shared ancestry and by the cuts above our heels. And when I slept, my dreams were filled with blood.

With Tink unwilling to discuss the Kin, and Gideon

unable to, I found myself spending more time with Elspeth. She knew every last detail of Kin life, and she was always ready to talk, without trying to drill the information into my skull the way Esther did. Elspeth's world revolved around being a Guardian—though, as she informed me one evening, she was considered too young to be fully involved in their day-to-day operations. She had a curfew to contend with, and Esther required that both she and Iris maintain straight A's. That put a few restrictions on being a teenage superhero.

"High school never really got in Mom's way," I mused. "She's been Morning Star since she was barely sixteen."

"She's *Lucy*," Elspeth said, as though that were the only explanation required. "It doesn't matter, though. I'm joining H&H as soon as I graduate, no matter what Grandmother says."

I could imagine what Esther would say. She probably already had Elspeth's Ivy League school picked out.

I took a sip of my cocoa. Elspeth had badgered me into doing more Christmas shopping, applying a heavy dose of guilt over Gideon's rejection and following it up with a pleading look that almost, but not quite, rivaled Leon's Hungry Puppy. After taking the bus to downtown Minneapolis, we'd spent an hour or so wandering around Nicollet Mall, then ventured to less crowded streets. We'd spotted a little café well away from the usual commotion of the city, and while I sat stirring the marshmallows around my cup of cocoa, Elspeth was on her second latte.

She was also still stuck on Gideon.

"I don't see why he won't go out with me," she said, running a finger along the rim of her glass. She wore the most perfect pout I'd ever seen, but she sounded sincere, so I didn't laugh.

"He's sort of a lost cause," I told her. I refrained from mentioning the number of times he'd called her insane, or that he'd offered to set her up with Stanley, one of his friends from the baseball team. Though Stanley was cute, only mildly obnoxious, and arguably the best pitcher in school, I doubted Elspeth would find the suggestion flattering. "Wouldn't you rather go out with another Guardian?" Esther would doubtless prefer that—though, since Iris was already dating within the Kin, perhaps Elspeth was off the hook.

"There aren't many Guardians my age," she said. "I'm the youngest. There's this guy a year older than me, but he's, well…" She grimaced. "And after that it's Leon. And after *that*—"

I laughed. "Okay, got it." And then I steered her on to non-Gideon topics.

Though she didn't yet work closely with the other Guardians, Elspeth knew a great deal about their business. She told me there hadn't been any confirmed bleedings in the past few weeks—but that may have been due to Guardian vigilance. They still weren't certain how the Harrowers were locating their targets, but the Guardians had taken to patrolling in shifts, reporting any signs of demon activity, and they were trying to establish their own system for detecting potential victims.

"Lucy's sort of a loner," Elspeth said, when I mentioned that Mom didn't seem to associate with the others. "Grandmother says that Morning Star always had to go her own way."

Except for having her very own sidekick, I supposed.

Dusk had faded into a cool blue darkness by the time we headed back to the bus stop. The air was chilled, and my breath formed little puffs as we walked. The storm had spent itself two days earlier, and most of the roads were clear, but bits of ice clung to barren branches along the streets. We'd wandered farther than I realized. Though the lights of downtown were bright around us, the streets felt unnaturally deserted. Empty cars sat silent and dark. The biting wind sliced against me. Elspeth, being a Guardian, didn't seem to notice the cold.

"We should've asked Iris to pick us up," I said, pulling my coat tight against me. Though she'd declined the invitation to come shopping with us, she did have a car.

"I think she's busy," Elspeth said. There was a little catch in her voice. She was still taking Iris's school transfer hard. I didn't fully understand the dynamic between the pair, but I knew that, despite being the tall, gorgeous Guardian, Elspeth idolized her older sister.

I gave her a smile. "Well, next time you drag me out somewhere, it had better be warm," I said lightly. I was terrible at navigating the skyway, but as soon as we reached it, I intended to head directly indoors.

Beside me, Elspeth had stopped. "Audrey, can we—"

I didn't hear the rest of her words. As I turned back toward her, I felt a sudden change in the air.

It wasn't like it had been at the Drought and Deluge, but it wasn't precisely different, either. There was no noise, no whisper crawling along my skin. No urgent, unrelenting alarm that ran through my veins. But the air around us had altered. A hush had fallen across the empty street, and the glow of lights from the surrounding buildings appeared muted and distant. Even the drone of traffic seemed to come from far away. My heart pounded in my ears. I heard the wind blow.

"Elspeth," I said. "Something's here."

A Harrower. I knew one was near.

An echo of Esther's words came back to me. *They revile the Kin,* she'd said, when I asked what the demons wanted. *And yearn for what we are.* Which meant either it planned to bleed Elspeth—or it wanted us dead.

I didn't intend to be an easy target. Not like the last time. I might not be a Guardian, but I remembered my mother's words. The throat. I would go for the throat.

Turning, I scanned the road, watching for movement.

"We'll be all right," Elspeth said. She sounded different. Gone was the funny lilt she sometimes affected, the giddy laugh that came so easily. Her voice was sharp, authoritative. "Stand back." She took a step forward.

And then something strange happened.

The change in the air became a change in her. Everything stilled. The light clung to Elspeth, the air around her shimmering. But it wasn't just the space around her. It was her face. It was her eyes, suddenly lit from within. It was her hair, waving around her as though it had come to life. And it was her hand.

The fingertips of her left hand began to glow. Softly at first, and in different colors. Her index finger was tinted lightly blue; red shone beside it, and a gentle color like lilac, and the yellow of honey, and the green of blooming summer grasses. I saw her veins through the skin of her palm, down her wrist, trailing toward her elbow. The colors pulsed and moved, blended and merged.

Leon had said Guardians had other resources, a weapon they carried with them. I hadn't understood what he meant.

Elspeth glanced at me, her eyes strange and ethereal. "We'll be okay," she repeated. "Just let me handle it."

The demon rushed forward.

It wasn't like the one that had attacked me at the Drought and Deluge. I didn't see just blinks and impressions: I saw it clearly. At first it appeared merely human. A woman, pale-haired, thin of figure, features nondescript. Then, as I watched, something shifted. The woman-image blurred. I saw blank eyes staring, long-nailed hands grappling for Elspeth. It moved quickly, contorting, bending, standing high above Elspeth and then slinking low as she repelled it, her left hand held in front of her as both weapon and shield. She went for its throat, but it evaded. There was something reptilian about the way it moved.

Then the Harrower stepped out of its skin.

Its movements were rapid, but I caught the blur of silver, rippling flesh, scales that flashed with a deathly gleam. Clawed fingers slashed toward Elspeth, and as it turned I saw the arc of jagged red teeth.

The Harrower paused and was human again. Just a woman with a wave of blond hair, hiding a secret beneath her skin. I watched as it took a wary step back.

"You picked the wrong girl for a fight," Elspeth hissed. "I thought you guys would've known better by now."

The Harrower lunged for her and caught air. Elspeth was on the ground, crouching, her left hand stretched out before her, even brighter now. The Harrower screeched, an inhuman sound that sent chills down my spine.

"You just don't know what's good for you, do you?" Elspeth panted.

Then she was on the offensive.

She moved quickly, so quickly she became nothing but a streak of black hair and long limbs, the glow in her hand flashing through the dark street. The demon retreated, then ran forward, its hands curving into talons again, abandoning its skin for scales.

I cried out a warning, but my shriek was cut off. An arm reached out from behind me, pulling me backward into sudden dark.

My first instinct was to scream as loudly as possible—
but a hand clamped over my mouth, silencing me. I struggled
blindly until it registered that someone was saying my name, and
the voice was a voice I recognized, and the place I stood in was
my own kitchen.

I bit the hand that covered my mouth.

Leon released me with a yelp of pain.

"What was that for?" he complained.

"For scaring the crap out of me!" I replied, hitting him in the
chest with my palm. He grunted, then leaned away from me to
flip on the overhead light. I blinked as my eyes adjusted to the
change. Mom had already left for the night, and the house felt
dark and empty.

"Did it hurt you?" Leon asked, frowning down at me. His
hand lifted to my shoulder, not quite touching.

I barely heard him; I couldn't hear much beyond the slam of my heartbeat. Somehow I managed to rasp out, "We have to go back. We have to help Elspeth."

Not that I wanted to go back. It pretty much topped the list of things I would prefer not to do, right along with being boiled alive and getting trapped inside a tornado. But Leon had brought me to safety and left Elspeth out there alone with a Harrower, and I couldn't ignore that.

Leon, apparently, could. "She can take care of herself," he said. "Right now I'm more concerned about you. Are you hurt?"

"I'm fine."

His fingers pressed against my arm, gentle on the fabric of my coat. "You're not fine. You're shaking."

"Of course I'm shaking!" I cried. "It's not every day I get attacked by a demon on the streets of Minneapolis." Though there was a strong possibility it was turning into a monthly event. "And Elspeth is still out there," I added. "Please. Go make sure she's all right."

Leon's frown remained. "I can't do that," he said.

"Why not?" I asked, stepping close to him. "That's what you do, isn't it? You're a Guardian. Go guard!" Hands clenched at my sides, I took a deep breath. "Leon. Please."

He looked at me a long moment before speaking. "You will stay right here," he told me. "You won't move." And then he disappeared.

I sat down at the table, laying my head against it. The house was quiet around me, and shaken as I was, the lack of noise was eerie, unnatural. It made my own breathing sound that much louder.

I closed my eyes, trying to think of comforting things. Gram's voice, the movement of her hands. The day she'd first explained to me the meanings of the Nav cards. "Your grandfather, Jacky, he was my Anchor," she'd said, her thumb grazing the surface of the card. "But I didn't need the cards to tell me that."

But my grandfather had died, killed by a Harrower when he tried to interfere in an attack. And Gram had lost her anchor. And when Gram died, I had lost mine.

"Elspeth is fine. The Harrower ran off before I got back there."

I looked up. Leon stood a few feet away, that same concerned crease in his brow, as though the line had been etched there.

"It wasn't my fault," I said, before he could accuse me of having thrown myself in the path of danger.

He surprised me. "I know. You weren't the target. Attacks against Guardians have been escalating."

"Oh." I sat up in my chair. My hair, unruly as always, had come free of its ponytail, and I had to fight it back behind my ears. "That sounds...bad."

"It's not good," he agreed.

Another thought struck me.

"That was what you meant by Guardian resources?" I asked, recalling the way Elspeth had moved, her body whipping through the night, the glow that spread from her fingertips and veins. The light in her eyes, the electricity along her skin and hair. "What Elspeth did—the light in her skin—that's how you fight?"

"You change when you're called. That's one of the changes."

When Leon didn't elaborate further, I asked, "Why were you out there, anyway?" Grateful though I was that he'd shown up, he'd probably scared me into sixty by appearing the way he did. "Does Mom have you following me? I promised I'd be careful."

He shrugged, cocking his head to the side. "It was getting late. I was just making sure you were okay."

I frowned. I wanted to be annoyed, but there was something rather deflating about being faced with good intentions. "You were looking out for me?"

Leon's gaze was unwavering. "I'm always looking out for you."

And with that, he vanished.

When I spoke to Elspeth later in the evening, she assured me she was fine. She hadn't been hurt, and sounded offended that I'd even suggested it.

"I didn't think a Harrower would attack so openly," I told her. "Or don't they care about being seen?" That was a distinct possibility, but it seemed to me that if demon attacks were a common occurrence on city streets, the rest of the population would have clued into it, and we'd be calling Minneapolis the City of Demons, not the City of Lakes.

Or maybe Demonapolis. That had a sort of ring to it.

"They normally don't," Elspeth replied. "Though humans don't really see them. It's an ability Harrowers have, clouding the senses."

I'd felt some of that myself, outside the Drought and Deluge: the fading lights, that rush of wind, a nothingness that crawled up along my skin.

"Demons just get better and better," I muttered.

Elspeth only giggled. I took that to mean she truly had escaped unscathed.

My next few days were a flurry of activity. Esther decided I'd had enough preparation and that it was time for me to meet other members of the Kin, as well as take my place within the community. She didn't, however, explain what that meant. I assumed from the frown she gave me that it didn't actually involve a laminated membership card and a sweatshirt that said SECRET SUPERHERO CLUB.

"Do we have Kin parties?" I'd asked during one of our sessions. "Kin dances? Car washes? Bake sales?"

Esther sighed and lifted her eyes heavenward. "You certainly are your mother's daughter."

Then she'd dragged me to a series of dinners with several dignified-looking older ladies, all of whom scrutinized me carefully, nodded, and agreed with Esther that I was, indeed, very much like their Morning Star.

It struck me as strange that the Kin referred to Mom that way, but Esther told me she found the name fitting. "The legend grew up around Lucy all on its own," she said. "But it is who she was meant to be. She was our light in a dark time. Even then, she was a force without parallel."

Personally, I thought that meant Mom should be in charge.

I was growing a bit weary of Esther claiming so much of my time. She seemed bent on not only teaching me about the Kin, but turning me into her version of a St. Croix. I told her I was perfectly happy as a mere Whitticomb, but she turned her sternest gaze on me, one I was certain would scare a Harrower back into the Beneath. And then I somehow agreed to attend two fund-raisers and a banquet during the upcoming weeks.

On Wednesday, my session with Esther was canceled, but I found myself at the St. Croix estate anyway. Iris had asked to see me after school, dragging me away from the lunch table to whisper that she needed to discuss something urgent with me. She wasn't like Elspeth, who thought the need for ice cream was an emergency, so I believed her. And there was that sense to her again, that clinging sadness that followed her step, some memory she couldn't flee. I told her I'd be there.

She met me at the front door and led me up the stairs to her room. The house was quiet. Elspeth had been cast in a play at school and had rehearsal that night, and Esther had gone out of town. Iris's room was on the third floor, and I trailed my hand along the banister as we picked our way up the steps. Portraits of past St. Croix family members stared down at me, faded and bleak.

"Do you have your Nav cards?" Iris asked, once we reached her room. I turned toward her. With her head tilted to the side, her long hair tumbled over her shoulders like some dark, deep waterfall.

"I always have them." I stepped into the room, and she shut the door behind us.

Iris's room was done all in blue. Not just dark blues, which might have matched her subdued nature, but blues of all different tones and shades. Her ceiling was the blue of summer lakes, an almost-green that seemed to shift as I looked at it. Her walls were a pale, dusky hue, and her bedspread the color of grape hyacinth. It left me slightly unnerved, as though I'd been dunked under water.

"Sit on the floor," Iris instructed, sitting cross-legged in front of me. Unlike Elspeth's room, which you couldn't walk into without stepping on old homework assignments or dirty clothing, Iris's room was clean, almost bare. Everything on her desk was neatly arranged.

"You want to do a reading?" I asked, pulling my Nav cards out of my book bag. I shuffled them idly while Iris smoothed a space on the carpet.

She looked up at me, her brown-gold eyes clear and focused. "Not just a reading. We're going to find the Remnant."

22

I frowned, pausing my shuffling. "How are we supposed to do that?" I'd considered the idea briefly, but I didn't think my Knowing would be of any use. Even with my cards, I couldn't just search blindly.

Iris peered at me through lowered lashes. "Has Grandmother explained the power that runs in our bloodline?"

Esther talked a great deal about bloodlines, about the value of connection and the bond of lineage, but she hadn't told me anything about powers specific to the St. Croix family. I shook my head.

Iris leaned toward me as she explained. "There's a trait among the St. Croix, something unique to us. Grandmother has it. My father had it, and so do I. We call it *Amplification*. It allows me to increase the abilities of others."

It took me only a moment. "Increase abilities. Meaning—"

"Meaning, maybe we can use your Knowing to find the Remnant."

I hesitated. "My readings aren't always accurate. Gram used to say having a Knowing doesn't make it right. They've been wrong before." My hands stilled on my Nav cards, feeling the texture of their surfaces, well-worn and comfortable. They still carried the faint smell of lavender from long years with Gram. "And I'm not certain it would work. I usually need to be near something to get a strong reading."

"That's why we amplify it," Iris said, her voice steady, her eyes intent. "This is important. I don't take much interest in the Kin —but I *am* interested in keeping us all alive. I'm not a Guardian, but I hear things. Grandmother is worried about a Harrowing. Or worse. But if we find the Remnant, Grandmother and the other Kin elders could seal her power. The bleedings would stop."

I understood Iris's worry, but I didn't understand her words. "Seal her power?"

She turned away, facing the window, so that I could see only her profile, the slope of her jaw and the hollow of her throat where the triple knot hung, catching the light. Her words were so quiet, I had to strain to hear. "It's not done often. It's what happened to your father."

I drew in a breath. No one else had been willing to speak about my father. When I tried to ask, the subject was changed; Esther's mouth would turn grim, and even Elspeth was reluctant to say what she knew. I had a horrible suspicion that that meant he was in prison. "You know about my father?" I asked.

Iris shrugged. "I don't know the entire story. Something happened during the last Harrowing. It had to do with Verrick, that demon your mother fought."

The name stirred a memory: Elspeth's voice going low and soft, the tremor of fear beneath her words. "The demon who knew about the Remnant," I said.

"Grandmother says he was the most powerful Harrower they'd ever seen. Until Lucy—stopped him."

I bit my lip. "And my father was hurt?"

"His powers were sealed. There's a ritual that's done—it has to do with blood from the five sacred spaces. You know about them?"

I nodded. Wrists, ankles, base of the throat. The places a Guardian's powers were centered, Esther had said.

"The ritual...it cuts off the life force of the Kin, seals the bloodline," Iris continued. "The old language had a saying for it. I can't pronounce it, but it's something about those who carry a sleeping heart, existing between, neither alive nor dead. Your father isn't Kin any longer. And he never will be again." She turned to face me, her eyes fixed on mine, then reached a hand out, pressing it against the back of my Nav cards. "But whoever the Remnant is, she probably doesn't even know she's Kin. It's not a part of who she is. Sealing her powers wouldn't even affect her."

I frowned. Iris's voice was strong, certain, but the idea unsettled me.

"It's the only way we'll be safe," Iris pressed, and this time her tone was low, filled with all that disquiet I'd felt.

After a moment I nodded slowly. "How do we do this Amplification?"

Iris hesitated. "To amplify abilities, first we have to share them. Then I add my power to yours." The light through the window haloed her face. With the tint of blue in the room and her hair fanned about her, she looked ethereal and mermaidlike. "It helps to be in contact," she said, moving close and placing two fingers on my elbow, leaving my hands free to shuffle the cards.

I wasn't certain how I felt about sharing my Knowing, but I nodded again and tried to focus. As I shuffled, a hum began along my skin. An image intruded, obscured and shifting before my eyes. I saw a series of flashes: rain rolling down pavement, silver in the light; a girl huddled on a street corner, her dark hair matted against her head; a pale streak through the night, a heavy hand reaching toward the slant of her shoulder, fingers gripping. The girl turned, her face catching shadow, her hair whipping about her.

Iris drew her hand back abruptly.

"Please don't look there," she said. "It's personal."

"I'm sorry," I said quickly. "It wasn't on purpose—it just happened."

"You need to focus." She placed her fingers back on my elbow, touching it lightly.

I closed my eyes and shuffled.

It wasn't the same, having a Knowing and sharing it. There was a difference in sensation. I didn't know if it was stronger, but I felt the change. I shuffled and didn't see Iris's images again. I thought of the Remnant, focusing on what I knew of her. *A Kin-blooded girl*, I thought, *who carries the powers of old*. I saw nothing but clean blank space, and began to lay out the cards.

The first card. Forty-eight, Sign of Swords.

I paused, my fingers pressed against it.

"Is something wrong?" Iris asked.

"It's not me," I said. "The first card—it's usually my card, Inverted Crescent."

"What does that mean?"

"I'm not sure." I placed card forty-eight in the center and set down the next two.

Card twelve, The Sisters. Card seven, The Beast.

"Are you getting anything?"

I shook my head. There was nothing. The cards weren't speaking to me at all, which may have meant the Amplification hadn't worked, just as I'd warned. Or maybe there was a pattern here I couldn't yet see.

I placed the next cards. Sign of Sickle. The Fig Tree. Year of Famine. Year of Flood.

An image flashed: a half-turned face. Light beneath me.

There was a chill in the air. Iris's window was closed, but I felt the wind pressing against the glass, the frost climbing upward. I shivered, laying out the next card.

The Grave Keeper.

Then I felt it. Not a sense or a Knowing, but an actual physical reaction, deep in my gut, down my skin, in my lungs, knocking the breath from me. Iris pulled her hand back, holding it against her as though burned. More images came to me—fleeting impressions, flickers, quick snapshots that left me dizzy.

A memory of Gram placing her hands over mine, her voice low as she said, *There are some places it's best not to look.*

An image of something old and cunning. A resonance from Beneath. Blood and heat.

Something watching. Something seeking me. Seeing me.

Speaking to me.

"Audrey. Are you okay?" Iris's voice broke into my reverie.

"We need to stop. We're not supposed to look there," I said, letting the rest of the cards tumble from my hands. They spilled onto the carpet, and the pattern disrupted.

The Remnant was hidden for a reason. And we weren't the only ones looking. I didn't know what it was—if I'd tapped into something, some sort of communal Knowing that existed beyond what I could sense or see, or if it was merely a product of Iris's Amplification. I felt exposed. Suddenly it felt as though there were eyes everywhere, watching us, waiting to see what we'd find. I covered the cards with my hands, closing out image and meaning. Gram always told me to treat my cards delicately, but this time I shoved them carelessly back into the deck.

It took a moment for the unease to lessen. I took long, filling breaths.

Iris was staring at me. "What happened?"

"We made a mistake," I said, giving her a shaky smile, the best I could manage. My breathing returned to normal, but I felt a flutter of nausea in my stomach. "The Remnant needs to stay hidden."

"It was our first try," Iris said. "Maybe we just need practice. Or maybe it's not the right time."

I shook my head. "I don't think so. But I have another idea." I shuffled lightly. My Nav cards had always been a comfort to me. They were meant to clear my frequencies, to soothe me and allow me to focus. They were meant to help. And they *had* helped: though the reading for the Remnant had frightened me, I realized there might be something else we could do.

Iris waited, watching me.

"We might not be able to find the Remnant—but maybe we can find the Harrowers' next target. Mom said she hasn't been able to stop the bleedings because most of the targets aren't even associated with the Kin. But if we could figure out who the demons will go after, maybe we could help them." Well, Mom could help them. I didn't feel like putting myself in the path of another demon any time soon—and I *had* made a promise.

"If you think it'll work," Iris said. At my nod, she moved forward again, placing her fingers back on my arm.

It was different this time. Different and immediate. Even

before I began to lay down the cards, I could see. Sense becoming shape, shape becoming image, image becoming knowledge. I heard a girl speaking on a cell phone, turning a corner in downtown Minneapolis. A light snow fell above her.

I set down the first card. Inverted Crescent.

"Good," I said, and continued.

Next card. Thirteen. The Garden. Iris's card. It was an easy connection to make: I could imagine Iris in a garden, sitting among flowers. Somewhere around her the hum of bees.

I set down the next cards, trying to focus. The Child. The Beggar. My fingers were light upon them, grazing the surface. I closed my eyes.

And suddenly I didn't need to focus. It was all there, like a line drawn between us. I saw the target. Her face, her name. Her favorite color was red. She played basketball on her school team, and softball in the spring.

Iris hadn't been kidding about her Amplification ability. It was so clear it almost hurt.

Anna Berkeley, age sixteen. She'd been working at a café somewhere close to Uptown, and now she was headed home. From Beneath, something watched.

I jumped to my feet, letting the rest of the cards scatter.

"You saw?" I asked Iris. I didn't know to what extent she'd shared my Knowing, but her eyes were troubled.

"Anna Berkeley," she said. "We should tell your mother."

225

Then she hadn't seen everything.

Hadn't felt the sudden screaming urgency that shook through my bones, as strong as the night Tink had been attacked.

"No," I said. "We have to go. We have to go right now."

Iris sped all the way to Minneapolis. The sky had grown dark, and a gentle snow fell. Headlights blurred before us. "You have a plan, right?" she asked, switching lanes to pass a slow-moving truck.

Not exactly.

Mom hadn't answered her cell phone or responded to her H&H pager, and Leon's phone had been turned off. Calling the police seemed like a great way to get myself tested for drugs. Our best option was to find Anna and warn her, somehow. We had to keep her safe until we could alert the Guardians.

We found parking a few blocks from where I'd seen her. Iris hesitated as she stepped out of the car, snowflakes melting in her black hair. Her eyes were round with worry.

"I'm not sure we can do this," she said, a slight quiver in her voice. Her gaze met mine, and I remembered that night at the Drought and Deluge. *I got scared,* she'd said.

"I'm not sure, either." Neither of us were Guardians. We didn't have my mother with us, we didn't have Leon, or even Elspeth. The darkening night was cold and quiet, and I felt that familiar tug of fear. But Anna Berkeley needed our help. "Let's just find her," I said, turning down the street.

I didn't know the area we were in. The roads were dotted with little shops and streetlights slowly blinking on. A couple of women clutching grocery bags shuffled past us, and an elderly man with a dog gave a warm smile. I nodded his way, my eyes darting past him. Anna Berkeley, I thought, searching for a tall, sandy-haired girl in a plum-colored coat.

"Are you sure this is the right place?"

I stopped, listening. We'd turned a corner, and I heard the jangle of Christmas music coming through the windows of a novelties shop. The road was empty ahead of us.

"Maybe we got the wrong street," Iris suggested. "Or the wrong time. If your Knowings aren't always right, maybe we should go back."

I didn't think so. The alarm I'd felt had been sharp, visceral, and very real—not simply the result of Iris's Amplification. The danger was near. That persistent urgency drummed in my skin.

"There!" I said, with a glance behind us. Two blocks down, I saw a hint of purple against a backdrop of snowbanks and bare branches. The girl stood with her back to us; she was too far away to see clearly, but I knew it was her. She rounded a corner and vanished from sight.

Swiveling, I ran in the direction she'd gone, Iris close on my heels. I had no idea what I would say—I needed to think of some lie, some way to warn her. Anything. It didn't matter as long as we caught her, brought her to safety. But as I ran, an eerie sense of déjà vu crept over me. It struck me how still the street had become, a hush in the falling twilight, cold air thickening.

This time when the demon attacked, I was expecting it.

That didn't mean I was prepared. I looked upward, toward the blur of dark, glassy sky. "Iris," I said, grabbing her arm. "I think—"

The Harrower knocked me away.

I stumbled backward, struggling to keep my feet. A rush of fear pulsed through me, but I ignored it. I wasn't a Guardian, but I wasn't helpless. *Fight back,* I thought. *Go for the throat.* His throat looked very human. No hint of silver or scales or claws on his hands. Except for my senses screaming that he was a Harrower, he could have been a man.

Regaining my balance, I aimed a blow above his collarbone. For half a second I felt the impact; then the demon jerked backward. I didn't hesitate, but pushed the attack. My first hit had taken him by surprise, but that wouldn't last. I hit again.

He was too fast. Before the blow connected, he evaded. My fist caught air. The Harrower stood unharmed. Watching me. Smiling.

Then I was on the ground, gasping. I hadn't even seen him move, but I felt a fist in my stomach and a sudden, wrenching pain as something sharp raked across my shoulder, through the cloth of my coat. The world grayed before me and nausea churned in my belly, even as I rolled on impulse, away from the demon's grasp.

He followed as I scrambled to my feet. A glimmer of light passed over him, and for one awful second I saw the flash of silver and scales and a wide, red-toothed grin. Then it was gone and he was human again.

I watched him warily, waiting for him to strike. Across the snow-bright distance between us, my gaze met his.

I know you, Kin-child, his eyes seemed to say. *And you know me.*

My heart skipped a beat.

I'd met this demon before. I'd felt the slice of his claws in my skin.

His smile grew wider. He would catch me, that smile said. And this time he would do more than bleed me. I looked into his face and saw death.

He inched closer, and with a small shock I discovered I could *read* him. I hadn't realized my Knowing extended beyond humans, but this demon—I could see into him. I didn't want to. I drew back, trying to block out what I felt. I sensed anger in him, and beyond that something cold and empty, like looking into the dark end of space.

The demon had talons again, and the talons were at my throat.

"No! You can't hurt her!"

Momentarily paralyzed, I didn't have the ability to react, but Iris's cry cut through me, severing whatever link the Harrower had formed, even as I realized I'd forgotten one of my mother's warnings. Harrowers rely on your fear of them, she'd said. I'd forgotten to focus.

The demon spun about, turning on Iris. His approach was slow, cautious, and he whispered at her, strange urgings I couldn't make out. A change came over her. Something dark and deadly flashed in her eyes, and one hand shot out in front of her, fingers curled. The other was pressed to her neck, cupping the silver of the triple knot.

. She wasn't a Guardian—she'd told me as much—but there was power in her. She flew toward the Harrower, quick and agile, striking out with her hand. Her attack took him by surprise. Her fingers latched onto the back of his neck, digging inward, then her other hand went for his throat.

Through his skin, his spine began to darken, ridges and bones turning blue, and then coppery, and then the deep, unforgettable color of blood.

The demon cried out, twisting in Iris's grasp. I rushed forward. I wasn't certain what I intended—pure instinct had taken over. But, even wounded and struggling, the demon was stronger than me. He lashed out as I reached them, shrieking and catching me by the shoulder. Iris's fingers tightened on his neck. His screech pierced the night, and for the space of a second, the sky around us seemed to shatter. There was a flash of light and then a sudden darkness, momentary but disorienting. Our surroundings flickered, colors blurring. The ground shifted beneath me. I didn't have time to process what had happened. The Harrower flung me away from him and at last pulled out of Iris's grip, his rage radiating out of him like a hot white star.

Pressing low to the ground, he slunk away and then leaped, his clawed, inhuman hands once again flashing toward me. I recoiled, blocking, but Iris was faster. She dragged the demon into the air with a strength I hadn't known she possessed.

Iris was more than a match for the creature. As I watched, her hands found purchase on his neck, holding, squeezing, twisting his throat. The crimson in his spine spread outward in thready veins down his back, along his arms, and then a sound like a sigh came from his body. He shook once in Iris's grip, and then went slack.

"Are you all right?" she asked, moving toward me. Her skirt was torn, her eyes huge. I nodded, knowing she had saved my life and not quite willing to admit she'd frightened me.

Instead, I turned slowly, trying to make sense of my surroundings. The street had changed. We no longer stood in the cool blue of evening or the warm lights of Minneapolis.

Bewildered, I blurted out, "What happened? Where are we?"

Iris turned away, black hair whipping about her.

"We're Beneath."

Minneapolis was gone—at least the Minneapolis I knew.

Around us, the world was skewed, distorted. The skyline had altered. The horizon was a smear of dust and darkness, and above us the stars had gone red.

Red stars. Red shadows. I'd heard that before.

The street had transformed. The buildings remained, the tar and the parked cars and the curve of the sidewalk below us, but they had changed, twisted somehow. Brick became bone. Gnarled trees jutted up from charred earth. The cars had lost their tires, their windows, their paint: they looked like metal skeletons covered in rust. At my feet, the ground was rough and unsteady, trembling on occasion, making it difficult to keep my balance. The snow, at least, was still snow, a strange and blinding white against the backdrop of decay.

Now and then, the real city flashed before me, an intrusion of sound and color into the space that surrounded us. I heard the turn of a motor, smelled exhaust. Then it was gone.

"It's my fault," Iris was saying, a hint of desperation in her tone. "I didn't mean to, it just happened. Because I touched the demon. Prolonged contact. I was sharing its abilities while I fought it, and I accidentally brought us here."

"It's okay," I said, telling myself to keep calm. "Just—just get us back out."

Iris didn't answer.

"You *can* get us back out, right?"

I didn't need a Knowing to read the fear on her face.

I clenched my hands into fists. "Right. Well, there has to be some way out of here." I looked around. Getting out might be an option if I had any idea how we'd gotten *in*. I pressed one hand against what used to be a car, then drew it back quickly as the substance flaked beneath my touch. It left a reddish film on my fingers, which I rubbed onto my coat. Above, the sky with its sinister, menacing stars felt low and oppressive.

"No wonder demons are so cranky," I said. "If I had to live here, I'd be in a bad mood too."

"Demons don't *just* live here. They live other places too. And there's more to it than—this. This is just the surface, in a way. A sort of passageway, or entrance. I've heard there are other places. Layers. Entire worlds Beneath."

"Come here often?" I joked.

Iris hugged her coat against her. "This is serious, Audrey. We shouldn't be here."

I nodded, scanning the area, trying to think. Mom and Leon hadn't told me anything about the Beneath, or how to escape it. What I did know came from scraps of information Esther had let drop, and my hazy memories of Gram's stories. None of it seemed very helpful. We were Beneath, between seconds and breaths, sun and shadow. The realm of the Old Race, long abandoned, corrupted by Harrower rage and gone to rot.

The realm of demons.

Everything I knew about Harrowers led me to believe they wouldn't be very happy to see us here. Not to mention the fact that Iris had just killed one of them.

I turned back toward her. "How did you kill that thing? That couldn't have just been training—Mom says most humans aren't strong enough. I thought you weren't a Guardian."

In the red glow around us, Iris's color was muted, her face vague, as though I were gazing at her through thick glass. She lifted her hand to the chain that circled her throat, resting one finger on the metal of the triple knot. "I'm not. I used this. It lets me share my boyfriend's abilities. It's made from his blood and skin."

Temporarily distracted, I gaped at her. "Did you . . . seriously just tell me your necklace is made from your boyfriend's *skin*?"

A giggle broke through her grim expression. "You should see your face."

"You put that thing in my hand!"

"It's not *just* that. It's a special kind of metal, made by the Kin. It's meant to enhance and preserve. He gave it to me for my birthday. As long as I have it, we're connected."

I couldn't decide if that was sweet or creepy. Possibly both.

But it gave me an idea. "Connected enough that he could come get us out of here?"

Iris hesitated. "It doesn't usually work both ways. And Kin powers don't work well Beneath. We'd need..."

"We'd need a Harrower," I finished for her.

Exactly what we didn't want to see.

"Well, we can't stay here," I said, a lump of panic forming in my throat. I heard the edge of hysteria in my tone and struggled to contain it. "We need to get out somehow. And quickly." Before something finds us, I thought.

Cautiously, quietly, I picked my way down the row of cars, surveying my surroundings, searching for movement. In the dim red light, every innocent shape appeared threatening. The ground beneath me shuddered again, and I noticed bits of scarred metal reaching up from dry, cracked soil. The buildings stood quiet, empty. All the doors were closed.

"What do you think we should do?" Iris whispered, following close on my heels.

Stepping farther into the street, I looked up into the blank glare of the stars. I shivered. It was cold here—not the cold of an icy Minnesota winter, but a chill that went deeper. I turned to Iris,

235

swallowing thickly. I kept my voice low. "Do you think you could fight another Harrower?"

"I wouldn't necessarily need to fight it. Just get near enough to share its powers—if it's one that's strong enough to breach the Circle. But I'm not sure I could handle one here."

"There has to be *something* we can—"

The ground shifted suddenly, thrusting upward, knocking me from my feet.

"Damn it," I complained. As I hauled myself upright, I saw a trace of blood on my palms.

Iris stared at me in horror.

"You can't bleed here."

Something sharp and metallic had dug itself in the skin of my left hand. I removed it gingerly, then drew back quickly as pain raced up my arm. I looked at Iris.

"Does blood attract demons?"

I had a sudden, terrible vision of Harrowers swimming up out of the night like sharks.

Iris tugged her scarf free from her coat, pushing it toward me to cover my hands. "You're the daughter of Morning Star," she whispered. "This place *knows* you, Audrey. It knows your blood."

Around us, the air rippled. The doors of every car blew open in unison, metal screeching in our ears, then slammed shut. A loud, unearthly keening rose up, filling my senses. Like some kind of alarm system for the Beneath.

Or some kind of awakening.

Iris and I stared at each other, our breath clouding the air. Red stars burned above us. I twisted about, searching the street for movement. The sky fractured once more. There was a flash of light, a moment of darkness. My surroundings shifted again, colors vanishing, leaving everything a pale, deathly gray.

Then, as abruptly as it had begun, the keening stopped.

I turned back toward Iris. "What just happened?" I asked, a tremor in my voice.

But Iris didn't answer.

She was no longer there.

Alone, I turned in slow, uncertain circles. The street had disappeared. Gone were the buildings, the skeletal cars, the knotted trees. There were no stars, no hint of sky. Cold, colorless sand shifted beneath me when I took a step, swallowing up my footprints. Everything was muted and dim. The only color that remained was the blue of my coat, the blood on my hands. Somewhere, a wind was blowing.

I called out for Iris, but my voice sounded harsh and loud in the echoing stillness. There was no response. I fell silent, worrying what else might hear me. What else might answer.

I told myself to remain calm. Panic wouldn't serve me. I needed to think. Harrowers moved out from Beneath, so there was a way. They crept out in places where the fabric was thin, pushing through the Circle and into the city. There would be some path to follow. There had to be.

But around me was only wasteland, emptiness spreading outward, dry, dead earth below the cold sand. I took a step forward, then another. Though I had no clear direction in mind, progress felt important. I walked, and kept walking; minutes, hours—I wasn't certain how long. I simply moved, stopping on occasion to check if my surroundings had altered, if I could discover some sign, anything that might point the way. Nothing changed. The emptiness continued around me unbroken. Briefly, I considered trying to reach out with my Knowing, but something told me I shouldn't try that here. I remembered Gram telling me there were places it was best not to look.

Even as I thought that, awareness crept over me. Not a Knowing. Something physical. The sort of awareness that makes your skin prickle and your heart freeze. I halted, barely breathing. I knew what that awareness meant.

This space was not mine, and it did not welcome me. But it wanted me.

In the stillness that surrounded me, the emptiness breathed. Something here was alive. Something old and angry, watchful, ravenous. It didn't have shape or name. But it knew me. Knew I was Kin. Knew my blood.

I turned, feeling the wind on my neck. In the low light beyond me, nothing stirred, but that nothing was bitter, full of craving.

As I stood there, the emptiness spoke to me. It whispered that I was forgotten. That I was abandoned. It whispered that this was what it was like to be left behind in the void. What it was like to know grief, to know wrath, to feel nothing but horror and hate bubbling up inside you in the blank space that should have sheltered a heart. To feel corruption eating up the light within until corruption was all that remained. To decay.

You are going to die here, the stillness said. *You are going to want to die.*

It was then that I realized I was no longer alone.

The first Harrower approached leisurely. It didn't walk upright, but crept, pulling itself forward, pausing, observing me. Here, Beneath, it had no need for disguise. I saw its face plainly. Gaunt flesh, silver and scaled, was pulled taut across its skull. Pale milk eyes blinked above an eager smile.

The second Harrower came slinking behind it.

I whirled, ready to flee, but I hadn't taken more than a step before I stopped short. The third Harrower was closing in from behind. This one was farther away, but moving faster. The click of its talons upon the ground was rapid, restless. At its side, the fourth progressed at an uneven pace, cautious and watchful. The fifth was running.

After that, I stopped counting. I glanced from side to side, but no direction was safe. Others were approaching now, and others beyond those, a thick net tightening. The nearest were slow, methodical in their advance; those farther away came hurtling across the distance, all of them moving closer, closer.

I knew, in that moment, that the voice had been right. I was going to die. I felt it with a certainty so deep that it pushed me beyond hope, beyond fear, beyond helplessness. For just a moment, I closed my eyes. I thought of Gram's voice, soft as she bent to whisper secrets. I thought of Mom sitting beside me in sweet summer grasses, leaning back to point out the moon. I remembered Gideon hitting a baseball up over the roof of my house, how it rolled so far we'd never found it.

These are the things I'll take with me, I thought.

I opened my eyes as the first demon reached me. I didn't scream when I felt its claws.

I fought.

I wasn't strong like my mother. No Guardian powers surged through my veins, no sudden swiftness to dodge blows, to counter and evade. No lights glowed beneath my fingertips. When the demon caught the side of my neck, I felt my flesh tear. Warm blood oozed onto my coat and steamed in the chill. But I fought. Frenzied, uncaring, I grappled with the demon, thrusting it away from me and then rushing at it, my hands seeking its throat. If I was going to die, I wasn't going to die easy.

The Harrower's skin was cold and hard. My nails couldn't pierce it, but I squeezed, digging my fingers as far as I could. This demon wasn't as strong as the others I'd seen, but it was strong enough. It tossed me backward and then launched itself against me. All around me, I heard the sounds of talons click-click-clicking

240

upon the ground. I rolled away as the demon sunk its claws into my arm. I didn't register pain. My hands went for its throat again, wild, ineffectual, unable to break its skin.

Teeth, I thought. Teeth might puncture it.

From somewhere above, I heard a man's rich chuckle and then a familiar voice, lightly accented, warm with amusement. "This vicious streak of yours is quite becoming, but it's like to get you killed. Allow me, please."

The demon was wrenched from my grasp. A silver form blurred past, dragging the Harrower with it. The two figures tumbled beyond my vision, and I heard a sudden, sickening snap.

I jumped to my feet and a hand caught at my elbow. Spinning wildly, I brought my arm up to fling away my attacker. Human fingers caught my wrist in a firm grip.

"Audrey," a low voice breathed.

Then there were hands on my shoulders, big hands, gripping me tightly. There were arms I knew, and white shirtsleeves, and a tie blown about in the wind. Dazed, uncertain, I looked up into dark blue eyes and an anxious face. Leon.

He drew me against him, wrapping an arm around my waist. "I've got you," he whispered, and I felt an instant of dizzy relief, even as the chaos roared around us.

Nearby, the other man's voice said, "No time for reunions, I'm afraid. We need to leave. You've attracted the wrong sort of attention, and the locals here aren't friendly."

Before I could respond, Leon tightened his grip on me, his other arm curving around my back. As I looked up, I caught the briefest glimpse of Harrower faces, dozens beyond us, a tide pushing forward. Some running, some creeping. Red teeth gleaming.

"Definitely time to go," the unseen man said.

A cold hand slid into mine. I sucked in a breath—and darkness closed around me.

24

Exiting the Beneath was not like entering it.

As that thick darkness engulfed my senses, the hand tugged me forward. Leon's arms remained securely around me, but I felt the ground give way beneath us. My throat was hot. I smelled blood. All around me were small explosions of sound. I heard music and whispers and a harsh, braying laughter. I caught the cries of animals—wolf howls and the hum of bees and the swift drumbeat of a bird heart. A high, broken wail found its way beneath my skin and settled there, so mournful and wild that I tried to pull back, to shake free of the hand that grasped me. The wind rose up, tearing its way into my lungs.

Then we were out.

I hadn't fallen. The sidewalk was solid under my feet, gray cement wet with snow in an empty street yellowed by lamplight. My hand had been freed, but Leon's arms held firm. Above, the sky was dark with clouds, but here and there, starlight pushed through. I didn't move. I didn't react to the pressure of Leon's hands against me, sliding down my arms, turning my wrists so he could see the cuts on my palms still burning red. I didn't react to him brushing the hair back from my face, or tugging me against him.

Then, finally, his voice broke through.

He was speaking.

He was saying my name.

He was telling me I was all right.

Relief washed through me, making my knees watery. I leaned forward, resting against Leon's shoulder. I told myself I would stay there only a second, but for that second, I simply stood and breathed.

Nearby, the other man spoke. "There now. Back in the land of the mostly living, with all limbs attached and in their proper positions. Nothing to it."

I pulled away from Leon and turned toward the voice. The man stood a short distance from us, his blond hair dusted with snow. Recognition sparked. I knew this man. Though I hadn't seen him clearly, I'd met him twice before. I recalled those green eyes and the trace of laughter in his tone. It was the same man who had rescued me outside the Drought and Deluge.

Frowning in confusion, I was about to speak—and then my mother appeared, yanking me away from Leon and into her arms. "Oh, thank God," she murmured.

"And here I was thinking you might thank *me*," the man said.

Mom ignored him, hugging me tightly against her. For just a moment, I Knew her feelings as strongly as if they had been my own: the choking fear that finally ebbed, that rush of relief at seeing me safe. Then her grip loosened, and she lifted her hands to my shoulders, stepping back to inspect the wound on my neck. Her mouth tightened.

I gazed down at my coat. The thick cotton padding had served as a peculiar sort of armor, though it was slashed open in places, tufts of white spilling out. The fabric was matted with blood where the Harrower had grazed the skin above my collarbone, but I didn't think the wound was deep. "I'm okay," I said.

Beside us, the man spoke again. "I wouldn't fret. I expect the damage isn't permanent." His voice lowered, the hint of amusement returning. "Fierce, though, isn't she? All full of ... fire."

Mom shot him a warning glare, but he wasn't looking at her. He was looking at me. His lips were upturned, his gaze intent. As our eyes met, something clicked into place. I tensed, recalling a flash of silver, the feel of a cold hand in mine. He appeared to be only a man—but he hadn't been a man, Beneath. "You're a Harrower," I said.

"You needn't worry. I've made my peace with the human community. You can call me Shane."

"He's neutral," Leon explained, moving beside me. His hand hovered near my shoulder. "Supposedly."

"I prefer *misunderstood*." The Harrower smiled again, an easy grin that left me a little bewildered. "I'm completely at your service, angel. Your mum and this fellow here came begging."

"I believe we came threatening," Leon retorted.

"Semantics."

Mom lifted a hand, cutting off their argument. She turned to Leon, her mouth a thin line. "I haven't been able to reach Ryan. I need you to go find him. Let him know the situation. We have some things to take care of."

Leon gave her a short nod and headed away, disappearing down the street.

The situation. I wondered if that meant Anna Berkeley. Or—

A jolt of panic coursed through me. I grabbed my mother's arm. "Iris. I forgot—Iris was with me. Beneath."

"I sent her home." Mom's voice was quiet, but I heard a note of anger in it, carefully restrained. "They brought her out first."

"You were the problem," Shane said. "You were drawn into a deeper level. Any further and we wouldn't have been able to find you. And it's lucky we reached you when we did. I expect you wouldn't be nearly so pretty if you came in several pieces." Before I could think of a response to that, he turned to Mom. "That's two favors you owe me now, and don't think I'm likely to forget."

She put one hand on her hip and shook her head. "I'm already overlooking the fact that my kid was attacked in your club."

Shane made a *tch* noise. "*Outside* my club, actually. And I notified the proper authorities."

Mom twitched. It was a good thing she wasn't near a streetlamp, or Shane would have shortly come into very close contact with it. "So that's why I have Detective Wyle breathing down my neck," she said. "You know, for someone who wants to keep all his internal organs internal, you could learn a bit more about diplomacy."

"Like rescuing your daughter twice now, maybe? Don't worry, from what I've seen of the good detective, the part of your anatomy that interests him is somewhat lower down."

Mom made a noise suspiciously like a growl.

"But let me give you a bit of free advice," Shane continued. "A token of my goodwill. On the subject of necks: you're going to have to get to work if you want to save his. He's running headlong into a threat he is ill-prepared to face."

"I've warned him already."

Shane's voice dropped to a whisper. "I don't think a warning will suffice." He switched his gaze to me. "Nice seeing you again, little Dark Star. Keep looking for that light." Then he turned down the street, disappearing into the swirl of snow.

I watched him go. Dark Star. He'd called me that before, outside the Drought and Deluge. *Not quite the bright shining star your mum is,* he'd said. She wasn't shining now. Her stance was rigid, her face grim. Worry had fled, and a deep fury had replaced it.

I swallowed. I'd broken my promise. "Mom—"

"Not now." She grabbed hold of my sleeve, tugging none too gently. Ignoring my protests, she steered me down the street, toward her car, then ushered me inside. A faint dusting of snow lay on the windshield. I waited for her to speak, to lecture me, or threaten to snap me in two like a soda cracker, but she just breathed, tapped her fingers on the dashboard, and started the car.

Silence was heavy between us as we began the drive. There was little traffic. The city felt empty, full of spaces and gaps. A memory of Beneath, I thought. I could see the layer of red shadows edging along the buildings, the places where lights ceased. With my thoughts in disarray, it took me several minutes to realize we were headed in the wrong direction.

"We're not going home?" I asked.

Mom didn't look at me. "I'm taking you to the ER."

"I'm fine," I said. The wounds on my arm and neck hurt, but the bleeding had stopped.

"This isn't a discussion."

At the hospital, our official explanation was that I'd been attacked by a dog, which involved a tetanus shot, several stitches, and Mom assuring the nurses that she'd already contacted Animal Control. She spent most of the visit talking on her cell phone, even when instructed not to, and vanished outside on occasion—so that her calls wouldn't be overheard, I supposed. A nurse tried to chat with me, but I didn't feel up to small talk. She patted my arm and told me I'd be better soon. I looked away, toward dark windows lined with frost. It felt as though a storm had passed through me, raging and wild, and now I stood in the aftermath, trying to assess the damage. Inside me, something had altered. Something had been pulled loose and rattled around and no longer fit quite right.

I closed my eyes and saw Harrowers: stark faces, red teeth. I heard the sharp click of nails.

I wondered how Iris was.

Mom was quiet during the drive home. When I tried to talk, she gave me clipped, one-word answers. I watched the streets blur past. The snow had stopped, but the clouds were dark and low, cloaking the moon. I felt like crying. I didn't know why; I hadn't cried Beneath, not when I'd stood alone in the emptiness, or when the Harrowers had circled me, or even when I'd felt that fierce, terrible certainty that I would die—but I wanted to cry now.

Instead, I asked about Anna Berkeley. Mom confirmed that she'd had Leon and Mr. Alvarez set up Guardian protection, but I could tell by the look on her face that the subject was a mistake.

"I tried to call," I said. "We had to get to her right away. We wouldn't have gone out there otherwise."

"You promised me!" Mom snapped. "I explained the situation to you in the hope that you would be able to make informed decisions. I expected more from you, Audrey. You're not a Guardian, and neither is Iris. What you did tonight wasn't brave or clever."

It hadn't felt brave or clever—simply necessary. I sighed, rubbing my forehead, and asked, "So, what, I'm grounded again?"

"No. That obviously had no impact." Her eyes were narrowed, her lips a thin line, and the expression on her face clearly meant she was assessing other options. Like sending me to a boarding school on the other side of the planet.

"I guess we're going back to secrets and cryptic answers, then."

"What do you want me to say? That it's all right for you to put yourself at risk? You could have been killed tonight."

"You could be killed *every* night," I shot back.

"Is that what this was about?" she demanded. "Trying to prove something?"

"It was about saving a life!"

She wasn't even listening to me. "I don't go out every night because I want to, Audrey. I do it because I have to. Morning Star is who I am. I can't change that."

I looked away, toward the haze of streetlights and the glint of new snow. I felt a tear roll down my cheek and brushed it away. "Why didn't you tell me about the Kin?"

Her eyes flicked toward mine, then away. "This isn't the time."

"It's *never* the time. I want to know."

Silence.

"You think I can't handle it," I said. "You think I'm still a little kid. Or that I'm too stupid to deal with it."

"You're not stupid, Audrey. You just don't think. There's a difference."

And then, just as she'd accused me, I didn't think about my next words. I just said them.

"I wish I had a father."

I'd never said that before. I wasn't sure I'd ever thought it before—but now I'd said it, and I couldn't take it back. I didn't even want to. The words just hung there between us.

Mom didn't hesitate. I heard a slight catch in her voice, but otherwise her tone was steady. "You know what? I wish that too. And it's just too damn bad, because you don't. You're stuck with me."

I didn't say anything. I knew I should have. I should have apologized, told her I was wrong, that I hadn't meant to say it. But I couldn't make the words come out. I *had* meant to say it; I was exhausted and angry, my body sore, my nerves raw, and I wanted to lash out. My throat felt tight.

We're all we've got, Gram used to say. *But we do just fine.*

But that wasn't true. We had the Kin. We had the St. Croix family. And once, I'd had a father.

And if Mom wouldn't tell me about him, I'd have to ask someone else.

The following afternoon, I went to St. Paul to find Esther.

She met me in the hall, her eyebrows arched as she looked me over. "What a lovely surprise. We don't normally see you here on a Thursday. I'll add another place at dinner."

"I won't be long," I said, keeping my voice even. "But I wanted to talk to you."

Her gaze met mine, and she gave me a slow, measuring look. Then she nodded. "Let's go into my sitting room."

I followed her down the hall, to the room with the delicate floral wallpaper and tidy furniture. She gestured for me to sit, then took the chair across from me.

"I heard about your little escapade yesterday," she said. "Well done."

Heat crept up my face. I couldn't tell if she was being sincere or not. "You're not going to yell at me?"

"We use our abilities to aid others. I won't lecture you. Thanks to your efforts, the girl has Guardian protection. Your instincts were correct."

"Someone should try telling my mom that," I grumbled.

"I imagine *someone* has. What is it you wanted to speak with me about?"

I took a steadying breath, gripping the arms of the chair. Across from me, Esther's face was impassive. "I want you to tell me why my mother kept the Kin a secret from me."

She raised her eyebrows. "You think she tells me why she does anything?"

"I think you know. And I think it has something to do with my father. With what happened to him—during the Harrowing. I want you to tell me what happened." I kept my gaze fixed on hers. Her eyes were very dark, more brown now than gold, taking on an almost reddish hue.

"Lucy won't appreciate my meddling. She keeps her secrets close."

"I'm her *daughter*," I protested.

"Why have you come to *me*, then?"

I didn't answer.

Esther folded her arms and gave me a shrewd look. "It is not a happy story."

"I didn't think it was."

She rose, turning toward the tall frost-glazed windows that flanked the room. From the back she looked just like Elspeth, except for the touch of silver in her hair. "I didn't approve of your mother and Adrian. You should know that."

I swallowed. Esther had grown very closed off, her tone unreadable. "Our Morning Star was never one to listen to anyone," she said. "She became a Guardian at the age of fifteen, and grew very powerful very quickly. She was reckless. I feared she would be a danger to Adrian. She was certainly a danger to herself."

She walked to the desk and bent, opening a drawer and retrieving her Nav cards. I watched her hands close over the deck, the absent way she shuffled them. Not like Gram, who had treated her cards with such reverence, letting her fingertips linger along the edges.

"We're doing a reading?" I asked.

"Hold on to these," she said, crossing the room and dropping the deck into my hands. "You may as well have them."

I crinkled my brow in confusion. "You're giving me your Nav cards?" Kind of pointless, I thought, since I already had Gram's.

"They were never mine. They belonged to your father. I use them from time to time, but Adrian was the only one in this family with any real talent in Knowing. Until you."

I shuffled twice and flipped the top card over. Inverted Crescent.

"That was his card, too," Esther said. I looked up at her.

For a second, I got a sense of him, some memory from Esther—a slow half-smile, laughter echoing. A sort of irrepressible buoyancy. Someone who knew joy.

Esther returned to her seat, crossing her legs and folding her hands together. "You know about Amplification, yes? Iris told you, I suspect."

I gave a short nod.

"It was Adrian's greatest gift. Lucy was an exceptional Guardian in her own right, but with him at her side, your mother was nearly unstoppable. She was a force of power unparalleled, at least in Kin history." Pausing for some sort of effect, Esther looked at me, then said, "*Nearly* unstoppable. Until the Harrowing."

I waited, listening. There was a soft knock on the door, but Esther sent whoever it was away with a curt dismissal. Outside, the last of the light had faded.

"Most Harrowings are organized. We sense them coming. There's a breach in one of the Circles, or a mass of powerful demons able to push through. They work together, hunting the Kin. Hundreds of them, sometimes more. But this...this was something else. This Harrowing was the work of only one."

"Verrick," I said. The word hung before me, as though it had been imprinted on the air.

Esther nodded slowly. "We don't know when exactly he came to the Cities. He was here long before any of us realized. Verrick was—different. He rarely went Beneath, kept himself separate from other Harrowers. His human form was without flaw. His aliases were simple, and he took care to avoid notice. In this way, he remained hidden and lay dormant for many years."

"What changed?"

"I can't say for certain. It may simply have been a matter of timing." She took a long breath, closing her eyes. "We knew by then that some danger was approaching. For years, we'd been watching for signs of a Harrowing, but we weren't aware of Verrick until he showed himself. He was cunning. It took us far too long to realize his true intent."

"He wanted the Remnant." When Esther nodded, I said, "But she wouldn't have even been born. Not if the demons are bleeding sixteen-year-olds. I thought they wanted her power, not to stop her existence."

"Verrick had information we didn't. His Knowing was strong, stronger than that of any Kin. He knew when and where the Remnant would be born—perhaps even her identity. He wanted us fragmented, the Astral Circle destroyed, so nothing would remain to impede him."

"Mom stopped him," I said. "She killed him. But why were my father's powers sealed?"

Esther turned back to me. Her face was blank, but she couldn't hide the grief in her tone. "Your mother battled Verrick many times before she defeated him. She was strong, but so was he. And though she wounded him, he always managed to escape. He recovered. He grew in power. And we sensed that this was worse than what had come before. That he was waiting for something. That he was planning."

"So ... your basic apocalypse," I said, shifting uncomfortably.

Esther threw me a look that meant she was not amused. "We lost a third of our numbers. Many of our people fled the Cities, seeking what little safety they could find elsewhere, among other Kin. Those of us who remained had little hope of survival. He was hunting down Guardians, one by one. Slaughtering them. And gathering his strength in the most brutal way imaginable. Whether it was something he learned or something inherent to him, I couldn't say, but Verrick had an ability other Harrowers do not. He wasn't just killing the Guardians—he was taking their power, their life forces, into himself. And he grew stronger with each Guardian he drained. Eventually, he caught your father."

At her words, an image shot through me: a young man's body bent, unmoving. From far off, I caught my mother's voice, a harsh, screaming sob—*Adrian!*

But he wasn't dead. They'd told me that. His heart was sleeping. "Mom saved him," I said.

Esther inclined her head. "Lucy fought Verrick off before he could finish draining your father. She brought him back here, to me." Her eyes clouded. She looked past me, into the dark distance beyond the windows. "We feared the worst, but Adrian surprised us. He recovered on his own. And then . . . then he began to grow stronger."

A tingling began on the back of my neck. "Stronger how?"

She lowered her eyes, trailing her fingers down the upholstered arm of her chair. "It was little things at first. His Knowing increased. He could tell Lucy where Verrick would attack next, and when. That was when we realized what had happened. Adrian was an Amplifier; he could share the powers of others. When Verrick began draining him, Adrian had attempted to reverse the process, to drain him back. A link formed between them. A connection that wasn't severed."

"A connection," I repeated. Dread pooled in my stomach. I knew where this was headed.

"It was Adrian who told us of the Remnant—that she would be born here, and soon, and that Verrick was preparing. Adrian's abilities as a Guardian grew, as well. In time it's possible he would have become powerful enough to defeat Verrick on his own terms. But we didn't have time. Too many lives had been lost already. An entire generation of Guardians—gone."

Like Leon's parents. I felt another tremor of grief from Esther, the weight of guilt. Not just for my father, but for all the others who had been lost.

"By then it had become clear to us that the connection went both ways," she continued. "Verrick made an error when he drained an Amplifier. And that was when we discovered the solution. To wound one was to wound the other. The way to weaken Verrick was to use the link: to seal both of their life forces. Permanently."

A ritual, Iris had said. Blood from the five sacred spaces. Life spilling out.

"So you sealed his powers, and then he just left?" I asked. I might not have a clear sense of my father, but I knew what he had left behind. I had felt it a thousand times behind my mother's eyes: a keen but quiet longing, fierce and hidden.

Esther shook her head slowly. "There was no other choice. It was for his own safety. Who we are as humans can't be separated from who we are as Kin. Sealing his life force meant sealing away that part of him forever. His knowledge." She paused, her voice unsteady. "His memories. He couldn't stay with us."

The sleeping heart.

Both living and dead.

Not quite what Iris had made it seem.

"He agreed to that?" I looked down at the cards in my hands. I'd been shuffling them absently, but the Inverted Crescent remained flipped up. His card, too, Esther had said. But no longer. Whatever ties he'd had to the Kin had been severed.

"He went to it willingly, though Lucy objected."

She would have. I knew my mother.

Esther's tone grew hesitant. "I can't tell you everything you want to know. But it's possible you can see it for yourself." She drew back in her chair, sighing faintly. In the dim light, she seemed less severe than I was accustomed to, almost vulnerable. "It's something that is rarely done, but you have the ability. You have to move past Knowing, into echo and reverie."

"I don't know what you mean," I whispered.

Except I did. She meant using my Knowing to see into the past, and I didn't know if I could. I'd had glimpses, flickers now and then—but those were things I felt rather than saw, like the

259

northern lights that lingered at the edges of every memory in Mickey Wyle's boyhood, or Iris's black shoes at her parents' funeral. I had never done anything close to what Esther was suggesting.

"It's about focus and control," she continued. "Like when you use your Nav cards. The significance is in the act. You clear everything else away."

"It's not that simple," I protested. "If I want to see the past —Mom's past—I'd need to have her here. My Knowings aren't nearly as strong when I don't have the subject with me."

Esther merely shrugged. "Perhaps usually. But this is your mother. She is a part of you. She carried you. Her blood lives in your blood."

"Her blood. Not her memories."

"That is why you use your Knowing."

I began to shuffle, and Esther rose from her chair, moving in front of me. Her hands settled on mine, halting their motion. I looked up at her questioningly.

She chuckled softly. "Use your Knowing—and my help. Did Iris mention that I'm also an Amplifier?"

I nodded mutely.

"We will do this together." Her fingers closed over mine. Tightened. "Focus." Her hands were cool and her veins lightly stained, ribbons of color that threaded down her left wrist. I could imagine a pale glow there, her knuckles bent. She was a Guardian, too, I remembered.

"Focus, Audrey."

"I *am*," I muttered.

Echo and reverie, I thought. Gram had never had me do anything like this. Once, she had sat before me and placed her hands over mine, a sort of connection, she said—the space where Knowing met Knowing—but that had been to help me clear my thoughts so that I could see the pattern.

This wasn't just a pattern. This was a history. Heritage. All the words my mother couldn't speak. Esther's Amplification was powerful, I could sense that, could feel my Knowing strengthening, but I still wasn't certain I could do this. I couldn't quite focus. I couldn't quite think—

Can't you ever be serious?

I jerked suddenly, searching Esther's face. She hadn't spoken. But—

It's like arguing with the weather, with you.

My mother's voice. A sound of laughter bubbling. And then, again, her piercing cry, all the strength of her powerful lungs within it. *Adrian!*

I closed my eyes. Opened them.

And for the first time in my life, I saw my father's face.

26

It wasn't like dreaming. I saw everything with a strange, sharp clarity. The dark, storm-battered sky. Picnic tables and tree branches glistening with rain. The light that grazed my parents' faces didn't come from above, it came from below. Fireflies in the grass. They stood near a lake.

My mother said his name, but I knew him before she spoke.

He had St. Croix eyes. Even in the semidarkness I could see them, dusty gold, their steady gaze on my mother as she stood before him. His curly hair was a rich brown, tousled by the wind that stirred up through the pines. He was tall and lean and had a crooked smile that was meant for mischief—except that now there was something a little sad about it, and the hand he rested on my mother's shoulder tightened when she said his name.

I looked at my mother. Her cheeks were red. It looked as

though she'd been crying. She looked so young and lost, her pregnancy—me—a swell not quite concealed by her baggy shirt.

"There's another way, I know there is," she said, staring up at him as clouds covered the moon. "We just have to find it. Give me time, Adrian. I'll find it, I swear I'll find it."

"We don't *have* time. We've been over this. Verrick is growing stronger with every Guardian he drains. This is our only chance, and we have to take it. We agreed—"

"No, *you* agreed," my mother snapped, jerking out of his grip. "You and Esther. You haven't let me find another solution."

"There is no other solution. You can't handle Verrick."

"I can handle anything." Her eyes caught a sliver of moonlight. She stood straight, her hands balled into fists at her side.

My father's voice was gentle. "You know I'm right."

She turned away from him, toward the lake, where the water was motionless and void of color. "I'll come to you after I defeat Verrick. I'll go with you. We'll start over. Leave all of this."

"You can't give up being Kin, being a Guardian. It's who you are."

"It's who you are, too!" She paused, relaxing her hands. She looked tired. "I'll have them seal my blood, too. And we'll leave together. I can't do this alone."

My father came up behind her, pulling her backward against him. One arm wrapped around her shoulders, closing the space between them. His hand rested near her belly.

"Lucy, I promise you. You won't be alone."

The vision—I didn't know what else to call it—sped forward.

My mother was farther away this time, standing in a hallway, her face half turned. She spoke to someone I couldn't see, though I recognized the voice. And I knew that hall, the pristine carpet, the walls painted in neutral colors.

"Verrick will be weakened, but so will you. Some strength will remain in him, and without Adrian, you're at a disadvantage."

"I understand." Mom's voice was flat. "I can do this, Esther."

"Timing is crucial. If Verrick realizes what has happened—"

"He'll go after Adrian. I know."

There was a pause, long enough that my mother turned to leave. Then Esther's voice, clear and cutting through the thick silence. "You really mean to go with him?"

"I do."

A blur of light. My mother strode down the hall, her face grim and determined—then she faded. A wind rushed up. The bright, vacant light of the hall became the muted light of stars and the dizzy yellow of headlights, streetlamps, office buildings. It was night, and she stood above the city, on the roof of a building. She wore a dark coat instead of a hoodie, and her long hair flowed free, but she was still Morning Star. She was there with a purpose. She took two large steps forward, then hopped onto the ledge, staring down at the city below. Traffic rushed past. Detached though I was, I felt a surge of panic as I watched her. She lifted her arms, spreading them outward, the wind billowing around her.

You could fall! I wanted to shout. I wanted to pull her backward, into safety, where a sudden gust was less likely to send her hurtling into oblivion.

A voice came from behind her. "You think you're clever, do you?"

Mom didn't turn. She didn't even seem to react, except for a certain tension along her arms, and the fact that her fingertips—both hands, not just the left—gained a faint glow.

"A noble sacrifice. He won't even remember you. But I wouldn't worry. You'll be dead soon enough, and I'll be sure to send him to you."

My mother finally turned, leaping off her perch onto the smooth tar of the roof. She bent slightly, her arms held in front of her, the glow spreading through her fingers, down to her wrists. At her throat, a third light began to pulse. "Seems like I've heard that line before," she said. "And yet, here I am, still living."

"A temporary circumstance."

"I'm ready, Verrick. I'm ready."

She was. I saw it in her eyes, the set of her mouth, the way she held herself. There was no hesitancy in her. No trace of fear or uncertainty. She would end this. Tonight. She stepped forward, and for the first time, I saw the Harrower she faced.

He looked like a man. I'd known that, I should have expected it, but seeing him there, his arms slack at his sides, his hair slightly rumpled, it felt incongruous that all of my mother's rage and hate should be directed at someone so benign in appearance.

She attacked. Faster than I could see or think, she sped across the roof, the shine at her fingers a sudden blurred arc. One of her hands shot toward his throat, burning the air behind her. Verrick deflected her, catching her wrist, tossing her backward. She caught his other arm and the two of them lurched forward, falling hard against the tar. I felt the wind rush out of her lungs.

But my mother was strong. She was fierce, and frightening, and something I had never seen. She kicked outward, away from Verrick, and crouched low. I heard her panting. The glow of her veins beat with her heart, colors churning at her wrists and jugular.

"Your powers are sealed," she said, her voice clear and carrying. "You really think you have the strength left to kill me?"

"You have no idea what my strength is," he said.

Beneath his feet, a ring of light began to pool, thick and bright and smelling faintly of blood. It rose around him, spreading outward until it surrounded them both—great waves of light, like a miniature aurora borealis. Its colors shimmered in the darkness, soft blues fading into greens, yellows, pale orange, a hint of violet, and a clear white light, warm and vibrant and strangely beautiful.

Only, there was something very wrong about this.

Glimmers of light, I thought. That was how the energy of the Astral Circle manifested.

Verrick had accessed the Circle. He was depleting its energy— draining it, the same way he'd drained the powers of all those Guardians he'd killed. Drawing its light into himself.

I felt my mother's heart lurch. All around them, the light continued to swell, fiery pulses that flickered and then dimmed as they rushed toward Verrick.

She launched herself against him.

He lifted his arm, and a shock of energy flew outward, hitting my mother just below the collarbone with enough force to knock her backward. I felt the impact rattle through her. She tried to lift herself upward, but before she could move, another blast caught her. Her head fell back against the tar. A trickle of blood welled on one cheek.

Verrick moved closer.

"I know what they call you. *Morning Star.* The light in the east. Some sort of godsend, here to guide and protect. But we know differently, don't we?"

He stood above her. The light that surrounded them was blinding, burning. My mother shut her eyes tightly, turned her face to the side, but I could still see him. Though his expression was blank, I felt the malice within him.

I'd seen images of demons in books and movies, in paintings hung in museums, in the bottomless depths of my own nightmares. I'd seen Harrowers before, the rippling skin that wasn't quite human, scales and claws, eyes that weren't eyes. I'd felt the malevolence and fury that stained the icy void Beneath.

None of that prepared me for Verrick's face. I didn't know if I believed in hell, but if one existed, he had surely crawled out of it.

It wasn't that he was hideous and distorted, some gruesome creature with horns and fangs. It was a sense of what moved behind his eyes: the final, gasping breath of a drowning child; a thousand moths crushed underfoot; bird wings caught on wires; the colors of blood and bone, muscle and fat; the last light of the cosmos suddenly snuffed.

It was something I'd felt before.

Something I'd felt as my hands covered my Nav cards, seeking the Remnant. Some trace of him left behind—seeking, also.

I began to understand why my father had made his choice. Why he had sacrificed himself, sealing his blood to weaken Verrick.

Your basic apocalypse, I'd told Esther, half joking.

Now this apocalypse stood over my mother. I wanted to tell her to run, to run and keep running and not look back. But my mother stayed motionless.

"You're no light," the demon said. "You're the black hole that consumes everything, heedless and without hope. You are nothing. Dozens of your Kin killed because of your weakness. And now your lover as well. I've fought you before. I've felt it. You crave your own destruction."

He knelt beside her, the Circle's stolen light washing over them both. His hand caressed her cheek, almost tenderly. "Let me end it."

My mother's eyes flew open.

Her hand flashed upward, her fingers latching on to the side of his face. Verrick jerked away, trying to escape her grip, but her hand slid to his throat and stayed there. The glow of her fingertips burned against his skin.

"You've fought me before," she said, jumping to her feet and dragging him with her. "You think I want to die? Maybe. But trust me when I say I'm taking you with me."

Around them, the Circle's light crackled and sparked, colors bending, writhing, weakening, fading. Even as he drew the light to him, Verrick struggled against my mother, clawing down her neck, her side, down toward the swell of her belly.

From one end of the roof to the other, they fought. Verrick broke free of her grip. A blast from his hand connected with her face, and she stumbled backward, somehow keeping her balance. She ran forward again, one hand catching his neck. Through skin and shirt, I saw his spine go red.

A sound burst from Verrick's throat, dark and wild. My mother didn't stop. He moved back and she advanced, pushing him farther and farther, until they reached the ledge.

"You can't end me," he choked out, gasping. "I'm bound to you. Bound to the daughter that sleeps beneath your heart. She carries her father's blood. Kill me and we'll meet again."

"I'll take that chance," she said, thrusting him forward, off the ledge.

And together they fell.

She should have died.

I knew that, and I felt her knowing it.

She should have died. She was ready to die. But she wanted to live. It radiated out of her, as brilliant and blinding as any sun in any solar system.

The ground rushed toward her.

As they fell, Verrick strengthened his hold on the Circle, dragging its energy with him. Light surrounded them both, so hot and bright that it seemed they were wrapped in flame. He struggled wildly against her, but she didn't relax her grip. Her fingers dug into his throat, twisting, squeezing.

And then it happened.

Verrick's body went slack against her. The light of the Circle vanished. It spun around my mother, burning into her, beneath her skin, so that for a moment her entire body seemed to shine. She cried out, wordless, afraid—and then it was gone.

My mother was alive, unharmed.

She'd landed on the street as though she'd been placed there, no shock of impact ripping through her. Though she was barely wounded, she reeked of blood. Verrick's body, still clutched tightly against her, disappeared Beneath. My mother didn't move. She just lay there on the pavement, staring up at the dizzy blur of city lights and the distant luster of stars. Tentatively, as though she were afraid, she lifted one hand and pressed it to her belly.

Finally she rose, pulling herself to her feet and looking around the street. The area was narrow and deserted, little more than an alley. On either side, buildings of steel and concrete loomed over her. A few cars moved past in the street ahead of her as a light rain began to fall. She headed for the intersection.

She caught a cab and asked to be taken to Lake of the Isles. The driver, seeing her injuries, gave her a long concerned look, but didn't question her. Pop music floated from the radio, and Mom leaned back against the seat, closing her eyes. The left side of her face was swollen and slightly bruised, and a smear of blood remained on her cheek.

She tucked one hand into a coat pocket and withdrew an envelope.

A fleeting expression of shock crossed her face. The cab was dark, but the ink of her name was easily visible on the white surface of the envelope. I didn't have to recognize his handwriting to know the letter was from my father. I didn't have to read the paper to know the words.

Lucy. You're asleep now. i can hear you breathing. i want you to know i meant what i said.

i won't be waiting. i've asked my mother to take me away after the sealing. i've asked her not to tell you where. You will say this is unfair. You'll say i'm making your decision for you. And i am. You're a Guardian, Lucy. You always will be. But i can't be anymore. it has to be done.

i don't know about religion or physics or the design of the universe, but i've heard it said that time is curved. i have to believe that somewhere there is a world for us. it isn't this one.

i love you, Lucy. Always.

She didn't cry. She didn't cry as she slowly folded the letter and placed it back in the envelope. She didn't cry when the cab reached its destination and she hastily thrust money at the driver. She merely stood there, breathing, looking out into the long empty darkness, where my father wasn't waiting.

Then she turned and walked back toward the road, away from the city, as the skyline receded behind her.

The vision snapped.

I was suddenly back in the drawing room. Esther sat across from me, watching me closely. I took in a deep, gasping breath.

"She didn't tell you she was pregnant," I said, trying to meet Esther's gaze. I felt out of focus and unsteady and overwhelmed, but I wanted to hear this.

"No. They chose to keep that information to themselves. And when Lucy returned to the Cities, she told us you were a year younger than you are, so you couldn't be Adrian's daughter. I should have investigated the matter—but, I suppose, I never believed she hated me enough to keep my grandchild from me."

"She doesn't hate you," I said softly. Mom might not have told

272

me her reasons for keeping the Kin from me, but I knew that much.

Esther cleared her throat. "Regardless, you're here now."

"She didn't go back," I said. "When she left that night, she didn't go back."

Esther's nod was slight, her eyes clouded. "No. She left. And she didn't just leave the Cities. She left us. She left the Kin."

My grandfather Charles, finally back from his business trip, drove me home. I remained silent during the drive, watching the snowy streets slide by. When I arrived at my house, I hesitated for a moment outside, standing on the sidewalk. There was ice along the stones, but Mom had put down salt to keep us from slipping. Though a dense cloud cover blocked out the moon, I could see the path easily. Only a few steps to the door—but I paused.

I thought of my mother leaving the Cities, the curve of her shoulders, how she didn't look back.

I thought of my father, the sadness in his smile, the promise he'd made her.

You won't be alone, he'd said. But she had been, all this time.

I wondered if she'd ever seen him again. Somehow, I didn't think so.

"It's too cold to be standing around out there. Get in here. I want to talk to you."

Startled, I jumped, almost losing my footing on the sidewalk. I turned to see my mother's face peering out through the window of the parlor, the glass pulled open and her nose pressed against the screen. The light was poor and I couldn't see her well; but, despite its volume, her voice wasn't angry or upset or even mildly annoyed. I gave her a quick nod and headed for the house.

She was seated on the sofa when I entered, her legs drawn up and a cup of cocoa on the table beside her. She'd forgotten a coaster again. Now that I could see her, I noted that wisps of hair had come loose from her bun, and there was a slight redness to her nose, as if she'd been crying. Her hoodie lay beside her but she pushed it aside and patted the cushion.

"Sit," she instructed, and even though I was somewhat wary of whatever it was she had to say, I obeyed. We sat facing each other, not speaking. Mom had pulled the drapes closed, but a faint light pushed through, into the room. I watched her face. Our eyes were the same, a deep brown without a hint of St. Croix gold, but hers seemed different now. She had no visible scars, but looking at her, I remembered the bruise that had bloomed on her face, the trace of blood on her cheek. Small, forgotten wounds.

"Esther called me," she said, and cleared her throat. "She told me about your visit."

I looked down, breaking eye contact. It had been an invasion of her privacy—looking into something that had been personal to her. Even if it was my heritage, my history, as Esther had put it.

"She said she told you about Adrian."

My mouth parted in surprise. Outside of the vision, it was the first time I'd heard her speak his name.

"Look at me, Audrey." I did, and felt tears blur the edge of my vision. "You asked me why I never told you about the Kin."

I nodded. My throat felt thick. I thought of the letter my father had left her. I wondered if she still had it.

My mother took a deep breath, keeping her eyes steady on mine. "My entire life, I've been bound to the Kin. Who I am, what I do. I was called as a Guardian when I was barely fifteen, before I'd even had a chance to fully form as a person. It was only three months after my father was killed, and suddenly I was so much stronger. I was angry, and I was powerful, and I was dangerous. I wanted to make the Harrowers pay. I thought I had this new destiny to fulfill, and nothing else could get in its way. I stopped going to school. My mother couldn't control me. The other Guardians couldn't control me. The rest of the Kin didn't even try."

She paused, watching me. I nodded again, and for a second I could see the girl she spoke of. I saw her at fifteen, a little younger than Elspeth but with so much more force; I saw the furious, haughty flash of her eyes, the certainty in her stance. Morning Star, young and bright and fearless, ready for anything. She was still there, behind my mother's eyes.

Mom leaned forward, taking one of my hands in hers. "It was hard, Audrey. And it hurt. My body heals quickly, and back then I thought that meant I could take any injury. I wasn't just

275

undisciplined, I was violent. And then—" She stopped, taking a breath. There was a catch in her voice. "Then I met Adrian. He changed me. He changed the way I saw the world. He made me a better person."

She didn't have to say the next part. I knew it already. I'd seen it. She just inclined her head slightly, acknowledging, and then said, "When I lost Adrian, I thought I'd lost everything. I wasn't angry anymore, but I felt cheated. I felt trapped." She pulled back, releasing my hand.

"That's why you left?"

"I never wanted you to feel that way," she said. "I wanted to give you a life free of the Kin. I wanted you to be young. I didn't want your life to be dictated by your abilities." She gave a short humorless laugh. "But I had to return. I was needed. And now the Kin have you anyway. Esther has you. Adrian wanted me to name you after her, you know—because, he said, someday I'd forgive her."

"Have you?" I asked. She'd named me Esther, but she never called me that.

One corner of her mouth tilted up. "I'm still waiting."

"I'm sorry I didn't listen to you," I said. "And I'm sorry about what I said."

Something passed over my mother's face, a brief expression swiftly banished. Something she didn't want me to see.

"Mom?"

She shook her head, her gaze sliding from mine. "I understand you're interested in the Kin, and I'll try to be more open about it. But putting yourself in danger isn't something I will ever be okay with. We're going to need to come to an agreement about this."

It was an evasion. She'd kept her tone steady, flat, but I'd heard what she meant to hide. A low ache, a dull sort of pain, and something akin to guilt.

"You need to tell me what's wrong," I said, panic prickling along my skin.

Mom still wouldn't meet my eyes. She busied herself fixing her bun, then retrieved her hoodie. When she spoke, her voice was firm, but she sounded distant. "I know you meant well. And you probably even did the right thing. I didn't want to tell you this. Audrey, Anna Berkeley is dead."

Friday morning brought with it another storm and another snow day. That was a small relief: I didn't think I could handle school. I hadn't slept well. I'd spent the night in a hazy, half-waking dream, where demons crept forth from black holes and wrapped their talons around slender throats while skyscrapers toppled in pillars of flame. A Harrower wearing a familiar face whispered that I was bound to him, and a distant voice cried out in pain. Nightmares, not Knowings, I told myself—but somewhere in that fog I'd glimpsed Anna Berkeley's face.

I thought she had Kin protection, I'd said.

She did, Mom told me. Two Guardians. Both had been killed.

And I'd been stupid enough to think I'd saved her.

Gideon called not long after I'd managed to drag myself out of bed, asking what my plans for the day were. I told him I wasn't feeling well and didn't think I'd be up for hanging out, but something in my voice must have alarmed him. He badgered me into a trip to the Belmonte house, threatening to invade and inflict all three of his sisters on me if I didn't submit. That made me smile, but as I moved through my house, my limbs felt weighted. There was a tightness in my chest, heaviness in my lungs. My thoughts slid down dark paths: Anna Berkeley, blood and talons, sharp red teeth. I wondered if she'd screamed.

Shaking myself, I pulled on a heavy turtleneck sweater to cover the bandage on my neck. My winter coat had been ruined, so I stole one of Mom's from the front closet before heading out the door.

I picked my way slowly down the street, where the sidewalks were covered with fresh snow, and tufts of white weighted the branches of all the trees. Gideon was outside his house, shoveling while he waited. Two of his sisters stood near a snowman and gave a cheery greeting. I responded with a halfhearted wave before following Gideon inside. We headed to the basement, where I kicked off my boots and flopped down on the bed.

"Weren't you wearing that yesterday?" he asked.

I glanced up. "So? It doesn't smell." And it was the only turtleneck I owned.

He shook his head at me.

I sighed, staring up at his ceiling. In fourth grade, he'd stuck about two dozen glow-in-the-dark stars there. Even though he'd removed them years ago, I could still see faded yellow outlines against the paint, and I remembered the countless hours we'd spent here watching movies and playing video games. From above, I caught the sound of low voices, the homey scent of his mother's Crock-Pot. Familiar things. Routines I knew. Upstairs, his parents would be reading the paper and drinking tea; his grandmother would be playing solitaire. In a way, the Belmontes had adopted me just as they'd adopted Gideon—but I no longer felt a part of them.

Seated at his desk, Gideon grabbed the baseball he kept there and bounced it between his hands. "Are you going to tell me what's wrong?"

I rolled to my side, looking away from him. "I'm just not feeling well."

"If you're going to lie, you could at least try a little harder."

I didn't answer.

"Seriously, what's going on?" His voice went quiet. "You've been acting weird for weeks. Your face is all puffy and your eyes are red. Either you've been crying all night—"

"Or I just walked several blocks through a blizzard?"

"—or you've been taking something."

I sat up, turning to gape at him. He was earnest, I realized, his face anxious, his brown eyes troubled. "I'm not on drugs," I said, scowling. "*God.*"

"Then what aren't you telling me?"

For a moment I just glared at him. Finally, I said: "Demons are running loose in the city streets."

He snorted. "Uh-huh. *Demons.*"

"You wanted to know," I answered, crossing my arms.

"I want to know why my best friend seems to have gotten a personality transplant."

"I *told* you I wanted to be left alone," I snapped. My throat felt thick. "And then you bullied me into coming over here!"

He looked stricken.

I opened my mouth to apologize—then started crying instead.

To Gideon's credit, he didn't flee the room. He came to sit beside me, saying, "Hey, hey, hey, it's all right." And, "Audrey, I can't help if you won't talk to me."

Uncertainty roiled within me. I did want to tell him. I wasn't accustomed to keeping things from Gideon, and I didn't like the way it felt. He'd always been a part of our secrets. Once he knew about Mom, there hadn't been much point in keeping the rest from him.

But this—

Mom's warning felt too close to home. *Humans who get mixed up with Harrowers have a tendency to end up dead,* she'd told me. Her father had been one of them. And it was so much more than that. It was Anna and Kelly and Tricia and those nameless girls I'd never seen. It was the dread I'd felt when the demons surrounded me, the certainty that I would die, the feel of claws at my throat. Nothing felt safe anymore, and I needed Gideon to be safe.

But if I couldn't tell him the whole truth, I could at least tell him part of it. "I learned some things about my father," I said. "About—his family. And why he left."

"And that's what's upsetting you?"

I nodded. "But I really don't want to talk about it, okay?"

He was silent for a long time. I wasn't certain if he believed me. Gideon was normally easy to read, but my senses were in chaos. Eventually, he shrugged, walked across the room to fetch a box of tissues, and handed it to me.

"Sorry for the meltdown," I sniffed.

He smiled and looked as though he were about to speak, but I was saved from any further questions by his phone ringing. He glanced down at it, let out a long-suffering sigh, and said, "It's the other one."

Gideon had various friends that demanded his attention, but only one other person pestered him as much as I did. He had to mean Tink.

"Answer it," I said. "Crisis finished, I swear." I headed to the bathroom to wash my face.

"She wants us to come pick her up," he told me, after he'd hung up. Tink had a license and a perfectly serviceable (though undeniably ugly) car, but she refused to drive if it even started flurrying. "She says she's trapped at home with nothing but ramen and ice cubes to eat. Do we rescue her?"

Tink would put an end to any Kin talk. If I so much as spoke the word, she pretended not to hear me.

"Yes, we absolutely rescue her," I said, with one final sniff. "I can't be responsible for that girl getting any skinnier. She's basically see-through as it is."

Then I grabbed my boots and headed for the door, not waiting to see if he followed.

Spending the day with Tink and Gideon calmed me. Tink refused to let me be morose. She didn't ask what was wrong, but I sensed she knew. We spent the afternoon playing board games and watching terrible movies while the snow piled up. By evening, I felt somewhat better, if still anxious.

When I arrived home, Mr. Alvarez was once again in the parlor, arguing with my mother. I didn't need to hear the beginning of the conversation to catch the topic: Mom was tired of waiting.

Mr. Alvarez disagreed. "You've said yourself you don't think Tigue is the real threat," he was saying. He didn't have his leather jacket with him, but his hair was spiked up again. I wondered how my mother managed to take him seriously.

She glanced at me when I entered the room and told me to head upstairs, but I caught a trace of blood on her shirt and chose to ignore her. I grabbed the first-aid kit. Instead of shooing me away as I fussed over the scratch on her arm, she kept her attention on Mr. Alvarez.

"This goes on much longer," she said, "it won't matter who's behind it."

"It does matter. If we don't take out the source, we'll go through this again next year. And the next year. And the year after that—until there are no Kin children left to bleed."

Mom's voice went deathly cool, sending goose bumps up and

down my skin. "Then I guess I just keep killing Harrowers until it stops."

"That's the spirit, Luce. If you can't solve a problem, beat the shit out of it until it goes away."

"It's better than sitting on my hands, which is all I've seen you doing," Mom shot back. I wondered how difficult it would be to scrape math teacher out of the carpet.

"Not all of us are Morning Star." I couldn't tell if that was meant to be sarcasm or not. Mr. Alvarez was strangely unreadable. Not that I'd ever really cared to try before, but standing there, I only got a sense of what I couldn't see, like staring into dark water. "We're on the same side here," he continued. "I don't like this any more than you do, but our options are limited. We don't just need to stop the bleedings, we need to stop the *hunt*. We can't allow them to find the Remnant, and right now, Tigue is the only link we have. We take him out, we're out of leads."

"So we do nothing, and in the meantime, innocent girls die."

"And if the Harrowers find the Remnant, even more will die."

"Oh, spare me. I know your reasoning. I just disagree." My mom sighed and rubbed her forehead with one hand. She'd finally grown tired of my attempts to plaster her with Band-Aids, and shook me away. Turning back to Mr. Alvarez, she asked, "You get anything out of Shane?"

He snorted. "About as much as you'd expect. He said he foresees bright futures for all of us—and that the greater Harrower community leaves him out of their fiendish schemes."

"You believe him?"

"I believe he's more scared of you than he is of them. And I don't think he wants a Harrowing any more than we do."

Mom made a noise of frustration. "We'll keep playing it your way—for now."

That answer didn't seem to satisfy Mr. Alvarez. He looked sterner than I'd ever seen him. "And how long will that last?"

Her eyes were dark, her voice cool. "That depends on Tigue."

Once Mr. Alvarez left, Mom ran to the basement to fetch a new hoodie. Her previous one was torn—though the wound, she explained, was human and not Harrower in origin. She'd interrupted a knife fight. I wasn't certain why she expected this information to make me feel better.

After changing her top, she went to the kitchen for a quick dinner of leftover mac and cheese. "You know," I said, following her, "if you killed Mr. Alvarez, I'd probably get out of a math test."

"He has a good heart," she said. Then, after a moment, she added, "Don't tell him I said that."

I laughed and chewed my lower lip. "How do you know Tigue isn't acting alone? I know you said he's not doing the bleedings himself, but couldn't he be ... organizing other demons?"

Mom hesitated. "I've fought a lot of Harrowers. More than I can count or even remember. Few of them are any sort of threat to me. Tigue is strong, the strongest we've seen since Verrick—that's why we've been focusing on him, even without solid evidence. But this ... this is beyond him. I've watched him for months now. I know his capabilities. We still don't know how the Harrowers are locating their targets, but I'm certain he's not the one doing it—on his own, he simply wouldn't have that power. Unfortunately, that means Ryan is right. We don't just have to stop Tigue. We need to stop whoever he's working with." Carrying her bowl with her, she crossed the kitchen and perched on the edge of the counter.

A thought had been troubling me ever since my vision. I swallowed thickly. "Could…could Verrick be his accomplice?"

"Verrick is dead, honey."

Images of the Harrower flashed before me. Light pooling at his feet, the scent of blood, the hate that burned inside him. *I'm bound to you*, he'd said. *Bound to the daughter that sleeps beneath your heart. She carries her father's blood.*

Kill me and we'll meet again.

"Are you sure?" I asked shakily.

Mom lifted her eyes to mine. She was silent a long moment before she spoke. "It's not Verrick. Supposing he were alive…he wouldn't ally himself with Tigue. Or anyone. He hated other Harrowers nearly as much as he hated us. He worked alone."

Sighing, I leaned back against the counter beside Mom. "That's good, I guess. But you still need to find Tigue's accomplice, then."

She held a hand up in front of me. "Stop. Stop right there. Stop what you're thinking. I'm not letting you anywhere near him."

I started to protest that I hadn't been thinking anything, but didn't finish. I *had* been thinking. It wasn't any sort of concrete plan, just the smallest glimmer of an idea. If they found Tigue's partner, they could stop the bleedings. No more search for the Remnant. No more threat of Harrowings. No more alleys and ankles troubling my dreams.

No more death.

"Audrey," Mom said.

"I know, I heard you," I said.

But I didn't stop thinking.

It was Elspeth who gave me the way to get near Tigue.

She showed up at my house Saturday afternoon to ask for a reading, with a quick apology for not calling first. I'd spent the morning online, searching the Internet for old newspaper articles and gossip magazines, following obscure information and vague references—reading everything I could find on Patrick Tigue. There had to be something everyone had overlooked, I reasoned. Some hidden clue, another Harrower disguised as a human, hiding within the Cities. Esther had told me that Verrick's human form and alibi had been without flaw; there could be others like him. I just needed to find who Tigue was connected with.

Most of what I found, I'd already known. Tigue had come to the metro area a little over three years ago, and mostly kept a low profile. He hadn't been romantically linked to anyone since his arrival—which was a comfort because, *ew*, really—and he hadn't been the subject of any scandals. Interest in him had declined in the past year or so, though his name popped up at fund-raisers and charity events. He donated money to hospitals, to children's programs, to homeless shelters, to the arts. Just like Leon had said: a model citizen.

Except for the part about murdering teenage girls. I kept digging.

When Elspeth showed up, she interrupted my research, so I explained what I'd been doing. I wasn't sure I'd be able to find anything on my own, I told her, but I wanted to try. And I couldn't do a reading. My Knowing wouldn't be strong enough without him close by.

"Well, if you want to get near him," Elspeth said, "just make Grandmother take you to the charity banquet on Wednesday. I have rehearsal that night, so I'm not going, but—"

"Tigue will be there?" My eyes snapped to hers. We were in my room, seated on the floor while I readied my cards.

She nodded. "He'll be there. He always attends those sorts of things. Though you probably shouldn't just go up to him and ask if he's been bleeding kids around the Cities."

I thought back. Esther had asked me to attend the banquet—as a proud member of the St. Croix family, she'd put it—but I'd managed to wriggle out of it by saying I had too much homework. She might get suspicious if I changed my mind, but I was willing to take the chance.

I didn't want Elspeth to know just how intent on my plan I was, however, so I focused on the reading.

"What exactly are we looking for?" I asked.

She hesitated. Her long hair, normally loose about her shoulders, had been pulled back in a ponytail. It made her look younger. "I've had some things on my mind. I just want to know what you see."

Elspeth was always easy to read, and now I could almost see the worry that hung about her, tinting the air. I gave her a slow nod as I began shuffling. I focused my Knowing on her: her usual lilting laughter and the frown she now wore; the memory of a glow in her veins; her favorite color—the blue-black of crows' wings—and her love of buzzing bees.

Then I laid out the cards.

My card, followed by The Garden and The Desert. Iris and Elspeth, inversions of one another. But I didn't need the cards to tell me that. I focused on the next three: Year of Famine. The Cutpurse. The Siren.

Elspeth was troubled, all right—but I wasn't certain why. The images I saw were from years ago: The accident that had killed her parents. The screech of tires. A road turned silver by the rain.

"You were in the car?" I asked. "When your parents died?"

"Iris and I were," she said.

Two more cards. The Blind Man. The Beggar. I saw the accident in a series of flashes. The wheels turned and skidded across the rain-slick road. Then the collision: Metal bending and shrieking, glass and bone shattering. Elspeth's choking screams. Then Iris, blood on her forehead, her vision cut off.

And—something else watched.

I pressed the last card to the floor, then looked up at Elspeth. "Was a Harrower involved?"

She shook her head. "No...it was just an accident. I don't remember a lot, but I think someone ran a red light."

I eyed her cautiously. "What's this about?"

"I don't know." She rocked backward on the floor, pulling her knees up against her. "I'm worried about Iris."

"What's wrong? Was she hurt?" I'd spoken to Iris on the phone Wednesday evening—she'd wanted to make certain I was all right—but the conversation had been brief, and I hadn't seen her since.

"She's not hurt. But she killed a Harrower, didn't she?"

Handily. It had been a little frightening to witness, but I didn't mention that. I just said, "We got in its way. It attacked us."

Elspeth's voice was low, without a trace of her usual gaiety. "It wasn't the first time she's killed one," she said. "Right after our parents died, something changed. She tried to hide it from everyone, but I knew. She went out at night, fighting Harrowers. She didn't even bring any weapons—she'd use their own powers to kill them. And she'd come home injured. I think for a while she wanted to die."

I recalled the sliver of memory I'd caught from Iris: A girl in the dark, shivering in the rain. A hand reaching toward her. *It's personal,* she'd said, and then she'd drawn back.

"Wednesday was different," I said slowly. "It was my fault, not Iris's. She killed the demon because she had to."

"You didn't see anything, then?" Elspeth asked. Her tone was nervous. "In the reading?"

"I saw the accident." *And something watching.*

She sighed softly. "She's okay, then."

"What exactly are you worried about?"

She didn't answer. Instead, she leaned forward on her hands, her eyes gaining that faint, familiar glint. "What was it like? Beneath? I've never seen it."

I stared at her. "Trust me, you don't want to."

"Iris wouldn't tell me, either," she lamented.

"How about this: it was dark, cold, and full of demons bent on killing me." I shuddered, rubbing my hands along my arms. "They nearly did, too."

Elspeth's little frown returned, and she nodded, touching my shoulder lightly. "I'm glad Leon was able to find you."

That made two of us. Though I supposed it was Shane who had actually found me, and I said as much to Elspeth.

She disagreed. "No, it would've had to be Leon."

I gave her a blank look.

"Because of the connection," she said.

"What connection?" I asked, feeling a trace of unease.

She regarded me curiously. "You haven't figured it out yet, Audrey? Leon's not *a* Guardian. He's *your* Guardian."

Elspeth's revelation wasn't just unexpected, it was incomprehensible. Leon? My Guardian?

She had to be joking.

I stared at her. "That doesn't make any sense."

Elspeth cocked her head at me. "It's pretty obvious. He knows when you're in danger. He completely freaks out if you're in trouble. He goes out of his way to protect you. And there's no other reason for your mom to have taken him in. An unfamiliar Guardian who just shows up out of nowhere? Lucy wouldn't have taken a chance like that unless there was a reason. Morning Star doesn't exactly need help."

I hadn't thought of that. Before I'd known about the Kin, it had seemed logical to me for Mom to take on another Guardian as her sidekick. But now I knew there were plenty of other Guardians in the Cities—and before Leon, Mom had always worked alone.

"But . . . why would I have a Guardian?"

"Well," Elspeth said, drumming her fingers against the floor, "Guardians are called to protect specific people when there's a particular gift, or a particular danger. But Leon and your mom might not even know why he's protecting you."

If they did, they were not inclined toward sharing that information.

I frowned. Esther had told me that most of our people had some level of Knowing, though it was often latent, deeply buried. And I didn't have any other abilities. I was hardly unique among the Kin. That seemed to rule out particular gifts.

Which might mean a particular danger.

I wondered if it had something to do with Verrick, the words he'd spoken as he stood with my mother atop Harlow Tower, the Astral Circle's bleeding light pulsing around them. If Mom was wrong, if Verrick was still alive, he was certainly dangerous.

I shivered. That was not a pleasant thought.

But Leon, my Guardian—

My unease deepened. "So he was just—what, *assigned* to me? Why him?"

"No one knows how or why we're called," Elspeth said. "You know that."

I thought of the night Leon had first appeared at the end of the driveway, the way he'd hopped off his motorcycle and stood in the clinging heat, watching us. His backpack had slumped to the ground at his feet. In the thin light of evening he'd seemed

293

just a little uncertain. As though he were as surprised to be there as we'd been to see him.

"Which means he didn't have a choice in the matter," I whispered.

It had never before occurred to me that Leon might not *want* to live as he did. That he might not have wanted to leave his home behind, to return to the world his parents had died in, to follow Mom into the dark of the Cities night after night.

"I wouldn't look at it that way," Elspeth said, her frown fixed on her face. "It's how Kin life works. It's part of who we are."

"But he *didn't* have a choice."

"No, he didn't," she agreed.

Other memories surfaced: How Leon had come to my side the night Tink was injured, quickly and without question, as though I had called him there. How he'd known to come home the night the Harrower attacked me. The way he'd lifted me out of the car, making certain I wasn't hurt.

How angry he sometimes seemed.

We don't always get to choose what happens to us, he'd said.

I hadn't understood, then, what he'd meant.

He didn't want to be here. He *had* to be here. Because of me.

"He never told me," I said. My face felt hot. "And neither did Mom."

"I'm sure there's a reason. You know Lucy—she didn't even want you to be Kin."

More secrets. More mysteries. More things kept hidden from me.

But somehow, this secret was worse than the others. I turned away from Elspeth as I felt my eyes sting.

"I'm *sure* there's a reason," she repeated.

I nodded, speaking softly. "There always is."

I didn't confront Leon. When I saw him in the hall that evening, before he and Mom headed out into the city, I turned and fled. I didn't care if it was cowardly. I didn't know how to act, what to feel. I wanted to ask why he was Guarding me, to yell at him for keeping it a secret—but mostly I wanted to apologize. To apologize that he was stuck with me, that he had to fight, that he had to protect me. I tried, once, when I saw him the following day, but I couldn't speak. My throat felt tight, my stomach knotted. Looking at him, I remembered the way he'd appeared Beneath, the concern in his eyes, how tightly he'd held me. Somehow, that made it even worse. For the second time in two days I hurried in the other direction. Then I hid in my room until he left for the night.

Instead of brooding over Leon and what he hadn't told me, I tried to focus on Tigue. I'd called Esther and said I wanted to go to the charity banquet after all. Though this included being coerced into two additional functions the following week, I agreed. Before she would allow me to accompany the family, however, she insisted

I be "properly attired." Then she sent me to a boutique where, she informed me, she'd already selected a few appropriate dresses. Since I didn't think Esther would be an ideal shopping companion, I dragged my friends along with me.

"I wish I had a rich grandmother," Tink sighed, watching me twirl as I tried on my dresses.

"I wish I had your dainty figure," I said.

"I wish I'd never been talked into this," Gideon lamented. He kept ducking out of sight whenever anyone walked past the store.

"Cheer up," I told him. "We'll go look at video games after this."

He frowned. I no longer had to wear a bandage—but he'd noticed my stitches.

"I accidentally cut myself," I said hastily, covering the wound with my hand. "It doesn't look *that* bad, does it?"

Gideon didn't answer. He just kept frowning.

I didn't dwell on it. I was beginning to form a plan for the banquet. I didn't need to get *too* near Tigue, I reasoned; I didn't need to let him see me or sense what I was doing. If I focused, if I tuned out everything else at the dinner, an answer might come to me.

Unfortunately, Wednesday brought with it other problems: I couldn't keep avoiding Leon. Since the deaths of Anna and the two Guardians protecting her, Mom was being extra cautious. She'd insisted not only that Leon drive me to the banquet, but that he also attend. He didn't seem too happy about the prospect. Since

I still didn't know what to say to him, I refrained from pointing out that, for once, he wouldn't be overdressed.

The night of the banquet arrived with flurries.

"More snow," I griped, mostly to cover how nervous I felt. Mom hadn't clued in to my plan—which, granted, wasn't much of a plan beyond hoping I might get some glimmer of Knowing off Tigue—but I felt a little guilty. Not that I believed it would be particularly dangerous. According to Elspeth, Tigue frequently attended fund-raisers and charity functions, and if he were in the habit of killing people during dinner, I doubted they'd keep inviting him. But that didn't mean Mom wouldn't build me a dungeon if she knew what I was up to.

As we drove toward the country club where the dinner was being held, the sky was low and gray, the stars neatly tucked behind a dense blanket of clouds. There was an eerie hush over the highways. Everything felt sleepy and quiet. After Leon parked, I sat soundless, studying our surroundings. Snow-covered trees jutted up out of the darkness. Gazing out across the grounds, I imagined how it must look in spring, vivid green and vibrant. Now, the blank white seemed stark and depressing.

I tugged my dress coat tightly around me. Beneath it, I wore a deep blue evening gown and a string of pearls Esther had lent me.

My grandparents were waiting inside with Iris. The reception would be followed by dinner, which would be followed by dancing, Esther told me.

I kept close to her side as she began introductions. A couple of other Kin were in attendance, and they smiled at me as we mingled, though I caught the haunting worry that lingered behind their eyes. I didn't see Patrick Tigue.

At dinner I did my best not to speak while chewing, and made certain I used each of my forks correctly. Iris sat across from me, smiling softly. She looked tired, and there was a light bruise along the slope of her shoulder. The fight with the demon, I guessed; she wasn't as quick to heal as Guardians were. Her necklace caught the light, a glimmer against her skin that didn't quite fit with the elegant cut of her rose-colored dress.

I'd been dreading the dancing, but it proved to be less of an ordeal than I'd feared. Most of the men and women I'd been introduced to were a blur of smiles and handshakes, but a few stuck in my mind, and I attached names to faces as I watched couples whirl. Though I searched the crowd, I couldn't find Tigue among them. I danced twice with my grandfather Charles, who told me fondly how proud of me he was. When I caught her eye, Esther gave me a short nod and a faint smile, which I took for approval.

Leon, I noticed, stood alone. He wasn't mingling with the other guests, though one or two of the Kin paused to greet him. He wasn't socializing; he wasn't dancing. He was Guarding. I felt a pang of guilt, recalling the night he'd tagged along to the Drought and Deluge. He'd told me he could think of any number of things he'd rather be doing—and now, here he was, stuck watching over me. Again.

His eyes met mine, and I gave him a tremulous smile. I threaded my way through the crowd toward him, hands clenched at my sides. That familiar, irritating knot had formed in my stomach again. Studying him, I tried to gauge his mood. He stood with an air of nonchalance, that easy confidence of his. He was well dressed as usual—better, even—but his tie was slightly crooked. I couldn't read his expression.

"You should dance," I said, feigning lightheartedness.

He lifted an eyebrow. "With you?"

For a second, annoyance overrode guilt. "Who else?"

"I'm just trying to be specific here," he said. There was a note of teasing in his voice, but I felt too out of sorts for teasing.

"Yes. With me. Specifically," I gritted out. His lips twitched upward. Ridiculously, I felt heat creeping over my face. To hide it, I let out an exasperated sigh and said, "See? This is why I never bother trying to be nice to you."

A perplexed frown flitted across his features.

"Forget it," I mumbled, twisting away.

He caught my elbow, and turned me back to him. Jerking his head toward the dance floor, he slid his hand into mine and tugged me forward.

"If you step on my toes, we're leaving," he said.

On the dance floor, his fingers rested gently on my waist. His gaze lingered on the stitches near my neck, but he didn't comment. Feeling strangely self-conscious, I didn't meet his eyes. Instead, I focused on the couples around us. I didn't recognize most of them, but nearby, I caught sight of Esther and Charles swaying, their heads bent close, barely the space of a breath between them.

Then, at the edge of the dance floor, I saw a man whose face I knew.

I tightened my fingers on Leon's shoulder. My breath felt heavy, like I was carrying stones in my lungs.

It was definitely Tigue. I'd looked through enough pictures of him in the past few days to recognize him on sight. I knew the cut of his dark blond hair, the little scar that tipped his chin, the set of his jaw. I studied him surreptitiously, taking in every detail. The suit he wore looked like it had been sewn right on to him. He seemed about thirty, attractive, muscular—and not in a scary way. There was something modest about his appearance, too, as though he didn't seek attention. Your eyes could slide right over him and forget him, unless you had a reason for looking.

A few other guests stood chatting with him, as though they found nothing disturbing about him at all. I supposed that made sense. Aside from being a probably-evil demon, he was well known in the Cities for his philanthropy. He exuded good manners, and he moved with an easy, careless grace. If I hadn't known what he was, I might have even liked him.

A woman I'd met earlier in the evening smiled flirtatiously up at him as he lifted her hand to his lips.

The other Kin, at least, avoided him.

Keeping my eyes pinned to him, I tried to focus my Knowing.

The room was busy and my frequencies were clogged, but I knew I could do it. I'd heard Tink through the tumult of the Drought and Deluge; I could find a way into Tigue, without Amplification, without my Nav cards. I gave Leon's shoulder a slight tug and turned us, shifting closer.

Leon gave a short laugh. "This doesn't really work if we *both* try to lead—"

He cut off when he saw Tigue. His reaction was more severe than my own. For half a second he stood frozen, but I felt the sudden racing of his pulse and heard him suck in a breath. Tensed, waiting, he took a small step backward. Then his hand clamped about my waist, drawing me with him as he turned and left the dance floor.

"Leon, wait—"

He ignored me, bringing us to the far wall, where the crowd was less dense. After a moment he released his grip on me and breathed slowly. Looking at him, I had a rare glimpse of Knowing, sensing his struggle to compose himself as his instincts screamed that danger was near.

"You know who that was?" he asked.

I nodded mutely.

His eyes searched mine. "Did you know he'd be here?"

Though I didn't speak, Leon saw the answer on my face.

"*Christ,*" he murmured, pulling away and running a hand through his hair. When he turned back toward me, his expression was caught somewhere between fear and fury. His voice was a hiss in my ear. "Is that the reason we're here? What are you playing at, Audrey?"

"Don't make a scene," I hissed back, glancing about me.

"Don't think I won't."

"You are completely overreacting."

He gave me his most stubborn look. "Get your coat. We're leaving."

"No!" I said, a little too loudly, then lowered my voice. "What do you think he's going to do? In the middle of a crowded room?"

"Audrey?"

Startled, I jumped and turned toward the voice. It was Iris.

She'd moved so quietly that I hadn't realized she'd joined us. She smiled when she saw me, but her hair was in disarray and the bruise on her shoulder seemed glaring in the light. There was a strange, unreadable look in her eyes.

"Are you okay?" I asked, grateful for the distraction. Beside me, Leon kept his silence.

Iris shook her head. "I'm fine, just a little tired."

"How long are you staying?" I asked.

I felt the pressure of Leon's hand on my shoulder, and turned to push him away—then stopped. A low voice came from behind me, and a chill formed in my stomach.

"Good evening, Miss St. Croix."

Iris inclined her head. "Good evening, Mr. Tigue."

I turned slowly, keeping my eyes lowered. My pulse drummed

rapidly under my skin, and Leon's grasp tightened as I raised my head and faced Patrick Tigue.

"I don't believe we've met," he murmured, gazing at me in a way that said he knew *exactly* who I was.

Close up, Patrick Tigue was good-looking, in a suave, charismatic sort of way. He looked clean-cut, and not at all like he was secretly plotting to bring destruction upon everyone in the room. His smile was broad, his skin a warm, sun-kissed tone, and his expression held not a hint of malice. He looked very human.

His eyes, though. I could see the difference there. They were blue and empty, like the flat surface of a swimming pool.

I kept my chin up and was glad that my voice didn't shake. "Audrey Whitticomb," I said.

He held his hand toward me, and I realized with a flare of alarm that he meant to shake mine. I stared directly at him, not speaking. My frequencies were jumbled, but I was getting a sense from him—indecipherable but strong. I lowered my eyes to his hand, the lines that crossed his palm, the smooth band around one finger.

The ring caught my attention. It looked silver, though it caught the light strangely. It was simple, unadorned. I'd seen rings like it before, but there was something familiar about it that I couldn't quite name.

"Miss Whitticomb?" His query was soft, but my eyes snapped to his. He was still waiting.

I swallowed and took his hand. His skin was warm, dry, and

not unpleasant. I looked up at him, and his eyes crinkled in faint amusement.

For the space of a second, my senses cleared. My Knowing shot through me, a beam of knowledge and understanding too fleeting for me to grasp. I pulled my hand away, cradling it against me. My gaze shifted from Tigue's as I caught something in his depthless eyes.

I know your mother, his eyes told me. *I know you.*

There are some places it's best not to look, I thought.

Some places look back.

A shudder ran through me. I drew away, trying to shake the sense that he was staring into me, through me, into the spaces of mind and memory. Into my history, into the dark of my dreams. Harrowers had abilities, I recalled. Just like Kin. And Tigue—he Knew.

I know your blood, he seemed to whisper.

"Let's go cool off," Leon said, pulling me away.

"It was nice meeting you," Tigue said, a crooked smile curving his mouth. His words lingered in the air, attaching to me like shadows.

As Leon propelled me away, I tried to organize my scattered thoughts. I felt off balance, and more frightened than I cared to admit. I'd sensed something in Tigue, something deeply hidden, a secret just out of reach—but I couldn't shake the feeling that he'd also sensed something in me.

Leon thrust a glass of water into my hands, and I downed it in long gulps, letting it cool my throat. Keeping my gaze at the wall, I concentrated on the music drifting behind us. Soft violins and the melancholy moans of a cello.

"Subtle, Audrey. Very subtle," Leon said. He grabbed my coat, and before I could protest, he'd thrown it over my shoulders, set my drink aside, and aimed me toward the door. We passed Iris, who gave me a troubled look but didn't interfere.

"Can you let Esther know I'm leaving?" I called to her, and saw her nod.

Outside, the snow continued. Huge drifting flakes caught the light, the sort of gentle snow that always happens in paintings. I couldn't enjoy it. My thoughts were in turmoil, and Leon's hand at the small of my back guided me toward the car, heedless of how fast I wanted to go.

We drove for a few minutes in stony silence. Leon didn't speak, and I couldn't seem to form words. Anxious and angry, I twisted my hands in my lap, wrinkling the fabric of my dress. Tigue had scared me, but I didn't want to think about that. I focused on my anger instead.

Leon kept his gaze determinedly forward. In the distance, the Minneapolis skyline loomed chilly and bright against the snow. The highway bent toward the city. The minutes dragged on. Now and then, I flicked a glance toward him, noting the tightness in his jaw, the tension in his arms.

Finally, I couldn't take it any longer.

"We need to have a talk," I said, trying to ignore the unease that roiled within me.

He didn't even glance at me. "Damned right we do."

"Because this attitude of yours? It's getting a little old," I said, crossing my arms and staring outward. If he wouldn't look at me, I wouldn't look at him. I gazed into the heavy darkness, watching as the lights of passing cars turned the falling snow gold. My throat felt thick; my face felt hot. "Look. I'm sorry, all right? I'm sorry you didn't have a choice. But I didn't have a choice, either. I didn't ask for this any more than you did."

I heard his breath catch. "What are you talking about?"

"I'm talking about you. Being my Guardian."

He didn't speak. When I chanced a look at him, I saw his lips part, but no sound came out. Eventually he let out a low sigh. "Audrey—"

"I get it, all right?" Now that I'd started, I couldn't seem to stop. "I know you have to look out for me, but that doesn't mean you get to dictate everything I do."

"We're not discussing this now."

My phone rang, but I silenced it, not bothering to look at the number. "I didn't ask to be your burden," I railed. "I don't even know why you're Guarding me, because—surprise, surprise—once again, no one thought to *tell me*."

Now he sounded impatient. "You're not a burden."

"Thanks, Leon. That's the sweetest thing anyone's ever said to me."

"What is it you want from me, here?"

"Nothing," I choked out.

His face was unreadable, his knuckles white against the steering wheel. "You want another apology? Is that it? I'm not sorry. I'm your Guardian. I'm not going to stop protecting you."

"I know. It's your duty," I snapped.

"It's not like that," he said. "I care about what happens to you."

"You have to. Isn't that how it works? You don't have a choice—the switch gets flipped, and now you're a full-time babysitter. Lucky you."

"You don't have any idea what you're talking about," he retorted.

"Because I'm just some dumb kid, right?"

"Because you don't know what it's like to be called!" he shouted, then lowered his voice. "I can't—I can't talk about this right now." There was a strange, panicky edge to his words, but I didn't have the chance to process that. Leon's phone rang. And, unlike me, he answered.

I slumped back into my seat, fuming silently. But my anger began to evaporate as Leon spoke.

"No, she's fine," he was saying. "She's with me. We're on our way back. We'll be there in a minute. What's going on?"

I fished through my coat pocket and retrieved my phone,

looking at the missed call. Mom. Apprehension stirred. I turned toward Leon, waiting.

"Yeah, I know—" He broke off, frowning. There was a long pause. "Understood," he said finally, and ended the call. Then the stern sidekick who always followed the rules and loved lectures on caution pressed his foot to the gas pedal and started to speed.

"Leon?" I asked.

"It's Tigue," he said softly. "He's got Iris."

We found my mother in the kitchen, surrounded by an assortment of weapons. She stood bent over the table, her hair pulled back in its customary bun, her hoodie draped over the chair beside her.

"What's going on?" I asked, rushing forward. Her explanation to Leon had been brief: Tigue had kidnapped Iris from the country club, and the Guardians were mobilizing. The details were confused. Someone had seen Tigue pushing Iris toward the door, but before anyone had realized what was happening, it was too late.

Mom glanced up at me, her expression grim. "We have to hurry," she said before returning to her array. She had knives and throwing stars and a length of chain, a few pieces of metal that might have been darts. Some of the weapons I couldn't even identify. Methodically, she took each weapon in her hand, then either returned it to its place or stuffed it into a bag she'd slung over her shoulder. "I spoke to Ryan. There's Harrower activity all over the Cities. The other Guardians have their hands full. I'm going after Tigue. Leon, I'll need you with me."

Leon nodded and started to speak, but I cut in.

"But what happened?" I asked. "Why did Tigue take Iris?"

Mom paused, weighing a knife in her hand. "We're not certain what his plan is. But if it's what we suspect—"

"You think she's the Remnant?" That hadn't occurred to me before: Iris was seventeen, a year older than the other girls who had been bled. But if Tigue had her . . .

I felt sick. I thought of Tigue—those blank eyes, the chill in his tone. I recalled the sense that he'd been staring into me, through me, that he had Known me. Known my blood. Iris had been beside us; perhaps his Knowing had given him insight into her, as well.

Or maybe it was just a guess. Maybe he planned to drag her Beneath, open her veins, let her bleed.

I closed my eyes briefly, trying to shake away the thought.

"We don't have a lot of time," Mom was saying. "We need to get to her." She grabbed her hoodie, sliding it over her head as her features darkened into a scowl. "And we have another complication. That idiot cop has gone to confront Tigue."

I blinked in surprised. "Detective Wyle?"

"He was here earlier."

"He found out about Anna Berkeley," I guessed. "He's going to arrest Tigue?"

Mom shook her head. "I don't think so. He's going alone on this one. He'll be lucky if he just loses his badge and not his life."

I swallowed, recalling the senses I'd had of him: Those blurred images, that hint of danger. His good intentions, how heavily the deaths had weighed on him. How desperately he'd wanted to help. Anna Berkeley must have been the breaking point. The darkness that chased him was leading him straight to Tigue. I looked at Mom. Her lips were pulled into a thin line, her eyes dark. "What's your plan?"

She didn't hesitate. "I take out Tigue. If whoever he's working with shows up, I take him out, too." Turning toward me, she took a step forward, placing her hands on my shoulders. "Don't worry, I'll make sure Iris is safe. I'll bring her back."

My throat closed up. I stood looking at her, frightened and unable to speak, then turned toward Leon. His face was blank; he looked entirely controlled, collected, like he hadn't been in a shouting match with me just minutes ago. I wondered if he was afraid, too. I wondered if he was afraid ever.

"Don't leave the house. We'll be back before sunup," Mom said, giving me a brief, tight hug. She dropped a kiss on my forehead, then turned and walked to Leon, who placed a hand on her shoulder and drew her close to him. His eyes met mine, but he didn't speak.

Then they were gone.

After they left, I headed to my bedroom, shutting my drapes before I flicked on the lamp. I changed into jeans and a sweatshirt, then sat on my bed with my legs pulled up against me.

Time moved slowly. Cars passed outside the house, their

headlights slashing through the darkness. My dress lay on the floor, where I'd discarded it, and I thought vaguely that I should hang it up, but I couldn't summon the will to move.

It was one thing to know, in an abstract sort of way, that my mother was out in the city, fighting crime and demons and whatever else lurked in the shadows. It was another thing to know exactly what it was she faced. To have looked into his cold, flat eyes and spoken his name.

Tigue. I remembered that flicker I'd sensed from him, the smallest glimmer, something I had almost seen.

I stirred from my bed briefly to gather my Nav cards. Both decks, my father's and Gram's. I shuffled them idly, first one set, then the other, but I didn't lay them out. Something told me I shouldn't try to do a reading for Patrick Tigue. Not now, even to try to get back the flash I'd seen. I had the eerie feeling that if I tried to look at him, he would look right back.

Mom would defeat him. She had defeated Verrick, and he was the worst Harrower the Cities had ever seen.

I continued shuffling. Images moved through me: the broad, straight line of Tigue's shoulders, the cut of his clothing, the smooth tone of his voice that said so much more than his words, that made me think of the cold empty of the Beneath. I thought of him near the dance floor, charming the woman whose hand he took. Bending toward her, reaching, reaching like he would for a girl on a corner in the rain, whose dark hair made a halo about her—

My mind skidded away from the image.

I thought back to the ring he wore. A loop of silver. The shine of it, the way light gathered.

Not a wedding band, I thought. But a way of binding.

I looked down at my hands. I'd been laying out cards and I hadn't even realized it. And I'd mixed my decks. They sat in disarray in my lap, except for the three cards I'd placed faceup in front of me. Inverted Crescent. The Garden. The Garden. One from each deck.

The light tap on my door made me yelp.

I felt my heart in my throat even as I forced myself quiet. The knocking continued, and I scrambled off the bed, letting my Nav cards fall all around me. Gram would have chided me. But Gram was dead.

I opened the door and stepped back as Elspeth stepped in. She stood shivering, hugging herself in the half-light of my room. Her dark eyes were huge and haunted. She didn't speak.

"Elspeth?" I whispered, almost afraid to speak.

"It's Iris," she said. Something slid into place.

And I knew what she meant.

29

It wasn't a Knowing. It was something I already knew. It was fragments aligning in an entirely different way: things I'd seen, words I'd heard, moments I should have understood. Connections I should have made.

It was the pattern emerging.

My mind rebelled.

Elspeth was speaking, but I didn't hear her. In the contours of her face I saw her sister's image: Iris smiling softly, Iris watching, Iris turning away. I remembered her huddled in the rain, blinking as a hand reached toward her.

It's personal, she'd said, when I'd glimpsed that moment. She hadn't wanted me to see his face.

But—no, I thought. No. That couldn't be right.

I sank down to my bed, where my cards were still scattered.

The same three remained faceup. I dropped my hands across them and flipped them over.

Elspeth was still speaking to me. Her eyes were wide, her brow creased with worry. "I can't talk to Grandmother," she was saying. "I can't tell her. So—so I came here. I took Iris's car, I—"

"Slow down," I said, trying to make sense of her words. "Start over."

"When I got home from rehearsal tonight, Grandmother told me that Patrick Tigue had taken Iris. Only, I don't think he did. I think…"

"You think she left with him," I whispered.

She nodded, hugging herself tightly.

I looked at my cards. The Garden. Iris's card. I realized now why Patrick Tigue's ring had seemed familiar to me. It was made of the same material as the triple knot she wore at her neck.

Other memories flashed through me. *It was a present from my boyfriend,* she'd said, handing me her necklace. And the way she'd fought that Harrower—she hadn't fought like a Guardian. She'd fought like a demon. Using a demon's abilities.

But I still couldn't fathom it.

"How long have you known?"

"I didn't. Not—not really. I wasn't certain." Elspeth took a long shaky breath, almost a sob. "It got bad after our parents died. Really bad. Iris wouldn't even speak to me for months. She wouldn't speak to anyone. I used to wait up at night, listening, hoping she'd come home." Another breath. I waited, my heart hammering. "And then—she got better. She started seeing some-one. She didn't tell me, but...I had an idea. I thought it would be okay. Some demons are neutral. We're not really so different, Harrowers and Kin. We come from the same place. And he helped her, he really helped her."

And she helped him, I thought, with growing horror.

I closed my eyes, trying to process. "There's something wrong here. I can't believe she would go along with—with what he's doing. Killing people. Going after the Rem—"

The words died on my lips.

The Remnant. She'd wanted us to find the Remnant. She'd placed her hand on me to reach out into the unknown and seek what she couldn't find.

And she could share powers. She could amplify them. Tigue wouldn't need another Harrower helping him. She could make him stronger all on her own.

She wasn't the Remnant. She was his accomplice.

"My mother went to save her," I said, standing. "She thinks Iris is a hostage."

Elspeth's face crumpled. "We have to help her. She doesn't want to be this way, I know it. He's tricked her somehow." Her voice went high and plaintive. "She's my *sister*."

"We'll help her," I said. "But you have to go home. You *have* to tell Esther. And then we'll figure this out."

She nodded once, quickly. "What are you going to do?"

"I'm going to find my mother."

I took Mom's car.

I chose not to think about the fact that both Elspeth and I were driving through the Twin Cities without licenses. On my growing list of catastrophes, losing my permit was nearly at the bottom. My mind was spinning. Mom had told me not to leave the house, and I'd broken promises to her before—but I'd tried calling both her and Leon, and neither had answered. They had to be told. Tigue had Iris with him. He could be pretending to use her as a hostage. As leverage.

I imagined Iris standing before my mother, pleading, pretending, distracting—and then Tigue swooping in from behind, a blur of scales and red teeth.

I shook my head. Tigue was using Iris; that much was certain. He'd confused her somehow. That was the only reason she would go along with this.

The road dissolved around me. The snow stopped, clouds scattering overhead. The highways rushed by in a blur of headlights. Beneath my coat I trembled, my heartbeat so fast and loud it drowned out the sounds of the radio and the engine and even the traffic. I'd printed out directions to the address and tried to calm myself by focusing on my destination, concentrating on exit signs and avenues. Small, easy steps, I told myself. Reach Tigue's estate. Find Mom and Leon. Tell them what I know.

I parked on the street a block or so from Tigue's home. Around me, the bright glow of streetlamps had turned everything yellow.

The road was empty, the houses dark and quiet. I hurried down the sidewalk, moving as quickly as I dared across pavement slick with ice. In the distance, a dog began to bark.

The neighborhood wasn't familiar to me, but I was close; I felt it. Awareness rang through my body, up and down my skin. I didn't feel the cold anymore, though I could see my breath billow in the air. Staring out into the empty street before me, I began to run.

I knew Tigue's house immediately. It was like the others: large and imposing, half-hidden by fence and shrubbery. But there was a difference, as though the Beneath clung to it, swallowing up its shadows. The gate was open. The windows were dark.

Slipping inside, I drew back against the gate before darting forward. My eyes had adjusted to the dimness, and I saw nothing but empty spaces and an expanse of snow, but my back tingled. I felt vulnerable, exposed.

I stepped carefully through the snow. The grounds were silent. At first, I didn't see anyone. The night appeared still, serene. The wind brushed past, but it was only the wind, and I stood confused, worried. Then something shifted. The light at the edge of my vision blurred. The feel of the air on my face altered, and I recalled that demons clouded the senses—that I could be staring at them and see right through them, that I had to look harder, to see what didn't want to be seen.

The night shimmered before me, and then they were there.

Tigue stood apart from the others, his hands held in front

of him, his chilly eyes dark and intent. He still wore his skin. Not far from him, two Harrowers were bent, no longer human in form, starlight grazing their scales. None of them moved. They were watching, waiting, their expressions secretive and sly. I didn't see Iris.

In front of Tigue, some distance away, I saw Leon. A demon crouched low before him. His coat lay discarded in the snow and his white shirt caught the moon, a beacon in the dark. His shirt-sleeves were rolled up, and along his left arm color swirled. I saw the glow of his veins beneath his skin, hues blending and twining at his wrist, radiating out from his fingertips.

The Harrower lunged for him, and he jumped back, graceful and confident in motion. His arm shot out, parrying. His hair was mussed, his face damp with sweat, and I heard the heaviness of his breath; but the world about him seemed to shine, light clinging to him.

My gaze slid from Leon to my mother, fighting nearby. Wisps of hair curled about her face, tugged loose by the wind. Both her arms were lit from within, her pulse flashing out in churning colors as she moved, faster than thought or reason. She bent and lunged, and a demon fell howling beneath her, its neck twisted in her grip. The Harrower fell slack, dissolving into darkness, and she moved again, quick and deadly through the snow.

"Ready to tell me what you've done with her?" she shouted to Tigue. "If this keeps up, you're going to run out of Harrowers."

"Oh, I think you'll tire long before that."

Three Harrowers lurched toward her, and as a cry strangled in my lungs, my mother reacted. She didn't even look. Her hand flung outward and three sharp objects flew behind her, splitting their throats. The demons gurgled and faltered and fell.

The glow at her fingers grew, and she sent a burst of light toward Tigue. He dodged, stepping backward.

A shot rang out through the darkness.

I flinched, turning toward the sound. I hadn't seen Mickey at first, but now that I did, fear clawed up my spine. He stood behind my mother and Leon, his body tense and straight, his gun raised. I got the same sense from him I always did, something quiet and sad, nearly drowned out by the adrenaline that radiated from him. I didn't need a Knowing to know how he must feel. He'd entered a world where demons melted out of shadow, and he had no powers to save himself, just a gun and what I hoped was perfect aim.

He was quick, at least. As a shape curved out of the darkness toward him, two more gunshots rang out in quick succession and found their mark. The Harrower didn't stop—but it slowed just long enough for Mom to turn and send a flash of light to finish it off. The Harrower hissed as it crumpled to the ground.

Mickey reloaded.

I pressed forward, trying to move soundlessly through the snow, but I hadn't taken more than a few steps before I froze. Through the long space between us, the motion of bodies and the careening light, Tigue's eyes caught mine.

Connection rippled between us, instant and violent. For the

briefest of moments, our senses collided. Knowing met Knowing. The barriers were gone; that cool facade he'd kept at the banquet disappeared. I felt the calm, deadly purpose within him. And he was reading me as I read him. He knew why I'd come, the message I carried. Something flickered in his eyes.

"You shouldn't be here," he said—not aloud but somehow directly to me; not in my ears but in my skin, in my blood. "This isn't the place for you."

Iris wasn't here, I realized. He'd sent her somewhere else. She was—

Waiting.

Somewhere.

Images flashed into me: Iris turned away, the dark fall of her hair. Snow at her feet. A tall building, empty and silent. City lights.

I knew the building. Harlow Tower. It stood in downtown Minneapolis, near the IDS Center. I knew its stark shape in the skyline, the huge revolving doors, the thick gold lettering that gleamed down its front. But I knew it for another reason, as well.

I'd seen it the way my mother had, standing at its edge before toppling over. It was where she'd defeated Verrick.

And now Iris was there.

For a moment, I caught the sound of her voice, frantic, frightened.

Audrey. I need you.

"You shouldn't be here," Tigue repeated.

I shuddered, unable to break the contact. "Mom!" I cried,

while I still could. "It's Iris! She isn't the Remnant. She's with him! She's the one who's been helping him!"

Sound exploded all around me.

Time stopped. I couldn't move. I couldn't speak, or breathe, or even think. My eyes were locked with Tigue's, and I watched in horror as his hands rose into the air. The Harrowers beside him shifted, and a blast of energy hurtled out of the darkness toward me.

In the same instant, just out of my vision, I felt Leon turn. I heard the air around us disrupted by his motion.

And then he was in front of me, his arms circling me, my face pressed to his shoulder. His body took the blast meant for me. I felt it hit him, shaking through both of us. His grip on me tightened and then weakened, and he slid from me, collapsing, dragging us down to the snow.

A scream tore from my throat as I saw red bloom around us.

"*Leon!*" I cried, again and again, struggling to make him move. My lungs felt raw and my hands at his back were sticky with blood. The glow at his fingertips faded; the light under his skin died out.

I looked up. Tigue had stepped closer.

"Audrey, don't move!"

I turned toward my mother's voice. She ran to us, crouching and stretching one hand out before her, the colors at her wrists burning and spinning. There was a sudden sizzle, a sort of hiss, and then a layer of light, thin and clear, formed around us. She was shielding us.

"Iris is helping him!" I cried. "She's his accomplice. She can share powers—she can amplify them."

Not just Tigue's powers, I realized. The Remnant's as well. Once they located the Remnant, Iris would be able to open the way Beneath anywhere, as Elspeth had said.

Or everywhere.

Mom's eyes met mine. My words hung between us, and I saw my own reaction repeated in hers: it was unthinkable. Her face was pale, and the color that stirred at her throat made her seem ethereal, more Morning Star than mother. But she nodded, and I felt an understanding grow between us, a thread in the darkness.

Without turning, her voice clear and resolute, she said, "Detective, I need you to get my daughter out of here. I'll cover you."

My gaze jerked toward Mickey. His gun was still drawn, and I saw him nod as he crept toward us. "No!" I cried, clutching Leon against me. I couldn't leave, not when he lay unconscious, bleeding, his breath little gusts against me. His body was warm, and I felt his pulse, but he hadn't stirred.

My mother spoke again, her voice cutting through my haze of fear. "Leon's going to be fine, I promise you. He's strong. The best thing you can do for him is get yourself to safety. Audrey—look at me. Audrey, I need you to trust me."

Lifting my eyes to hers, I felt my panic loosen its grip. I took in a shaky breath and nodded. I moved backward, away from Leon, even as I felt Mickey reach for my hand. His voice was low in my ear.

"We gotta go."

I nodded jerkily, letting him help me to my feet. Without speaking, we turned in the snow and ran.

Detective Wyle hadn't brought his usual car.

I hadn't figured him for a pickup-truck kind of guy, but something about the vehicle told me it wasn't his anyway. The interior smelled like leather and smoke and greasy fast food, and the voice that crackled through the radio was so strained and tinny it sounded like someone dying.

"No wisecracks, kid. And buckle up."

I wasn't exactly in the mood for wisecracks.

No demons had attacked us as we fled across the snow, but I knew I'd feel safer once we were in motion. All around us, the night seemed to listen. I held my breath as Mickey shifted into gear and flicked on the headlights, twin beams slicing through the darkness. I watched his hands on the steering wheel. There was a slight tremble in his fingers. No matter what he might have speculated about my mother, nothing could have prepared him for what he'd seen tonight.

"I guess you know, then," I said. "About my mother." And demons. And the Kin, probably. Even if he didn't know everything now, he was smart. He'd eventually piece it together.

"She's Morning Star," he said. His voice was husky.

"She's more than that."

He didn't hesitate. "I know."

"What are you going to do?"

"Right now, I'm getting us out of here. We'll wait at your house." He pushed down on the gas.

"No," I said. I wasn't going home. I wasn't sitting still. I couldn't. Leon's blood was drying on my hands and clothes. Across the length of the Cities, battles were being fought, Guardians and demons, my mother and Tigue—and somewhere, Iris stood waiting.

"No?" Mickey echoed. "Wasn't really expecting an argument, here."

"We're going to Harlow Tower," I said. "I have to find my cousin."

Audrey, I heard Iris say. *I need you.*

Elspeth's plea came back to me: *We have to help her. She doesn't want to be this way.*

And I realized I knew something Iris did not.

That familiar alarm woke inside me, my frequencies screaming. Memories flashed before me: Rain and tires and the bend of wind around a car, cold eyes watching. Eyes I recognized.

I turned toward the window, trailing my fingers along the glass. The streets were quiet and still, but my Knowing was loud within me. I saw Iris atop the tower, the metal gleam of the triple knot at her throat. Snow swirled around her, blown up by the wind, melting in her hair, along her skin. Her eyes were closed.

I can do this, I told myself. Iris will listen to me. We'd stood together in the cold of Beneath and I'd seen into her history, the hidden places where her grief still slept. She could break free of this. She just needed someone to guide her.

And there was a reason my Knowing had grown so clear and insistent. Out there, in the dark of the Cities, Iris was seeking me. Calling to me.

She wanted me to find her.

Harlow Tower was dark when we arrived.

"I thought they usually left lights on," I said as we approached the front of the building. The sidewalks had been swept clean of snow and dusted with salt, but I picked my way carefully across the cement, my heart hammering against my ribs.

"I still think this is a stupid idea," Detective Wyle mumbled. "When some nut job summons you to a remote location in the middle of the night, the smart decision is not to go."

Stupid wasn't the first word he'd used. I hadn't wanted to tell him about Iris, but he wouldn't agree to drive me without an explanation—and he hadn't been willing to let me go alone. It was an echo of everything I'd felt from him before: a genuine sort of goodness, a desire to help. But I remembered, also, the shadow I'd seen at his back when I'd given him his reading. That danger felt nearer now, close, creeping upon him. The sense grew stronger with each step we took toward the building. A darkness looming. Before I faced Iris, I was going to have to get rid of him.

We walked up to the glass. The revolving doors would be locked, I knew, but if Iris was here, one of the doors had to be open. I moved to the side door and reached for the handle. Mickey stopped me.

"Hold up," he said, easing the door open. "Let's leave the breaking and entering to me."

He stepped in first, cautiously, and I followed. My eyes went to the staircase that led to the skyway, and then to the elevators. The guard at the front desk lay unconscious in his chair. He didn't wake when we approached, but his breathing sounded steady.

Mickey peered over the edge of the desk. "She must've disabled the alarms," he mused.

"She left the cameras," I said, shifting uncomfortably as I stared into the round black eye of the surveillance equipment.

"She didn't want company, but apparently doesn't care who sees her. This is your cousin, you said?"

"Someone will take care of it," I murmured, certain suddenly that I was correct. The Guardians must be accustomed to taking care of things like this. My mother couldn't have gone unknown as long as she had without using a few tricks.

Mickey grunted. "Right. You know where we're supposed to go next?"

I hesitated, shoving my hands into my pockets. That *we* was a problem.

"The roof," I said, after a moment. "But just me. You need to stay here."

"Yeah, that's gonna happen."

I drew in a steadying breath and took a step toward him. "Detective Wyle," I said, meeting his eyes. He looked older now than when I'd first met him. Or maybe it was simply that his expression was more severe, and my own abrupt understanding that his rugged-tortured-soul act wasn't really an act at all. He'd seen his share of darkness, too, even if it hadn't come in the shape of demons. Maybe it was worse for him seeing what humans did to humans.

But I still couldn't let him come with me. He had to stay behind, for his own safety.

"My mother sent you away to save your life," I said. "Not just to protect me. Tigue would never have let you live."

He didn't flinch. He didn't speak, either, though a muscle in his jaw tensed.

I didn't have time to argue with him. I took an unsteady breath, feeling that sharp pang of Knowing, the truth of what I was about to say. "If you go up there with me, you'll die."

My eyes flicked to his. I didn't force my Knowing toward him—the insistent, undeniable certainty of what I felt. I just waited, and watched his eyes, and hoped that somehow he would understand.

"And what about you?" he asked.

"She doesn't want me dead," I said. "She wants something else."

I didn't know what it was, but I felt the strength of her seeking. Urgent, desperate, willing me to her.

He stepped back, running his hand through his hair. "I can't claim to understand all of this, but I believe you."

I didn't give him a chance to change his mind. Whirling, I ran for the elevators.

Iris had left everything unlocked. My way to her was unbarred.

A strange sort of calm came over me as I slid the door open and stepped out onto the roof. The wind was icy and sharp against my face, stinging my eyes. But I wasn't afraid. Not even when I saw Iris standing at the far end, in the exact place my mother and Verrick had fallen.

"You got my message," she said as I moved forward. "I'm glad you came."

"You've been calling to me. You weren't expecting me?"

"Hoping, let's say."

My shoes were cold and wet, shifting through the snow. I walked slowly, careful not to slip or lose my balance. The wind grew, slicing across my cheeks.

"I came to talk to you," I said, peering across the darkness to where she stood. I couldn't see her clearly. She was half turned,

329

her body concealing something. "Iris, you should stop this. We should just go home."

Then she moved, and my heart fell into my stomach.

Beside her, at her feet, a body lay crumpled. Even from this distance I knew who he was. I knew that dark hair, the curve of his shoulder, the way he kept his arms tightly against him.

She had Gideon.

Why did she have Gideon?

I rushed forward, intent on reaching him. Iris stopped me, thrusting her hand into the darkness between us.

"Stay where you are, Audrey. He's my insurance. He's been very worried about you, you know. He stopped me at school yesterday, asking if I knew what was wrong."

"What have you done to him?" I demanded, my eyes on the snow around him, just the barest hint of red in the white.

"Don't worry; he's only sleeping—for now," Iris said. "We have time to talk."

Speech was impossible. I stared. I knew I should tell her something, that I should talk about Tigue, and how his eyes had been the ones watching the night her parents died, and that he was just using her, and that she could come back home and the Kin would forgive her and everything would be all right—but I couldn't. Images flashed through me: Iris at Gideon's door. The worried tremble of her smile as she asked for his help. Gideon following her out into the darkness. A blur of silver. Demons in the street.

Now I saw Gideon crumpled at her feet and I couldn't breathe.

And there was something else.

Something about this place.

I could feel my heart pounding, the movement of blood within me. For a split second, my vision blurred.

"Pay attention," Iris said.

"What do you want with me?" I asked, trying to keep myself steady. My pulse wouldn't slow. "Why did you call me here?"

"I want the Remnant," she said, her voice cool. "I thought you'd figured that out."

"And you think I can tell you how to find her? We already tried that."

"No. Only one person in the world knows who the Remnant is. Her Guardian."

A horrible thought struck me. Guardians. Particular gifts. Leon bleeding before me. "It's me, isn't it? I'm the Remnant."

"Don't be a moron, Audrey. If you were the Remnant, we'd have taken you already."

I frowned, inching closer to her. I could see her clearly now. She wasn't alone on the ledge. Two demons bowed at her side, her hands touching their skin. She was sharing their powers, I realized. The triple knot glowed faintly orange, burning against the flesh of her neck. A trail of smoke made a chain at her throat.

And her eyes—

Her eyes had lost their warm St. Croix glow. Now they were lifeless, the pale milk white of a Harrower without its skin.

Dread pooled in my stomach. I didn't even know who she was anymore.

"Only one person knows who the Remnant is," she repeated, digging her fingers deeper into the skin of the demons beside her. "But seventeen years ago, someone else did. He knew she was about to be born. He knew when. He could find her."

My eyes flew to hers.

"This is the real reason your mother kept you hidden from the Kin. It's why I transferred to Whitman—to find you. Your blood is special, Audrey. It's the blood of Adrian St. Croix."

My breath hissed in through my teeth. I knew what she meant. "Verrick is dead," I whispered. But even as I said it, I knew it was untrue. I'd felt it. I'd sensed it myself—in my dreams, in my readings.

"Wrong," Iris said. "He didn't die when your mother defeated him. Not completely. He fell Beneath. Now he is . . . elsewhere. Waiting. Your father's blood sealed him. Yours can release him. But you have to do it willingly—the same way Adrian did."

Gaping, I nearly laughed in horror and disbelief. "Are you completely *nuts*? You can't release Verrick." He'd been frightening enough as a memory. Just the thought of him conjured up the dread I'd felt. To meet him in reality, to see his face that wasn't a face, with everything that moved unseen—Iris couldn't want that. No matter what.

"I'll share his power. And he'll share his knowledge with me."

"You've spent too much time Beneath," I said. She must have

been there before, I realized. In its many layers and ways, the void pressing in on her—twisting her, changing her. "You think he'll just wake up happy to see you? You'd never survive."

"I will. It doesn't matter. Nothing matters once I find the Remnant."

My eyes dropped to Gideon again, motionless at Iris's feet. "Why are you doing this? For Tigue? He's tricked you. You have to know that. He was there! He was watching you the night your parents died."

"He saved me!"

Her voice was harsh in the stillness, something wild and broken and full of pain. For a second her eyes flashed, showing that hint of brown and gold, and I caught wisps of memory: The smell of roses, her shoes clapping hard against a funeral parlor floor. I saw her reach for Tigue in the rain, I saw him pull her against his body. The way the night melted around them, a sense of security, heat to beat back the cold.

I was wrong. She had known. She'd known all along.

"I was supposed to die that night," she said, and now her voice was soft. Numb. "Elspeth would've survived, but not me. And it wasn't an accident. It was my fault. I caused the crash. I killed my parents."

"That's not true," I said, taking another step toward her. "I saw it. It was raining. The other car ran a red light. What could you have done?"

All emotion had left her voice. "I was practicing my

333

Amplification, toying with borrowed Guardian powers. I sent a pulse through the car. My mother couldn't control it. I killed them. Patrick saved me. He pulled me free when everything was burning."

"To use you!" I shouted. "He must have known what you could do. He wanted you to amplify his powers, to help him control the Remnant."

"You really have no idea, do you? He isn't controlling me. He loves me. He's doing what I ask, not the other way around. He's not the one who wants the Remnant. I am."

Shock jolted through me. I stared blankly at her. "Harrowers don't love."

"What the hell would you know about it?" she sneered.

"You expect me to believe this was all your idea?"

"It's *our* idea."

"You can't really believe that." I felt sick, and stupid, and hot with anger. Kelly. Anna. Tink. Me. All those other deaths. I couldn't breathe. And my blood was still rushing, seething, loud in my ears.

"You killed them," I choked out. "You killed all those people."

"No. Harrowers did that."

"But you let them! You let them kill their way through the city. You let them bleed me." Somehow, that seemed worse than everything else. That she had claimed to be my friend and left me in the darkness of that alley to feel the burn at my ankles, my life force draining. "And—your sister. You had a demon attack your own *sister*."

"That wasn't one of mine," she protested. "I didn't want it to happen like this. Things just got out of control. And don't forget, I saved your life."

"Your demon friends couldn't have been too happy about that," I jeered, an ugly feeling gripping me. "You killed one of their own."

Anger sparked behind the white of her eyes. "This is pointless. It doesn't *matter*, Audrey. When I have the Remnant, everything will be undone."

My breath caught. "What do you mean?"

"The Remnant has more power than you can even begin to imagine. She can open gateways. Holes between here and Beneath."

"You mean to bring a Harrowing."

"Not a Harrowing. Time works differently Beneath. It can turn seconds into decades. And the Remnant—her power works both ways. She creates passages, don't you see? With her powers Amplified—she could even cut a hole through time."

Everything about me stilled. "You *are* insane," I breathed. "Listen to yourself. You really think that's possible? Tigue is deluding you!"

Iris shook her head. "It will happen. I'll make it happen. And then all of this will go away."

"You plan to bring back the dead." It was incomprehensible.

Of all the things I could have imagined—this was not one of them. "Your parents."

"I'm going to fix things. I'm going to make things right again." Her tone went hard. "But first, I need to find her. And for that, I need you to unseal Verrick."

"I wasn't planning to do it before," I said. "And I am definitely not going to do it now."

"Then your friend dies," she said, withdrawing a knife from the pocket of her coat. She slid one foot through the snow to touch Gideon's neck. A noise escaped him, almost like a whimper, but I didn't think he was conscious. "Do you think I'm bluffing?"

"I think you're crazy!" I shouted. My vision blurred again. Something here—

Something was stirring within me.

"None of this matters, Audrey. It will all be undone." Iris dropped her knife to the ground and kicked it toward me. "But not unless I find the Remnant. So can—we—please—hurry?"

I stared at the knife. It had stopped about a foot from me, its silver edge gleaming in the snow. I bent slowly, my fingers curving toward it. She would kill Gideon. I believed that now.

"What am I supposed to do?" I asked softly, taking the knife in my hand.

"It's a ritual. We start with five cuts. They don't have to be deep. This won't kill you. You need to bleed from the five sacred spaces. Wrists, ankles, throat. Be careful of the arteries."

Soundless, nodding, I held the knife to my left wrist. I pressed the point against it, not quite enough to break the skin.

I couldn't do this. I couldn't unseal Verrick.

His face swam before me, and all the horror that lived behind it. The hunger and need that filled me with dread. His last words echoed up and down my skin. *We'll meet again.*

"It's useless," I said, keeping the knife at my wrist. "My mother will find you before you ever reach the Remnant."

Iris shrugged, unconcerned. "Patrick is keeping her busy."

"I've seen Verrick. You can't control him," I argued. "You know he won't just let you use his powers. He didn't work with *anyone*. He'll take the Remnant for himself. There won't be anything to stop him."

She tapped her foot against Gideon's neck. "I want to see blood, Audrey. Show me your blood or I'll show you his." Her demons had gathered close to her again, and I felt other Harrowers around me stir, pressing close.

I winced, slipping the edge of the knife into my skin, then held my hand up for Iris to see. A single bead of blood welled up in the cut.

Heat poured through me.

Blood, I thought.

Bloodlines—

"That's one down," she said. "Four more and I'll let him live."

I moved the knife to my other hand. "Why here?"

"Don't ask stupid questions. This is where it all ended. Where he fell. This is where he must be unsealed. I know you saw it."

"Then you must know what happened," I said, pricking my other wrist. It felt as though my pulse was moving faster now, faster than was even possible—but the blood dripped out slowly. "Even with his powers sealed, my mother barely defeated him. He nearly destroyed the Circle. He'll kill you. He'll kill us both as soon as he's unsealed, and then he'll take the Remnant. You won't be able to undo anything."

Iris sighed. "I didn't want it to happen this way, believe me. But you left me no choice."

"Me?"

"At the banquet tonight—I knew you were close. I knew you would find out about Patrick and me. He told me what we had to do."

"Of course he did," I scoffed.

Rage brought the gold back into her eyes. "Stop stalling, Audrey, or I kill Gideon and move on to someone else. Would you prefer it if I went through all of your friends?"

I lifted the knife to my throat. Made a slight cut. I felt the warmth ooze out onto my neck.

"Two more. You're doing well."

I crouched and rolled down my socks. The scar of my first bleeding was still there, a thin white line marring my skin. I closed my eyes and nicked it.

"There's more to it than just bleeding me, right?" I asked, feeling nausea rise in my stomach. "It can't be that simple."

"One step at a time. We start with blood."

"I think I'm going to throw up."

Iris rolled her eyes. "Stop being so melodramatic."

"I'm not kidding. Something really weird is happening to me."

It wasn't just nausea. It wasn't just blood. It wasn't just heat. My body felt strange, sensation running down my skin, in my bones, as though every part of me had begun to breathe.

"It'll be—" Iris broke off, gasping, as the air before her shimmered and the two demons fell back, tripping over Gideon in their haste. A surge of relief flooded through me and then evaporated as I realized the shape that appeared so suddenly in front of her was not Leon or my mother—but Patrick Tigue.

It didn't take a second glance to realize he was in bad shape. His skin had gone pale, sickly—was beginning to ripple. For a moment I could see through him. His body was being pulled Beneath. With a sharp breath, he slumped forward. His arms went around Iris, clutching her tightly.

His word was soft, but the wind carried it to me.

"Sorry—"

Iris's voice went low and soothing. "Shh," she murmured, her hand in his hair.

"They're on their way. It has to be now."

And then he simply faded.

Iris didn't scream. She didn't sob or wail. She stared at me across the blank distance between us and lifted her arm. "We're taking it all back," she said. "We're going to make things good again. Now, Audrey. Right—*now*."

I pressed the knife against my other ankle, barely touching it, my hand shaking, my vision pulsing. I made the final cut.

For the second time that night, the universe stopped.

The city around us went dark. The sky, the buildings, the world below. We stood under the vanishing stars. Everything else dissolved—no movement of cars in the streets beneath us, no lampposts, no shadows of clouds passing over. Just the blank, empty, endless void of space.

I looked up. The sky was bare, save for a single point of yellow where the moon should have been.

A pinprick of light in the darkness, I thought.

Where all hope begins.

I had seen all of this before. The city dead around me, vacant and silent and cold. The dark of the buildings. It was my dream called into life.

I'd dreamed of destruction—but as Gram liked to say, just because you had a Knowing didn't make it right.

I stood, dropping the knife. I looked at my hands. They were glowing. Not like a Guardian's, not with colors that shone at the fingers and wrists, but a shine beneath my skin, vibrant and pulsing and hot.

I faced Iris. I understood, now, the vision Esther had shown me. My mother falling, the arc of light that wrapped her body, rushing beneath her skin, the sudden hush. How she had lived. The Astral Circle was diminished, but its power wasn't lost. Verrick had weakened it, but he hadn't destroyed it.

The Circle had saved my mother—and she had saved it. Its light had hidden within her. In the unformed, sheltering flesh of the child she carried.

It was in me, a part of me, in my blood, singing through me. Leon wasn't just guarding me; he was guarding the power I held.

And here, at the center of the Circle's power—here, where my mother had fought and fallen—I could release it.

I looked down.

Fire.

Fire in my hands.

The light was blinding.

It was hot, unbearable. It burned me.

It flowed out of me like flame, angry and merciless, ripping its way through my skin, spreading outward, everywhere, a flood released.

Around me, Iris's Harrowers shrieked and squirmed, their bodies buckling as they clawed their way back into the cold emptiness of the Beneath. The light rushed toward Iris, dragging her down to her knees. For a single moment she looked up at me, frightened and surprised—and then her eyes went blank again. Her face washed clean of emotion, and she turned away. Her body flickered and then vanished.

She wasn't Kin anymore. She wasn't my cousin. I didn't know who she was, or what. She'd gone Beneath.

And still the light kept coming. It poured out of me, boundless and violent. But even as it swelled, it didn't leave me. I felt myself moving with it, a part of it, moving through earth and air, soaking up shadow. And I felt connected to everything. I felt the city, the motion of engines and tires and feet, of doors opening, of throats trembling with sound. I smelled soil and snow, grease, garbage, sweat, breath, heat. I felt the earth, and everything beneath and Beneath.

The Astral Circle's strength was renewed, and I was a part of it. It was a part of me.

Finally, the light ebbed and then vanished. The Circle was unseen once more. I walked across the roof to where Gideon lay. I knelt, pressing my hand to his cheek, watching the steady movement of his breath.

"Audrey!"

Turning, I jumped to my feet. My mother stood at the door to the roof, panting, her hair floating about her. Her arms whipped around me, holding me fast. She reeked of sweat and blood, but I didn't care.

"Where's Leon?" I asked.

Mom pulled back, brushing my hair from my face. "He's fine. He brought us here, but Detective Wyle is taking him to the hospital. You're okay? You're not hurt?"

Shaking my head, I turned toward Gideon. "I'm worried. I think Iris did something to him."

He moaned then, his eyes beginning to open. I crouched beside him as he lifted a hand to his face.

"Gideon?" I whispered. "Are you okay?"

He turned aside. He wouldn't look at me. "I want to go home."

Gideon was groggy as we brought him home, and didn't manage to say much beyond, "I told you she was creepy." I'd suggested we take him to the emergency room, but my mother assured me he was fine, and Gideon himself seemed reluctant. We dropped him off at his house, and I watched him disappear inside. I'd asked if he wanted me to come in with him, but he told me all he wanted to do was curl up in bed and sleep.

"He's had quite a shock," Mom said. "Just give him time."

She had to meet with Esther and the Kin elders—not to mention she had Mickey to deal with—but she dropped me off at Hennepin County Medical Center so I could check on Leon.

I didn't like seeing him there, in that sterile room with its bright fluorescents and hospital smell. I stepped through the door slowly. Mom swore he would be fine, but I couldn't stop seeing him as he'd appeared before me, shielding me; I couldn't help feeling the shock that had run through us both, remembering how he'd slumped forward and then gone still, and how his blood had welled beneath my hands. Everything in the hospital —the nurse's station beyond the door, the scrubs and white coats, the charts and monitors—served as a painful reminder that Leon had been injured because of me. He might have been killed—because of me.

Not exactly something I could make better with a get-well card and balloons.

He appeared to be sleeping when I entered his room, so I kept my footsteps light, creeping toward the chair at the side of his bed. I stopped beside him, pressing my fingers against the bed rail. Peering down at him, I took in the dark circles beneath his eyes, the evenness of his breathing. His face had lost a little color. I was reaching forward to brush aside a stray lock of hair when he abruptly sat up and caught my wrist.

Which is how it happened that the first words I spoke weren't an apology, as I'd intended. They weren't words thanking him, either, or even asking how he felt. Instead, I yelped and jumped back, mumbling out gibberish. Then, as I tried to steady my breath, I said, "You are really determined to give me that heart attack, aren't you?"

He shrugged, pushing away that wayward lock of hair himself. "I'm helping you hone your abilities. Shouldn't you have *Known* that was coming?"

"Well, I'm glad you're feeling better," I grumbled, not nearly as nicely as I'd planned.

"You know Guardians. We heal quickly." Then his face darkened, that little frown of his appearing. "You did something amazing tonight, Audrey."

345

I thought of Iris disappearing Beneath, and Elspeth, and who would tell her. There was a catch in my voice as I said, "So did you guys."

He'd done something I wouldn't ever be able to thank or repay him for. And the worst part of it was, he didn't even have a choice. I took a deep breath. "Leon—"

He must have guessed what I was thinking. He lifted a hand to silence me, then shifted in the bed, sitting so that we were at the same level, eye to eye. And he put on his most serious expression, the one usually reserved for lectures, or when someone criticized his baking. His voice, though, was soft. "It's not what you think," he said. "Being your Guardian."

It took a moment for his words to sink in. Then I stepped back, frowning down at him. "You want to have this conversation *now*?" I eyed him suspiciously. "You're all drugged up on pain medication, aren't you?"

"I'm completely lucid, I swear," he said. And then he gave me a crooked smile that crinkled his eyes and made my heart do that alarming little flip-flop thing again.

To cover the heat I was certain was stealing up my cheeks, I turned away, mumbling, "Yeah. Uh-huh."

He caught my hand, drawing me back to him.

"You need to hear this," he said, and though his voice was quiet, it was firm. He kept my hand tucked into his, but I couldn't meet his eyes. He let out a ragged sigh. "I won't lie to you, Audrey. I didn't want to be a Guardian."

I wasn't sure I wanted to hear the rest of this, but Leon wasn't done.

"My grandfather—I think he knew I'd be called. Even though he took me away from the Circle, he spent years preparing me. Most of my childhood. And I hated it. I had plans. I knew what I wanted to do with my life, and it didn't involve the Kin."

The opposite of Mom and me, I thought. I wondered if I'd have felt differently if I'd grown up knowing everything about the Kin.

"When I was called, I thought I'd been cursed," he continued. "I rebelled. Or thought I did. It was months before I came here to find you, and even then I kept telling myself I wouldn't stay. But that changed. And—would you look at me, please?"

I shook my head mutely. I kept my eyes focused on our hands, on the thin material of the sheet he lay on, on the little scar that hooked his wrist—anything but his face.

He sighed again. "It changed. *I* changed. It's been years since I felt that way. This is who I am. Being a Guardian—being *your* Guardian—it's important to me."

I chanced looking at him. "Then why didn't you tell me?" I asked. My voice sounded small, far away. "Why not tell me instead of just—getting angry?"

I didn't think there was a power in the universe more devastating than the Hungry Puppy, but Leon managed it. He withdrew his hand and glanced away, his entire face transforming. He didn't look like a hungry puppy now; he looked like a kicked one.

"Because it's also scary as hell," he said, letting out a shaky breath. "I don't... I don't always know how to deal with it. It's not just wanting to protect you. It's *needing* to protect you. It's physical. And I can't shut it off. It's always there."

I stared at him in horror. "So you're trapped," I whispered. This was the worst thing yet.

He looked about as panicked as I felt. "No—that's not what I'm saying."

"What *are* you saying?" My throat felt tight again, and my lungs. My heart wasn't just flip-flopping anymore; it was thrashing like it wanted to jump right out from beneath my ribs and find a deep, dark hole to hide in. Sort of like I did. I kept waiting for Leon to say something, anything, but he just stared at me. That familiar worry crease appeared in his forehead. Twice he seemed about to speak, then didn't. Each time, the frown deepened.

I couldn't take it anymore. "I have to go," I mumbled, beginning to turn away.

My words finally spurred him into action. "Audrey, wait," he said, and he caught me a second time. But he didn't just grab my hand. He sat forward, gripping me by the shoulders, and tugged me to him. "What I'm trying to say is—"

Later, I would tell Tink it was perfect. That it was the sort of kiss you see in movies, with soft lights and spinning cameras and some pop singer crooning a ballad in the background. That it had been like gravity: me swaying into him, his hand curving around the back of my head, our faces tilting. That it was inevitable, inescapable, a force beyond our control.

In reality, it wasn't perfect. It wasn't even close.

Injured though he was, Leon was stronger than he realized. I lost my balance when he pulled me toward him; I ended up crashing against him, and not even in a sexy way. Then my mouth missed his. As I grappled with the side of the bed, trying to regain my balance, I slipped again. I would've ended up on the floor if not for Leon's arm circling me. And then he started *laughing*. Laughing so hard that, when he finally managed to tangle his hand in my hair and drag my mouth to his, he was still laughing as he kissed me.

But I didn't care that it wasn't perfect. I didn't care that our background music consisted of whirring hospital machinery and a janitor pushing a cart down the hall, or that we were in a room that smelled like applesauce and latex gloves and disinfectant. I didn't care that it took us three tries to kiss—really kiss—or that the metal bar of the hospital bed was digging into my ribs. This was what I'd been waiting for. What I'd been wanting. What I hadn't wanted to admit.

After a while, Leon broke away, sighing softly as he pressed his forehead to mine. "This is a problem," he said.

I couldn't stop grinning. "You worry too much."

"You don't worry at all," he replied, and the slightest hint of his stern expression returned.

I decided to take Tink's advice. To shut him up, I leaned

forward and kissed him again. I didn't stop. I dragged my hands through his hair, that dark hair that curled at the ends, and then I climbed up onto the bed beside him. And I went right on kissing him until his heart monitor began beeping and the nurse rushed in.

Leon was discharged from the hospital the following morning. If the doctors thought something was strange about his rapid recovery, they didn't mention it. They sent him home with pain medication and instructions to take it easy.

The next few days passed quickly. Details about the Harrowers' attack trickled in, and for once my mother didn't try to keep them from me. There had been incursions scattered throughout the metro area, Harrowers creeping out from the Beneath to prey upon the vulnerable Cities, their assault cut short by the revival of the Circle. Several Guardians had been hurt— including Mr. Alvarez, who assured me his minor injuries would *not* delay our precalc exam. But since Tigue's death, the Twin Cities had gone quiet. With the Astral Circle at full strength, few Harrowers would be able to emerge from Beneath. Demon activity was minimal, and in Minneapolis, at least, things were returning to normal.

I tried to put other thoughts out of my mind: the knowledge that the Remnant was still out there, in need of protection—and the certainty that Verrick, wherever he was, definitely wasn't dead.

There were other matters that needed more immediate attention.

Elspeth was inconsolable. She refused to go to school. She refused to eat. She spent most of her days sitting up in her room, crying, and wouldn't let anyone near her. I waited outside her door a few times, knocking gently and letting her know I'd be there for her whenever she wanted to talk.

We'd heard nothing from Iris. I hadn't expected to. I didn't know where it was she'd gone, but I didn't think she would be coming back. Esther didn't speak of it, but I saw the worry and grief in her eyes, the hint of words she wouldn't speak.

Then there was Gideon.

He wasn't happy with me, and I couldn't exactly blame him. Though, as it turned out, he was angrier that I'd kept secrets from him than about the fact that my creepy cousin had kidnapped him, dragged him across the city, and used him as a hostage in her attempt to force me to unleash an unspeakable evil upon the land.

"I can't believe you didn't tell me," he said, when I'd forced my way into his house after he wouldn't return my phone calls.

I took a long breath. I should have told him before, I realized —regardless of my mother's warnings and my own fears. I would tell him now. I would tell him everything. About the Kin and about Harrowers. About the Circle and the Beneath and the power that ran through us all. He wasn't Kin, but he was a part of it now, bound by another kind of heritage: those who had seen too much. He'd seen demons; it was time to show him the other half.

But Tink was the one I told about Leon.

"I thought you hated him," she said, when I called her Saturday night.

"So did I."

She laughed. "You are such a mess."

This from a girl who wouldn't date a boy if he had hazel eyes, wore sports jerseys to school, or was color-blind. In ninth grade I'd spent an entire month telling Tommy Ferguson what color shirt Tink had on.

Before I could mention this, she squeaked into the phone. "Oh! I almost forgot. The weirdest thing happened last night. I was at the Drought and Deluge—"

"I can't believe you went back there," I said, though I supposed it shouldn't have shocked me. She'd wanted to go to the Halloween party, after all—and she'd just broken up with her exchange student. "Who did you get to go with you?"

"*Greg,*" she groaned. "Let's not talk about that. Here's the weird thing. The owner came up and asked me to give you a message."

I frowned. "Shane? What did he say?"

"Something about how he was glad to see you 'found your shine.' And then he called you a star or something. Like I said, it was weird. He was pretty hot, though."

"You know he's a demon, right?"

"It's just an observation."

"And *I'm* the mess?"

Instead of a ready comeback, Tink turned serious. Apparently, it was a night for confessions.

"I lied to you," she said. "About the night I was attacked. I remember everything. And I know that you came for me. You put yourself in danger to help me. I haven't forgotten that." Then she was lighthearted again. "But I'm still not running off to join the Kin." Like we'd progressed from cult to circus—and, in Tink's mind, the latter was worse.

I didn't argue with her. I didn't tell her it was a part of her, whether or not she wanted it to be. That I could sense it in her as clearly as in my mother or Elspeth, that I could see it in the way she moved and the way air settled upon her, that it might even be the reason we'd first become friends. An unspoken thread between us. Kin drawn to Kin.

"Tink has to find her own way," my mother said, when I asked her about it. "Just like the rest of us."

I nodded, following her out onto the front step, where she sat down with a cup of cocoa and gazed out into the quiet street. A light snow was falling, hanging in the air. Around us, I felt the presence of the Astral Circle, shielding us from Beneath.

"The Cities will be safer now, right?" I asked, sitting beside her and taking a sip of her cocoa. I watched a little frown flit across her brow.

"Safer," she agreed.

But not safe. Though the barrier had been strengthened, some Harrowers would still push through. The Circle protected us, but it was not absolute.

I chewed my lip, drawing little circles in the snow with the edge of my mitten. "I've been thinking about something," I began.

Mom looked at me expectantly.

"Releasing Verrick—unsealing his powers. That would have unsealed my father, too." I'd felt that as I'd stood atop Harlow Tower, watching my blood spill out. I hadn't been able to process it then, but I thought of it now. The ritual would have brought my father back. Woken the sleeping heart, that laughing boy who had vanished so long ago. I glanced at Mom. She'd turned slightly away, facing down the road. Snowflakes caught in her pale hair. I felt the sadness she carried—a dull ache she had learned to ignore. "Do you still miss him?"

"I miss who he was. I miss who he made me." She turned to me, and I saw the shine of tears in her eyes. "But I have you. He would have been very proud of you."

I hesitated. "Will you tell me about him?"

She took my hand, squeezing it. A little smile crossed her face. "I can try." She laughed softly, shaking her head, and lifted one hand to wipe the moisture from her eyes. "If I can figure out where to start."

"Tell me how you met," I suggested.

This time, her laugh was loud. "No, you don't want that story. I was horrible to him."

"Horrible how?"

"I put him in the hospital."

No wonder Esther had disapproved. I grinned at her. "Okay, now I *definitely* want that story."

"Later," she said, and refused to say more. Instead, she told me the things my father had loved: Rain, she said, especially thunderstorms; wet grass and red autumn leaves, greasy popcorn, the smell of old books. He loved winter, cold soundless nights and the fall of snow. And the Kin. He'd loved being a Guardian.

"I wish I could have known him," I said.

There was a catch in her voice, but her smile remained. "I wish he could have known you."

I leaned back, looking up at the low, cloud-filled sky and the swirl of snow that drifted through the air. Down the street, Christmas lights blurred, colors shining and bright. I took deep breaths, filling my lungs.

I turned back to Mom.

"I want to begin training," I said. She started to respond, but I lifted a hand to stay her. "Just to be prepared. Even if I'm never called, I'm still Kin. And..." I paused, thinking of Iris, and the light that had poured from my veins, and the connection I still felt to the Circle—the power that bound us. I didn't know what the connection meant, but it was there, within me. "I'm ready."

It was a long moment before my mother spoke. When she did, I heard a slight tremor in her voice. "This is what you want?"

She gazed across the darkness at me. Her eyes met mine, and for a moment, I saw both Morning Star, fierce and defiant, and the girl she'd once been, before she'd been bound by duty and shaped by her own myth.

"I'm ready," I repeated.

Mom nodded, another soft smile touching her lips. "Okay," she said. "But not tonight."

I leaned against her, resting my head on her shoulder.

We sat on the steps and watched the snow fall.

Acknowledgments

The first thing I need to acknowledge is that there are far, far too many people who belong on this page to ever list them. Nevertheless, I will attempt it. Completing this book was a long process, and I will be forever grateful to the tireless efforts of a number of people. Specifically:

My brilliant agent, Caitlin Blasdell, who has my deepest thanks for everything she does; without her support and guidance—and especially her hand-holding—I would be utterly lost. My awesome editor, Abby Ranger, who challenges and encourages me in equal measure, and who frequently assures me that I'm not nearly as neurotic as I think I am. Two others who helped this book along the way: Laura Schreiber, whose insights are invaluable, and Ari Lewin, whose enthusiasm I cherish.

The friends who kept me sane, and didn't complain (at least to my face) about midnight brainstorming sessions and e-mails that were nearly novels in length: Sarah Bauer, Brinson Thieme, Patricia Reinwald, and Leah Raeder. The amazing individuals I've had the great luck to know as both teachers and writers: Bill Meissner, Mary Logue, and the wise and wonderful Sheila O'Connor, who told me to be brave.

And finally, my parents, who taught me to chase my dreams, and always believed I'd reach them. Even if my mother did seriously ask me, "Is this a kissing book?" (And made a face when I answered.)